Brink of
Death

Books by Brandilyn Collins

Eyes of Elisha

Dread Champion

The Bradleyville Series

Cast a Road Before Me

Color the Sidewalk for Me

Capture the Wind for Me

HIDDEN FACES SERIES

BOOK ONE

Brink of Death

BRANDILYN COLLINS

ZONDERVAN™

GRAND RAPIDS, MICHIGAN 49530 USA

Brink of Death
Copyright © 2004 by Brandilyn Collins

Requests for information should be addressed to:
Zondervan, *Grand Rapids, Michigan 49530*

Library of Congress Cataloging-in-Publication Data

Collins, Brandilyn.
    Brink of death / Brandilyn Collins.
        p. cm. — (The hidden faces series ; bk. 1)
    ISBN 0-310-25103-6
        1. Courtroom artists—Fiction. 2. Trials (Murder)—Fiction.
    3. Women artists—Fiction. 4. Witnesses—Fiction. I. Title.
    PS3553.O4747815 B75   2004
    813'.6—dc22

                                                                    2003024008

Interior design by Beth Shagene

Printed in the United States of America

04 05 06 07 08 09 10 /❖ DC/ 10 9 8 7 6 5 4 3 2 1

For my son, Brandon,
who brings me great pride and joy.

Acknowledgments

This story could only be written with the help of some very patient people. Many thanks to these kind folks, who proved invaluable to me:

Les Caldwell, retired sheriff's sergeant, who granted me an interview as the story was being built, then read the completed manuscript to catch any glitches regarding the law enforcement characters. Les's wife, Marilyn, who also read the completed manuscript and caught numerous typographical errors.

Guy Ottsman, retired deputy sheriff, and Bill Osborn, retired sheriff's detective, for their willingness to be interviewed.

Mark Collins, my husband and a private pilot, for going over all the details relating to flying.

Jacqueline Clark, my dear friend who serves in the chaplaincy programs of numerous California Bay Area law enforcement departments, for guiding me with the character and duties of Gerri Carson.

My editors, Dave Lambert and Karen Ball. The two best in the business. What more can I say?

One more important note. *Forensic Art and Illustration*, by nationally renowned forensic expert Karen Taylor, serves as the basis for my fictional textbook *The World of Forensic Art*. For purposes of this story, I moved some of the information and chapters of Ms. Taylor's book around, but in general the concepts and procedures of forensic art noted within these pages are attributable to her excellent text.

"I tell you the truth,
whoever hears my word
and believes him who sent me
has eternal life and will not be condemned;
he has crossed over from death to life."

JOHN 5:24

Prologue

The noises, faint, fleeting, whispered into her consciousness like wraiths in the night.

Twelve-year-old Erin Willit opened her eyes to darkness lit only by the green night-light near her closet door, and the faint glow of a streetlamp through her bedroom window. She felt her forehead wrinkle, the fingers of one hand curl, as she tried to discern what had awakened her.

Something was not right.

An oak tree lifted gnarled branches between the streetlamp and her window, its leaves casting eerie spider-shadows across the far wall. When she was younger, Erin had asked that a small lamp on the desk by that wall be left on at night. Anything to dispel the jerking dance of those leaves. Lately, she'd watched the dark tremble across the posters of pop stars on her wall with no fear at all.

But not tonight. On this night the shadows writhed and twitched.

Erin listened.

Vague sounds from her dad's office on the other side of her wall took form. A drawer slid open. Contents rustled.

Her heart tripped over itself, then scrambled for balance. There was nothing unusual about the sounds. Anyone working in the office could have made them. Someone paying bills, like she'd seen her dad do so many times, making no noise or movement until a pen was required or a piece of paper . . . until a drawer was opened to pull out a file. Erin knew how quiet her dad could be when he worked in his office. She was used to the creaks of his chair, the plunk of his briefcase on the desk.

The shadow-leaves on her wall skittered across the face of a male star, transforming his features into the thrust forehead and sunken cheeks of a half-human. Erin pulled her eyes away.

She raised her head from the pillow, listening more intensely. Her breath stalled midthroat, making a little click as her mouth sagged open. More noises. It couldn't be her dad. He'd flown his plane just that afternoon to visit his sister in San Diego, who was sick.

Maybe Mom was in the office. She had a second desk in there, which she used when she helped Dad. Erin glanced at her radio alarm clock. Nearly twelve-thirty. Mom never worked that late. Besides, the sounds were stealthy, secretive. Like someone sneaking around in a place they weren't supposed to be.

Erin's heart staccatoed once more, then ground into a steady, hard beat. *Whoosh, whoosh, whoosh,* echoed the blood in her head. All other sound ceased, drowned out in the adrenaline rush. Erin gripped the hem of her pajama top, straining to hear. She held her head off the pillow until her neck ached. *Whoosh, whoosh, whoosh.* She could hear nothing more.

She bit her lip, then laid her head down.

Erin inhaled deeply, willing her heart to settle.

She'd imagined the noises. Just like she'd imagined the ghosted death-dance on her wall. She forced her gaze to the trembling silhouettes, eyes boring into them until she could discern the pattern of individual leaves. See? Just shadows from an old tree.

A muffled thud emanated from the office. A drawer closing. Then a soft thump against hardwood floor. A footfall.

Primal instinct reared its head. Erin wanted her mom— now. Her mother meant safety, security against all harm. Mom was sleeping upstairs in the master bedroom suite—so far away. But Erin had to go. She would turn on every light between here and there.

Trembling, Erin pushed back the covers and slid out of bed. Cool conditioned air slithered around her shoulders. She stood rock still. What if some predator in the next room had sensed her movement? She could almost visualize a massive beast's shining nose sniffing the air, smelling her fear.

Oh, she *was* thinking crazy stuff now.

She edged forward. The dark leaf images tremored on her wall, warning her: *Don't go, don't go!* The undefined shadow of her own form hulked across her desk and wall, obliterating the oak silhouettes. Erin crept across her bedroom carpet on soundless feet. Reaching the door, she placed her palm against the cool metal knob.

Another sound from the office. A light bump.

Erin's resolve crumbled. She couldn't do this! She should lock her door, jump back in bed, and jerk the covers over her head. Dive deep, deep down in those warm folds.

But then what? Hide panic-stricken and vulnerable until Whoever It Was came for her?

No way! She had to get to her mother. As she opened the door, she'd see the gleam of light from the office. She'd just peek into the room, see her mother there, working late.

Maybe with a cup of tea resting on the coaster that never left her desk. "Sorry to wake you," Mom would be saying seconds from now. "I couldn't sleep and I had some paperwork to do."

Erin could almost hear the lilt of her mom's voice. Could almost see her face, bathed in the glow of the desk lamp. *Please, Mom . . . please be there.* Erin held her breath and twisted the knob. She pulled the door open a crack and peeked through.

No lamplight spilled from the office. The darkened hallway was lit only by a night-light like the one in Erin's bedroom.

Maybe the office door was closed. Sure, that was it. That was why the sounds had been so muffled. Erin eased her own door farther open, slipped her head out. A short hallway to the office angled off the main hall that ended at Erin's bedroom. She couldn't see the office entry without venturing farther from her room.

Don't be so stupid! Go on out there. If she could just step out, she'd see the office light illuminating the bottom of the door. Heralding her mother's presence on the other side.

A sudden glow spilled from the office and swept over the hallway, like the weakened edge of a flashlight's beam. A shuffle and a small thud followed, another drawer opened and closed. Erin froze. Mom wouldn't bump around in a darkened office with a flashlight.

Hideous images from Erin's childhood sprang into her head—from gruesome imaginings of a toddler's boogeyman to visions of the murderous Freddy Kruger. The latter images were the most terrifying. Freddy was not a surreal monster. He was real, a man with a killing machine for a heart. Erin suffered nightmares for a week after the back-to-back horror movies illicitly watched at her friend's house. The lamp on her desk was on that whole week, just like when she was little.

Her mom tut-tutted. "That's why I don't want you watching those movies."

Moms were right about some things.

Mom. How could Erin get to her? If Erin ran down the hall, Freddy would hear her, maybe *see* her. He'd come after her. Freddy loved coming after his victims.

Erin hunched, half in and half out of her doorway, stilled by indecision. And fear.

At the other end of the house, the entryway chandelier flicked on. Erin flinched, every nerve tingling. Freddy had to see the light! Had Mom come to investigate the noises? Surely she couldn't have heard them from her bedroom. Maybe she'd come downstairs for a glass of ice water. Maybe sheer maternal instinct had pulled her from bed and toward her panicked daughter.

Down the hall, Erin's mom glided into view, a pink summer robe tied about her waist. She stopped to turn on the hall light, rubbing one of her eyes. No fear on her face, no tension racking her limbs. Erin's shoulders eased. If her mom wasn't scared, then there was nothing to be frightened of. The mere sight of Mom's calm features whisked Erin back to when she was three years old, huddling in her mother's lap.

"Hush, hush now, there's no one there; you just saw a shadow."

See? Nothing to be afraid of.

Reality rushed back, chilling Erin to the bone. This time she *had* seen something. She *had* heard noises. Noises that couldn't be explained away by any amount of soothing.

Go back, Mom, go back! Erin wanted to shout. *Freddy's in the office! Run!*

She opened her mouth, emitting only a gurgle. At that moment her mother saw her in the doorway.

"Erin, what are you—"

Her mother's eyes shifted toward the office. Her expression pinched; then her features shifted into a frozen mask.

Help, God. She saw Freddy. Help!

"N–no!" Mom's voice quavered. "Erin, get back!"

Instinct flooded Erin, pushing her toward her mother. No matter the distance separating them, no matter what lay between, her mom's arms still meant safety. She flung her door wider, drawn forward by a force she couldn't resist. Her mom threw out both hands. "No! *No!*"

Time leapt into a nightmare dance, whirling before Erin's eyes. A dark figure—*Freddy!*—sprang from the office hallway. A man dressed in black shirt, black jeans. Not too tall but muscular, built like a truck. He lunged toward Erin's mom and shoved her hard. She bounced off the wall, then lashed out, pummeling him with her fists. *Move!* The word screamed through Erin, telling her to creak her knees into action, help save her mom. . . .

But her muscles turned to stone.

The sights and sounds pounded Erin, wrapped squeezing fingers around her head. The man warded off her mom's flailing arms with one hand and hit her in the face with the other. Mom reeled into the wall. She came back with a scream, kicking.

Erin stared as her mother became a creature she didn't know, violent and keening. Arms and legs lashed out, intertwined, as man and woman struggled to the death. Then

Erin's mom sagged, unable to keep up her battle. The man wrapped gloved fingers around her throat and squeezed. Her hands flew to those fingers, clawing, clawing. Her eyes bugged, her mouth dropped open. Strangled sounds spilled from her bluing lips. The man flung her then, across the hall and into the kitchen, out of Erin's sight. Erin heard a sickening crack, then the thud of her mom hitting the tile floor.

Nauseating heat gushed through Erin's veins. Her mouth opened to scream, but only a desperate whimper escaped. The man turned and, for the longest second she'd ever experienced, locked bright-blue eyes with hers.

It isn't Freddy, it isn't Freddy, it isn't Freddy.

That one distinct thought ran in her head. Even as Erin's brain shut down, she knew she stood at the brink of death. The hallway dimmed and the world spun around her; black spots ate away at the perimeter of her vision. The spots grew and gobbled and crawled. Like cockroaches.

Erin's mind slipped away, down a long dark tunnel, peering back at her granite and soon-to-die earthly form.

Run, run! Lock the door! But her brain's final plea was too late. Far, far too late.

The man drew himself up, breathing hard. The sound was muffled. Erin slid farther into the tunnel. Still he stared at her.

The cockroaches ate up the walls and ceiling and floor. Ate right to the man, then fed on his arms, his toes, his head. Erin's knees gave way.

As she fell, her elbow hit the door frame hard, sending shock waves up her arm. Cockroaches scurried and swarmed. Then covered her world in blackness.

Monday, July 21

Chapter 1

V*ic stands behind me with his arms around my waist, pulling me against him, his chin on the top of my head. I lean back into his solid body, my eyes closed, drinking in the sense of security and warmth. My nostrils fill with the woodsy scent of his cologne. How long it has been since that smell washed through me like a warm wave! I see no one else, the scene filled with the power of the two of us. Sheryl is blissfully absent—a blustering wind invading someone else's marriage, ruining someone else's life.*

"The kids need us together," Vic whispers, and I feel his breath wisp through my hair. "Let's try again."

The kids need him, yes. But can I forgive him after all he's done to me, to us? I need him, too. I love him still.

And I hate him.

My mouth opens to answer . . .

A sudden howl swoops over us—a monstrous, black-winged bird, hurling blasts of air against our faces. I cringe, digging fingers into Vic's arms. His skin shimmers . . . breaks apart . . . evaporates. I am left alone, helpless. The bird beats away to hang in the air. Its curved beak opens as it glares at me, its eyes cold and obsidian. I swivel away, hands shielding my head. The monster screeches, screeches . . .

Wails ripped the night. My eyes flew open, mind hovering between dream and reality. The manic bird, the feel of

Vic's arms—so vivid one second ago—faded into oblivion. But the screeching remained. Slowly the sounds registered.

Sirens.

I turned my head to check the digital clock, a superstitious voice within whispering that the hour would make a difference. Sirens at noon could spell tragedy. Sirens after midnight . . . madness.

In my defense, I don't think I was fully awake.

The numbers glowed red in the darkness. Twelve-fifty, past the bewitching hour.

The sirens grew closer, one falling as another rose, yowling like wounded beasts. The final lingering shrouds of my dream dropped away. I pushed up on my elbows, veins pulsing, senses alert.

They were coming up Barrister Court.

I hauled myself from bed, tapped the base of my touch-sensitive lamp twice. It flicked on to medium power. The sirens writhed in my ears like hissing snakes. Red and blue lights flashed through the sheers on my window, tainting them the colors of blood and water. Surely the bearers of these sirens had taken a wrong turn. My father's house—I still couldn't think of it as my own—lay at the left end of the cul-de-sac, bordered by forest. Where could the sirens be going?

I raked back the sheers. Two black-and-white Sheriff's Department patrol cars and an ambulance careened to a halt outside the Willits' house across the wide street. *The Willits. What could be happening at the Willits'?* I shook my head to clear it. In the next instant I found myself jerking open a dresser drawer, pulling out jeans and a T-shirt. I threw them on with barely a thought, fingers trembling.

All sirens fell away. The ensuing silence was deafening. Car doors slammed, voices intermingled. For a moment I felt frozen, watching the scene. Then before I knew it, my feet were racing out of the bedroom and down the hall toward Kelly. At her door I tried to gather myself, force calmness into my expression, knowing that I failed miserably. I crossed the threshold of my twelve-year-old daughter's room.

"Mom!" Kelly sat up in bed, clutching the covers, her voice pinched and trembling. "What's going on?"

"I don't know, honey." I hurried to hug her. "They've stopped at Erin's house. You stay—"

"Erin!" The name burst from Kelly's mouth, and her eyes teared up. Erin was her new best friend—the girl who'd reached out to her when we moved to Grove Landing one month ago. Kelly sprang from her bed. "I have to go see—"

"No, Kelly." I placed firm hands on her shoulders, speaking rapidly. "Stay here. We can't get in the way. Just let me see what's going on first."

I heard bare feet ascending the massive curved wooden staircase that ended not far down the hall. My younger sister, Jenna, materialized in the doorway, clad in her cotton summer pajamas. A second later the thud of Stephen's feet echoed in the great room, one floor below. The feet trotted across the hardwood floor before I could stop my son. The front door opened and banged shut.

I slipped past my sister, knowing I had to stop Stephen from getting in the way of the officials dealing with whatever nightmare had befallen the Willits. A fifteen-year-old with a mind of his own would hardly be welcome. "Jenna, will you stay with Kelly? I'm going to see what's happening."

"Yeah, sure. Go."

I scurried down the stairs, fear for the Willits mingling with a selfish fear for myself. Traces of my dream snagged against my memory, like gauze over splintered wood. Vic making promises . . . then disappearing. For the millionth time I wished him back, despite all he'd done. I wasn't made to be without him. To raise two kids alone. Always so many crises to handle, and goodness knows I wasn't good at coping with any of them.

The soles of my feet smacked against the oak steps. How much faster I moved than the first time I'd descended that staircase, when I was sure I'd fall right through it. It was custom-made and ridiculously expensive, each polished step seeming to float with no backing, connected only by gnarled, thick logs on either side, and similarly sized handrails. By the time it reached the second floor, fourteen feet down, it turned one hundred eighty degrees. Certainly not the kind of stairs for small children. But perfect and fitting for my father's executive mansion of a log home.

Hitting the bottom of the steps, I ran across the great room to the front door—a good thirty-five feet. At the entryway I stopped to slide into the open-back shoes I'd left there, then flung myself outside.

Barrister Court is the width of two normal streets, designed for use by both cars and the private planes owned by each of the twenty-four homeowners of Grove Landing sky park. Across the street and down, I caught sight of the Willits' next-door neighbors, Al and Sandy Edinberger, emerging from their house. Other figures ran up the road, but I couldn't make out who they were. Radios crackled from the patrol cars. The flashing lights pulsed against trees, the road, the frightened faces of the Edinbergers as they cut across their yard toward the scene. A new siren wailed up the street, another patrol car carving out a parking place behind the ambulance. A deputy sheriff sprang from the car practically before the engine died. He headed for a rubbernecking Stephen, a few feet from the Willits' front yard.

"Back, please!" He held up both hands.

"Stephen," I called as I trotted down the front walk, "come here!" My voice sounded weak. Stephen ignored me. No surprise there.

Al Edinberger met me in the middle of the street. "What happened?"

I shook my head.

The memory hit then, clear and cold as ice water in my face. Erin at our house that afternoon, hanging out with Kelly: "My dad's gonna fly the plane to San Diego around two. Wanna come with me to say goodbye to him?"

Dave Willit was gone. Erin and her mom were alone in their house.

I brought a hand to my mouth, thoughts swirling as I surveyed the scene. Sweet Erin. And Lisa, so kind, so accepting of me and my motley crew. She had a manner about her that drew me in—an openness, a sense of embracing life as if each moment held new wonder. Lisa had brought over cookies as we were still unpacking, Dave and Erin trailing behind. She oohed and aahed over the house, noting with a pixie expression that she'd wanted for so long to take a peek inside once it was completed. Yet her words seemed void of the implication that my father had been less than neighborly to not invite her over, and she wouldn't hear of my apologies on his behalf.

The medical team and two sheriff's deputies had disappeared into the Willits' wood-shingle house. The paramedics carried a gurney. A tense silence fell over our street, punctuated only by the disembodied voices from the radios and nervous whispers among gathering neighbors. Had I slipped into some *Outer Limits* episode, where characters wait in a time warp for gruesome news?

I shifted from foot to foot. Stephen huffed. Shadowy figures moved across the windows of the Willits' lighted kitchen. None of them looked like they could belong to Lisa or Erin. More cars drove up, more figures of authority raked a look at the house, then strode up its steps. Three men in plain clothes, two dressed in jeans, as if they'd been pulled from bed. And a woman with short, curly, graying hair who looked to be in her fifties, in civilian slacks and shirt but sporting a vest with "Chaplain" on the back. A badge hung from a cord around her neck.

The deputy sheriff securing the area told us to retreat to our side of the street, out of the way of the responding vehicles.

"What's going on?" Al Edinberger demanded.

"We're not sure yet, sir. We have to finish checking things out."

Al shook his head and muttered under his breath. Stephen and I exchanged a grim glance.

I rubbed my arms. The July day had been hot, hot, but nighttime brought a chill to the air. The ebony sky, pocked with stars, hung low and threatening, a witch's face thrust toward earth to observe human tragedy with sneering delight. I fidgeted, tapping knuckles against my chin. Kelly and Jenna appeared at my side, dressed but without shoes. Kelly was crying. I put an arm around her shoulder and drew her close. As each minute ticked by, I knew with more certainty that something terrible had happened.

Think good thoughts, think good thoughts.

The night's events held an irony I couldn't deny. I'd moved from the San Francisco Bay Area to Grove Landing, northeast of Redding, California, to get away from the traffic, the crime, sirens in the night. Yet in all my years there, never had something like this happened on the very street where I lived.

Someone inside the Willits' house opened the door. I stared up into the entryway, trying in vain to perceive what lay beyond. Kelly dug her fingers into my arm, rising on her toes, neck craned. In the froth of light just inside the door, two paramedics appeared, carrying the gurney. As they crossed the porch, I frowned, willing my eyes to discern who lay upon it. I caught sight of white-blond hair, too light to be Lisa's. "It's Erin." The whispered words felt dry upon my tongue. The chaplain woman followed the gurney through the door. She took a few catch-up steps and drew near its side, taking Erin's hand. The group faced a long flight of stairs. Like many of the other homes in Grove Landing, the Willits' main level rose above a large garage with ceiling high enough to hangar an airplane.

"Erin!" Kelly cried. But her friend was unable to hear. Before I could stop her, Kelly broke away, bounding across the street toward the Willits' lawn. She hit the grass and nearly tripped, swaying into the deputy sheriff. He caught her, soothing, "Hey, hey, it's all right. You've got to stay back now."

"She's my friend, she's my *friend,*" Kelly protested, struggling. I ran to her side, pulling her away, apologies spilling from my mouth even as my eyes remained locked on Erin's pitiful figure being brought down the stairs.

"Keep her back, all right?" The deputy sheriff meant business.

"I'm sorry, I know she shouldn't—"

"Erin!" Kelly's cry tumbled through the night.

The rear paramedic stepped off the final stair onto the front walk.

"Almost there now, we're almost there," the chaplain told Erin. My jaw hung askew as I watched them make their way toward the ambulance. When they were no more than a car's length away, Erin turned her head to focus empty eyes upon Kelly.

"Erin, are you okay? What *happened?*"

Erin blinked, then let go of the woman's hand, her arms lifting toward Kelly like weakened magnets. Kelly rushed past the deputy sheriff and he let her go. I could see the trembling in Erin's limbs. Kelly reached for Erin's hands, grasping them hard in her fright. Erin's mouth creaked open but no sound came.

Think good thoughts, think good thoughts.

But my mind raced down terrifying paths, imagining, filling in the blanks. There were so many cars. Where was Lisa?

"Erin?" Kelly bent to hug her friend, then pulled back to study her.

Erin's cloudy gaze traveled over Kelly's face. I could almost feel the wrenching of the young girl's mind. The answer finally came, words like parchment paper, thin and dry and wrinkled at the edges.

"My mom . . . my mom . . ."

Something about the sound of her own voice, perhaps the words yet unspoken, broke through Erin's shock. Her mouth mushed into a wailing cry, her brows knitting. Her keen rose in the eerie night as her hands covered her eyes. Kelly leaned over to hug her again, the two girls' sobs intertwining until I could not tell where one's ended and the other's began.

The chaplain rubbed Erin's leg. She turned to me, her eyes full of empathy, then exchanged a glance with the deputy sheriff. He motioned for me to join them.

"I'm Gerri Carson," the woman said, "with the sheriff's chaplaincy program. You're a friend of Erin's family?"

"A neighbor." I pointed toward our house across the street. "Annie Kingston. What happened?"

She looked again to the deputy sheriff, as if asking him to answer.

"Erin needs to go to the hospital and have a bump on her head examined," he explained. "She's probably okay, but she fell and blacked out for a moment. When she woke up, she called 911."

I fought for understanding. "And Lisa?"

He took a deep breath. "An intruder got in the house. They struggled. She . . . didn't make it."

I stared at him, my mind going numb. "Lisa's *dead?*"

"I'm so sorry," Gerri said.

The words made no sense. This was simply not possible. Not here, not tonight, not someone I knew. "How can you be sure? I mean, maybe she's not really . . . maybe she just . . ."

Gerri's hands gripped my own, steadying me. A moment passed before she answered. "I understand."

I closed my eyes, tried to regulate my breathing.

"The detectives and paramedics did all they could for Mrs. Willit, Annie. But she could not be revived."

I turned away, the news wriggling through my stomach like an eel. Bending over the gurney, I tried to hug both girls at once. Erin let go of Kelly and clung to me, as if my very motherhood could bring back what had been ripped away from her.

"Would you like to ride with me to the hospital?" Gerri's voice remained calm. "You could be a comfort to Erin."

I thought of the ambulance. Such a frightening journey for a young girl. "Can I ride with her instead?"

Gerri hesitated.

"There's not much room in there," the deputy sheriff put in. "But under the circumstances—"

"She can go," one of the paramedics said, nodding. "We'll make room."

"Okay. Thanks." With Erin holding my shirt, I could not straighten. I eased her hands away and laid them over her chest. She grew quiet again, then still, as if her mind had slipped away to some distant place.

Jenna trotted over as the paramedics loaded Erin into the ambulance. Somehow I managed to form the words to tell her what happened.

"I'm going with her. I, uh . . . I can't think, Jenna."

"The kids, Annie." Jenna remained calm, as she always did. Capable, unflappable Jenna—a world and a half apart from me. "I'll take care of the kids."

I nodded.

"Isn't Erin's father gone?" Jenna pressed. "She said something to Kelly about him going to San Diego?"

"Yeah. To visit his sister after she had surgery. Something like that." I glanced at the ambulance. Erin was in place. I needed to follow. "I have to go." But I couldn't seem to move.

Jenna nudged me. "Go. I'll talk to the neighbors. Somebody needs to get Dave Willit; he'll be in no shape to fly himself home."

"Not you! We need you to take care of the kids."

"Okay, okay, not me. I'll be here. You just go. I'll . . . I'll talk to somebody about Dave and then bring the kids to the hospital, okay? Kelly will want to see that Erin's all right."

"Yes, good." My sister started to leave. A burst of clear thought fizzled in my brain, a single firework against muddied sky. "Jenna! See that lady?" I pointed at Gerri Carson's back. "Talk to her about getting Dave home."

I turned to climb into the ambulance, my legs shaky. The door slammed behind me.

Chapter 2

Somehow I managed to balance beside Erin's gurney as we sped toward Redding. The ambulance siren rose and fell like the wail of a mourner, wrapping itself around my soul. Somewhere behind us trailed Gerri's car. Jenna too would be following soon with Kelly and Stephen. The sounds and sensations meshed in my head like a metal net, weighting my ability to think. All I could do was hold Erin's hand and whisper empty reassurances. In the space of an hour our rural sky park, cut out of the forest and gentle hills just south of Lake Shasta, had become a place of horror and fear. Lisa Willit was dead. Her killer had escaped into the night.

A killer who could have entered any one of our homes.

Why had he chosen the Willits' place, way at the end of the road?

I knew that the sheriff's detectives were already at work in the Willits' house, laboring against the clock to gather evidence. With a decade of trial coverage as a courtroom artist, I had enough knowledge of crime scenes to picture all too vividly what would happen next. Not to mention my over-the-top imagination, which is known to flash full-color slides and movies of any subject upon the screen of my mind, like a projector in warp speed. This strange and ever vigilant quirk of mine is enough to drive me crazy.

In the past year I was astonished to see something akin to it when I stumbled across a new forensic series on television. The grimly detailed "flash" scenes in the show were innovative to TV but nothing new to me. My mind had subjected me to that kind of abuse for years. In fact, as I viewed that television show, I was convinced the writers had peeled off the top of my skull and peered inside.

Now the scenes flashed hard and fast, full of details that my mind added of its own accord . . .

A close-up of a roll of yellow crime-scene tape; the hands of a deputy sheriff slowly unwinding it to cordon off the Willits' property. There's a cut on the deputy's right index finger, the whitened outline of a wedding band now removed . . .

A plainclothes deputy in the Willits' house, leaning to examine a vague smear on the kitchen wall . . .

The form of a killer, phantomlike, fleeing into swirls of gray, consuming fog . . .

As if these pictures weren't enough to clog my brain, my father's features rose before me. For a burning second I felt almost glad he was dead. I'd loved him, feared him, revered him, disliked him. Finally I'd grown embarrassed of his cunning abilities in the courtroom, where he wooed juries as well as he'd wooed his mistresses over the years. The "ultimate defense attorney," he'd been called. Trent Gerralon was known for getting criminals—like Lisa's murderer—off free.

Though he was dead, my father's work lived on. If Lisa's killer was caught and had the bucks, he could always turn to my father's partner, Sid Haynes, who was still in the Bay Area. Sid had managed plenty of his own successes in the courtroom, including the much watched Edgar Sybee murder trial, which he'd taken over upon my father's sudden death. Another acquittal, of course.

I hoped whoever had killed Lisa was penniless. Only the rich afforded attorneys like Gerralon and Haynes. The rich with blood on their hands.

Stop it, Annie.

My father was my father. I should not malign the dead. Silently I apologized to his memory.

"I don't want to go to the hospital." Erin's feeble voice chased away my thoughts. "I want to call Daddy; I need to call Daddy . . ."

A paramedic soothed her, his large hand dark against her hair. He looked so young, with a long, angular face, one eyebrow slightly higher than the other. "Don't worry, somebody will talk to your dad. He'll get here as soon as he can."

"But I don't want to go—"

"We're just going to check you out, Erin. Make sure you're okay. You hit your head pretty hard when you fell."

"I'll stay with you, Erin." I stroked her forehead. "I promise not to leave you."

I exchanged a glance with the paramedic. He shook his head.

Without warning my brain popped in another sequence of film and turned on the projector. Up flashed a gruesome image of the scene now occurring in the Willits' house. A close-up of Lisa

lying where she fell, all privacy stripped away in the presence of exploring, exacting strangers. Her eyes are open and fixed, lips parted, spittle down the side of her mouth. Her colorless face

*lights in the flash of an investigator's camera. A few feet away a
plainclothes detective squats to view injuries, pointing without
touching to a contusion on her face . . .*

I squeezed my eyes shut, forcing the scene from my head.
How I wished I knew a god worth praying to.

We reached the hospital. I jumped out of the ambulance
and tried to keep out of the way. The emergency room reeked
of the clean of antiseptic, the dirt of disappointment and
shock. The angular-faced paramedic wheeled Erin toward a
room, detailing her vital signs and injuries to the attending
physician as I followed.

"I'm Doctor Strang." The physician held out his hand to
me. "You are . . ."

"A neighbor. Her dad's out of town right now. She needed
somebody."

He nodded. "You can stay near her as we examine her, if
you like."

"Thank you."

In the small examining room, the paramedic, doctor, and
nurse transferred Erin to the bed, their movements smooth
efficient. The paramedic gave me a wan smile as he left. "I
hope she's all right."

Erin had fallen again into an eerie calm and lay staring at
the ceiling. I stayed as close as possible while the doctor
looked her over. He was probably in his forties. Thin lips,
deep-set eyes. Small ears. My gaze fell to his hands, his
scrubbed cuticles, as they gently probed and pushed.

"Let's see how well you can bend and straighten this." He
coaxed Erin's left arm to move. She winced. "That hurt?"

"Yeah." Her voice sounded void, dead.

A sob rose in my chest. I turned away, forcing it back down, the dull beige wall of the room blurring. I could not bear to think of the pain Erin would face from losing a parent. My own children had lost their dad two years ago, and they'd been reeling from the emotional upheaval ever since. But they had not lost him to death. In those two devastating years, I often thought Vic's death would have been easier.

How naïve I had been.

Gerri Carson slipped into the room. One look at my expression and she took me aside. "Your family's going to be coming soon. They'll be in the waiting area. If this gets to be too much, you should go out there with them. I'll stay with Erin."

"No, no." I firmed my lips. "I don't want to leave her yet."

"Okay."

I took a couple of deep breaths as I studied the chaplain's face. She wore no makeup, this being the middle of the night. But for some reason I guessed she wasn't the type to wear it anytime. Her cheeks were plump like her body, her mouth wide, as if it had been stretched through smiling over the years. Something about this woman struck me. The way she stood, her face, her entire demeanor, spoke of calmness and peace. But it was not the peace of detachment, for her gray eyes were full of warmth and compassion.

"Did Jenna talk to you about Erin's dad?" I asked.

"Yes." Gerri flicked a glance over my shoulder. "The next-door neighbors—the Edinbergers, I believe?—they happened to have the contact information for Mr. Willit's sister. Sounds like they've watched over the Willits' house before, when the family's been down to San Diego. The police in that area are being called. An officer will go to the sister's house in person to tell Mr. Willit what happened. Meanwhile your neighbors are talking about who'll fly down and bring him home."

"Good news about that elbow, Erin." Dr. Strang's voice brought us back to her bedside. "Looks like it's only bruised." He looked at me. "I want to do a CT scan of her head to check for concussion. But we're waiting for contact with the father for approval."

"Let me see how that's going." Gerri crossed to the doorway. "It shouldn't be long; the detectives are aware you need to talk with him."

Long minutes passed. When Dr. Strang left the room, I stood by Erin's side and stroked her forehead. The girl lay dry-eyed, staring upward. Finally Gerri returned. She nodded at me, then spoke to Erin. "We've talked to your dad, honey. The doctor wants to take a picture of your head, and your dad said that's okay. It won't hurt. I can stay with you if you like."

No response. A single tear rolled down Erin's temple. I wiped it away.

"You want to go see your family now?" Gerri half whispered to me. "They're anxious to talk to you. I'll stay with her."

For a moment I fought with my conflicting loyalties. "Okay. Thanks." I squeezed Erin's shoulder. "Honey, I'm going to tell Kelly how you're doing. Then I'll be right back, okay?"

With a final, tugging look at her, I left the room.

Chapter 3

The emergency area was quiet—an antithesis to the whirl-wind I felt inside. With forced concentration I listened to the faint squeaking of my shoes against the tile floor as I headed toward the waiting room. On the way, I passed Dr. Strang talking to one of the detectives I'd seen at the Willits'. I caught the words *question her* and shivered. Erin was in no shape to be questioned anytime soon.

In the waiting room Kelly was sitting next to Jenna on a worn couch, her head on her aunt's shoulder. Stephen sprawled opposite them, his legs spread wide and one arm thrown across the back of the chair. He looked bored to tears. The fluorescent light cast a yellow-beige sheen on his scalp through the buzz cut of his hair, reminding me how much I hated his insistence on being nearly bald. Just because all his scurvy pals back in the Bay Area wanted to look like members of the Aryan Nation didn't mean he had to follow suit.

"Mom!" Kelly rushed to me, her eyes red. "How is she?"

"She's okay, honey, she's okay." I told them what had happened.

"Those sheriff people were everywhere on our street when we left." Stephen sniffed. "Killer's probably hiding in the woods behind our house."

"Shut up, Stephen!" Kelly pressed both hands over her ears and flung herself back on the couch.

"Thank you for your learned opinion." Jenna shot a hard look at her nephew. "Just what we need right now."

I surveyed my son, aware of the accusation behind his words. His dark, close-knit eyebrows were raised as he awaited my reaction, and he flexed his jaw to one side—a sure sign of his rebellion. I had seen Stephen do that a lot lately. Somehow I'd lost him in the last year. The pain from his father's abandonment had seeped like muddied waters into his soul. He'd stopped talking to me, turned to less-than-desirable friends and, I feared, drugs. Then I'd forced the move from the Bay Area, away from those friends. He hadn't forgiven me for that.

I ran a hand through my hair and turned to my sister. I had no energy to deal with my son's testiness. "What happened with getting Dave back here?"

"We had to find somebody who hadn't had a drink in the last eight hours. You know Wesley Darrel, lives off the taxiway?"

I shook my head.

"He said he goes to the same church as the Willits. He's got a Beech Baron that'll get him down to San Diego fast. He took Bryan Carney, a flight instructor who's familiar with all kinds of planes. Dave will come back with Wesley, and Bryan will fly Dave's plane back."

"Mom, I want to see Erin!" Kelly scooted to the edge of the couch.

"In a little while, honey. I'm going with her in a minute while they do the CT scan." I placed a palm on Kelly's cheek, reveling in her warmth, her health. Then I slipped away.

Turning the corner outside the waiting room, I nearly ran into a detective. "Oh! Sorry."

"My fault." He towered over me. I stand five feet five, so most men seem tall. But this guy had to be at least six three. "I'm Detective Ralph Chetterling. You came in with Erin Willit, right?"

"Yes. Annie Kingston." I looked up at him, that familiar feeling of defensiveness crawling up my spine. Even after his death, Trent Gerralon's legacy lived on within me. Those who had taken the pledge to fight for the law, to wipe criminals from the streets, didn't tend to respond too fondly when they heard my father's name.

"You know her pretty well?"

"Only since we moved to Grove Landing. But she's been over to our house a lot. She and my daughter became close friends pretty fast."

Chetterling nodded. He stood with feet planted apart, toes out, one hand resting on his hip. His big face seemed cut from a block of stone. His eyes were dark brown and small, his mouth thin. Large nose. His countenance reeked with the authority of his badge.

"Are you here to question Erin?"

"Yes. Soon as she's done with all her tests."

"Um, could I just say . . . I don't think she's up to it."

"I understand. But we have to do this as soon as possible. She's our only witness. Our progress is going to depend on what she can add."

"I know, but—"

"Ms. Kingston." He softened his voice. "I know all this is a horrible shock to everyone involved. But in a homicide, the first seventy-two hours are crucial. Still, I can assure you we'll do everything we can to take care of Erin. Gerri Carson, you met her?"

I nodded.

"She's a great help to victims and very knowledgeable about what they need. She'll be right with Erin the whole time."

"I want to be there, too. I won't get in the way, but I think Erin needs—"

"No problem. Anything it takes to make Erin more comfortable, we're willing to do. Okay?"

I crossed my arms, suddenly cold. "Okay."

The faint shush-shush of a rolling gurney sounded from down the hall. I turned to see an attendant wheeling Erin away for the CT scan. I hurried to catch up. Gerri came out of the examining room. "Are you going?" I laid a hand on the woman's arm.

"If you'd like."

"I wondered if you'd talk to my family. My daughter, Kelly? She could use some help."

"Absolutely." Gerri gave me a firm smile.

During the CT scan, Erin made not one sound. I shivered as I watched the girl's brain, her life center, reduced to flat pictures on a computer screen. Medical technology could be so cold.

The doctor said all the pictures looked normal.

"Physically she's okay." He watched Erin's face across the room as he spoke with me. "I see no reason to keep her. I know the detective wants to question her as soon as possible. She's able to walk. You want to take her back downstairs?"

I bit back my opinions about Erin being interrogated. "Sure." Crossing the room to where she lay, I placed a hand on her shoulder. "Honey, you're all done at the hospital now. The doctor says you can go."

The girl's eyes fluttered closed. I waited, watching her face. The light eyelashes against her faintly freckled skin; the mouth that smiled so quickly, now weighted at the corners. "Erin?" I smoothed her forehead with my fingers. "Can you get up and walk now? I'll take you down to see Kelly."

Without a word Erin sat up, then swung her legs to the floor. She let me help her stand, then hesitated for a moment, feeling for her balance. Doctor Strang followed us out of the room.

"I want to talk to my dad." Erin clung to my hand.

"Okay, honey, okay."

"I'll be calling him." Dr. Strang punched the down button at the elevator. "He's waiting to hear results of the scan."

Back at the registration desk, the doctor picked up an extra phone. Kelly was waiting in the hall and ran to meet her friend the moment Erin appeared. The girls hugged one another, Kelly's brown hair crushing against Erin's blond head. Chetterling hung nearby, talking in low tones with Gerri. Glancing at him, I felt a wave of frustration. Yes, he had a job to do, but couldn't it wait until morning?

"Mr. Willit?" the doctor said into the phone. "Dr. Strang here."

The words brought Erin's head up. She pulled away from Kelly and surged toward the phone, snatching it from the doctor's hands. *"Daddy!"* She sagged over the counter, the phone pressed to her ear, and burst into sobs. Gerri slipped to her side, patting her on the back.

Kelly began to cry. Stephen and Jenna popped out of the waiting room.

Detective Chetterling walked over, his face creased in sympathy. Quietly he told Jenna and me that he would now be questioning Erin.

There was no point in arguing.

The next five minutes blurred into colors and snippets of sound, like a movie tape forced through the reel. Gerri assured me they wouldn't push Erin any more than she could handle. Erin sobbed into the phone. Jenna talked to the detective about taking Erin home after the questioning. Chetterling spoke to Dave on the phone, obtaining permission to talk with his daughter. Details followed—who would go where and do what. I would ride with Erin in Gerri's car to the Sheriff Department's North Substation, where Erin would be questioned. Jenna would take Stephen and Kelly home.

"Lock all the doors, turn on the alarm!" I demanded. It would be the first time we'd used the alarm. Like too many homeowners, we'd planned to use it only if we left the house overnight. Apparently, the Willits had made the same horrible mistake. "And all of you, sleep in one room!"

"I'm not sleeping in anyone's room but my own," Stephen declared.

I whirled on my son. "Stephen, I'm not hearing it, you understand?"

Minutes later I was helping Erin to Gerri's car, trying not to think that my family was returning to a neighborhood disturbed by the sounds of investigating detectives, their slamming car doors and crackling radios.

A neighborhood that was no longer safe.

Chapter 4

We sat in a cramped office at the substation, an overhead light glaring far too cheerily for the darkness of this night. Detective Chetterling had pulled his chair out from behind the desk and placed it before Erin's. In his hands were a notepad and pen. Gerri and I were on either side of Erin, my hand on the girl's knee. She slumped in her chair, focusing empty eyes on the scuffed floor as she answered questions. Her fingers worked at the hem of her T-shirt.

"Okay." Chetterling shifted his position. "You told me you heard sounds from the office, like someone was opening drawers, looking for something."

"Uh-huh."

"And when you peeked out into the hall, you saw a beam from a flashlight, right? When you first saw the man, was he holding the flashlight?"

Erin picked at her shirt. "No."

"You're sure?"

"Yes."

I looked for clues on the detective's face. Hadn't they found a flashlight in the house?

"All right." He made a note. "I'd like you to think again about what he was wearing. Tell me what you remember."

Erin's foot raised from the floor, then plunked back down. "Black."

"Black what?"

"Black shirt."

"What kind of shirt?"

Erin shrugged. "I don't know."

"Did it have long sleeves or short sleeves?"

"Long."

"Any buttons?"

"Um . . . I don't think so."

The detective wrote in his notepad. "Was the shirt tucked into his pants or on the outside of them?"

"Outside."

"Okay. What did the bottom of the shirt look like?"

Erin seemed not to have heard. Finally she sighed. "It was all one length, like a T-shirt. But with long sleeves."

"Good, Erin. Now tell me about the pants."

"Black."

"Do you know what kind they were?"

Erin frowned at the floor.

"Were they tight or loose?"

Fear flicked across her face. She drew back, mouth twisting. "I think they were jeans."

Chetterling asked about the man's shoes. Erin faltered, three times saying she didn't know. Then she blurted, "The shoes were black." Minutes later she remembered something else. Whatever the reminding picture in her head, it was enough to cause her limbs to tremble. "Black gloves."

I slid an arm around her, exchanging a glance with Gerri. An intruder, clad all in black. Whoever he was, he hadn't planned on being discovered.

The detective let Erin rest for a moment. "Now, Erin," he said gently. "I need you to tell me exactly what happened between him and your mom. I know this is hard to think about, but it's very important. Okay?"

Erin drew in her shoulders, then gave a slight nod.

Prompted by Chetterling, she told them of the assault. Of a horror so unimaginable, I felt the dread of it in the pit of my soul. The detective led Erin to focus on how her mother fought back. Had she scratched the man's face? His hands? Had she bitten him? Had Erin seen any marks on the man?

She couldn't remember.

Finally, those questions complete, Erin looked exhausted and broken. For the first time during the interrogation, she began to cry. Gerri fetched her some tissues from the bathroom.

One more important part of the interview remained, Detective Chetterling said. At the house, Erin had told them a little about what the man looked like. They needed to talk about it some more. So the people looking for this man would be able to find him soon.

"No." Erin shook her head. "No, no, no."

"Please try, okay? We just want you to try, that's all."

Erin turned and buried her face in my chest. I held her, locking eyes with Gerri. Sorrow creased the woman's forehead. I saw her mouth one word. *Jesus.* It seemed a prayer rather than a curse.

After a minute Erin pulled back and said, "His eyes were blue! I saw them when he looked at me like he was gonna kill me. They were bright blue!"

A startling thought sped through my mind. If Erin had looked into the man's face, why *hadn't* he killed her? It was a miracle she was alive.

Erin threw herself back into my arms and gasped muffled words into my shirt. "He had . . . blond . . . hair."

"What kind of blond?" Chetterling pressed. "Light blond, yellow blond?"

"Y–yellow."

"Good, Erin. What else can you tell me about his hair?"

Erin shook her head vehemently. Chetterling looked to Gerri, defeat pulling at one side of his mouth. "Would you get Mike in here now? I think I heard him come in."

Gerri nodded and rose. Chetterling moved behind the desk and turned on a computer.

"You have a computerized Identi-KIT?" I asked.

Surprise flicked across Chetterling's face. "Yeah. You familiar with it?"

"Enough to know what it is." I hesitated, one hand rubbing Erin's back. "You don't have anyone who can draw composites?"

"Used to." Chetterling watched the computer screen. "Andy Garisinsky. Great guy. A deputy sheriff. He was killed a year ago in the line of duty."

My eyes closed. "I'm so sorry to hear that."

There was too much tragedy in the world.

Gerri returned with another plainclothes detective, apparently in his thirties. One side of his brown hair stuck out, uncombed.

"Erin, I'm Mike Haller. I would like you to help me figure out what the man you saw looked like. We have a computer we can use and it's not hard. Would you sit beside me at the computer? I'll show you what to do."

She stared at the floor.

Chetterling leaned back in his chair and rubbed his eyes. I pointed to myself, seeking his permission. He gestured with his hand. "Go ahead."

"Erin." I squeezed her shoulder. "Let's go over there and sit down, okay? I'll go with you."

Zombielike, Erin allowed herself to be helped from her chair to a different one at the computer. For the next fifteen minutes Haller tried his best to get Erin to choose from eyebrow shapes, noses, mouths. As different components were chosen, they could be put together to create a face, modifying and perfecting as the process went along. But Erin would point to nothing, even though she fixed her gaze upon the screen. Finally Haller leaned back with a sigh and shook his head.

There was nothing left to do but let Erin get some rest. Haller shut down the computer, suggesting to Erin that maybe they could try again tomorrow. Then he left.

"Erin—" Gerri knelt before the girl—"I'll bet you could use a trip to the bathroom. I'll show you where it is."

With no expression Erin trailed Gerri out the door.

"Don't you find it surprising," I ventured when they were out of earshot, "that the killer let Erin live?"

Chetterling inhaled. "Yeah. I've been thinking the same thing. Maybe he just couldn't bring himself to kill a young girl. It's a question worth thinking about." He opened his notepad to a new page and jotted in it. "Okay, I need to ask you some questions, too. As we're doing with all the neighbors."

"I don't know what good I'll be." I sighed. "I didn't see or hear anything."

"Before we get to that, can you tell me anything about what Dave Willit does for a living? He apparently works out of his home."

"He owns commercial real estate. You know Shasta Station in south Redding, that strip mall with all the shops? He owns that, and another one on the north side, I think. Maybe some other places, too."

Chetterling wrote in his notebook. "Ever hear him or his wife mention trouble with a tenant?"

"Nothing. They didn't talk about his work. The only reason I know anything is because I noticed he worked from home and asked Lisa what he did."

Vividly the memory of that conversation jolted through me. Lisa

leaning against the beige granite kitchen counter, the back of one hand resting upon her hip. Wearing a pink T-shirt that sets off her light skin and hair. Behind me the coffemaker sputters, the aroma of the warm liquid seeping into the air. "So tell me about you," Lisa says, smiling. To her right on the wall hangs a hand-painted plaque that reads, "As for me and my house, we will serve the Lord." I wonder about that. I can hear Erin's voice filtering from her bedroom down the hall as she chats with Kelly . . .

My throat tightened. "And one more thing. Lisa helped him do the secretarial stuff."

"Okay." Chetterling nodded. "What about any unusual activity in the area the last few days? See anybody driving or walking around that you didn't know?"

"I don't know too many people in the neighborhood yet, so I couldn't say who belongs and who doesn't."

"I see. How long have you lived at the house?"

"About a month. It was my dad's second home. He had a heart attack about four months ago and passed away. I live there now with my kids, Kelly and Stephen."

"You're divorced?"

"Yes. Two years ago."

"Where is the children's father?"

"Dallas. He . . . married the girl he took up with when we were still together." Bitterness crept into my tone. "Then his company transferred him."

Chetterling wrote in his notepad, showing no reaction. "How about your sister that I talked to at the hospital. Jenna, right?"

"Yes. She still lives and works in the Bay Area, but she flies up on weekends." The Bay Area was about four hours' drive from Redding but less than an hour in the plane.

"Are you a private pilot, too?"

"No. My dad was. Jenna got her love of flying from him."

"And your mother?"

I focused on the black night through the room's single window. "She died when I was sixteen."

"I'm sorry." Chetterling let the words hang in the air for a moment. "You said your sister comes up weekends. Why didn't she return last night?"

Oh, wouldn't Jenna love that question. "Her work's been cut to four days a week, Tuesday through Friday. She's not happy about it but there's nothing she can do. She works in Redwood Shores, on the northern border of Silicon Valley, for a software company. Jenna's in their marketing department. But, well, you know how hard the tech industry's been hit. She's lucky to have a job at all."

Chetterling wrote down my answers. "All right. Back to the neighbors for a minute. Didn't you visit your dad during the years he owned the house? Enough to get to know them?"

I hesitated. "I only came up twice. We weren't all that close."

The detective remained poker-faced. "Why did you move here?"

"I was tired of the pace of the Bay Area. Just wanted a change."

He jotted in his notebook. "All right. Do you work?"

"No, not since we moved."

"What did you do in the Bay Area?"

A long sigh escaped me. Where were Gerri and Erin? "I was a courtroom artist for ten years. I covered a lot of trials. That's why I know about the Identi-KIT. You hear lots of stuff over the years through testimony. Get to know things about police work."

He studied me. "You know faces."

Footsteps sounded outside the door. "Yes." I tried to smile. "It goes with the territory, I guess—always studying features."

Chetterling smiled at Erin as she and Gerri stepped through the door. Erin's eyes drooped. As horrific as the night had been, sheer exhaustion was taking its toll. I looked to the detective, pleading on my face. "Can I take her now?"

"Just one more thing. Your father's name?"

I suppressed a cringe. Of all the questions to end on. I pushed to my feet, forcing myself to look the detective in the eye. "Trent Gerralon."

His eyebrows rose. "Gerralon? The defense attorney?"

I crossed to Erin, feeling the detective's gaze upon me. It was not just my imagination—distaste had seeped into his tone.

"Yes." I made no attempt to keep the defiance from my voice. "But don't worry. I didn't like him, either."

# # # #

Twenty minutes later I sagged in the backseat of Gerri's car, Erin already asleep on my shoulder. Detective Chetterling's card was stuffed in my pocket. "Call me anytime if something comes up with Erin," he'd told me. Gerri had also scribbled her cell phone number, apologizing that she'd run out of business cards in her wallet and had forgotten to replace them.

The digital clock on the dashboard read 3:58 a.m. We drove through the silent streets of Redding, the peacefulness surreal. Streetlamps washed against the car windows like spotlights over a prison yard. Did Lisa's killer live in town? He could be out there somewhere, skulking by night, pounded into anonymity by day through the beat of traffic and thousands of feet.

"I'll be around tomorrow," Gerri said quietly. "I'll be checking in on the Willits, and I'd also like to see how you're doing, if that's all right."

"Sure. Thank you."

We turned off Skypark Road and rolled up Barrister Court. Lights were still on in the Willits' house, cars parked out front. I averted my eyes from the yellow crime-scene tape, my mind projecting another sequence of sadistic slides. Gerri made a U-turn in the cul-de-sac and drew up to the curb in front of my father's rambling log house. Even on this horrendous night, it pulled at our eyes.

"Your place is so beautiful," Gerri said.

Your place. I could not get used to that. "Thanks."

Gerri turned to gaze at Erin, no doubt wishing, as I did, that we didn't have to wake her. "Let me help you get her out." She turned off the engine.

I summoned my energy to focus on one final task for the night: leading Erin inside without allowing her a glimpse of the violation that had befallen her home.

Chapter 5

Stupid. Stupid, stupid, *stupid!*

The man swayed through his expensive house, kicking designer furniture, punching a hole in the wall with his fist. He could smell his own stinking sweat. It dripped down his head, down his armpits in rivulets that reeked of his own *stupid* fate.

"Aah!" He bashed the wall again, ignoring the pain to his knuckles, then swore in the dimly lit room. His frightened cat sprang from her hiding place to scramble across his shoes toward the kitchen. Furious, he lashed out a foot, catching the feline in its side. It let out a wail, tumbled over, then shot underneath the couch.

That's right, cat, you'd better hide. I find you, you're dead.

He prowled around the living room like a caged lion, then threw himself on the couch. The perfectly coiled springs underneath him whined in protest. He hoped he'd sat right on top of the cat. He hoped the couch bottom had sagged enough to kill the worthless beast.

Stretching out his arms, he pummeled the back of the couch with both fists. How could he have been so clumsy in that house? Especially after his business and personal responsibilities had made him wait so long to get up there. He'd been smart enough to get in, oh yeah. Smart enough to find the house in the first place. Then he bangs around in there like some one-handed idiot. And the few things he gets a good look at don't begin to fit his needs.

So the snoopy woman shows up. And her kid. And he panics. He, who never panics about anything. Calm and cool, that's how he's known. Can handle anything. And watch out to those who cross him.

So why'd he do it? He could have just run past the woman, slipped into the night.

But not really. *Chill out, man. How far would you have gotten while she was calling the cops? You needed time to get to the car, race like a demon out of there. You did what you had to do.*

He grimaced, narrowing his eyes at the plush weave of his carpet. He'd just had the whole house recarpeted last month. A few small stains here and there and he'd decided to replace it all. Pristine—that's how he liked his surroundings.

Now he'd have to fix the holes in the wall. Repaint the room. As if he didn't have enough to worry about.

It was all that woman's fault.

Was she dead?

He hadn't meant to kill her, just slow her down for a while. He felt a chilling smile tug at the corner of his mouth. Well. Maybe he had. He held out his hands, fingers spread and curved, and stared at them. Remembering the power in those hands as they'd crushed neck cartilage. So easily done. So . . . satisfying.

His hands returned to fists, sinking into the couch cushions.

Well, good for him, but he hadn't gotten what he wanted, and he needed it. Badly. He could count on only one small thing, one favor in this whole rotten universe that had turned against him since the day of his birth: they wouldn't know it was there. He'd have to be oh so careful next time. No doubt trigger-happy cops were all over that area. But then, he'd eluded 'em for years.

And he always would.

Always.

Jail was not an option, not now, not ever. He'd kill anybody, he'd die himself before he spent time in a prison. Small. Dark. Claustrophobic. Like the closet his daddy had put him in every time he was bad. Every time he wet his pants or fell asleep watching cartoons or didn't hold his head just right. Oh, and hadn't his daddy shoved him in that closet, laughing. Cackling like a clown. And wouldn't the guards at a jail do the same thing. Smirk at him, snicker and snort when he begged to get out, when he pleaded to feel the air.

One night in a jail cell and he'd go stark raving mad, start tearing off his own skin.

But there was another reason, even more important than himself. His little sister needed him. Stuck away in that nursing home, unable to move the paralyzed body their father had left her with. Couldn't even feed herself. Could talk only with painstaking effort. And the pneumonia she'd suffered in the past two months. He'd been scared to death he'd lose her. But the way she smiled at him when he visited every day. Her pinched face would light up like the sun. She thought he was still in his old line of work, hobnobbing with the elite. It would kill her to hear it was all a lie. That he'd ended up in jail.

And jail is what could happen to him if he didn't get what he needed. If he didn't retrieve what was never meant to exist in the first place.

Brink of Death

He cursed again into the night, swearing vengeance on the man who'd begun this cosmic fiasco. Oh, the guy was safe enough for now, but just wait. The fool's day of reckoning would come.

After he'd gotten what he needed from that house.

And may the gods help anybody—*anybody*—who stood in his way.

Chapter 6

My eyes opened as if they were weighted. I aimed a slow look at the clock.

Shortly before seven.

Was it only six hours ago I'd awakened as sirens screamed in the night? Running a hand across my face, I turned to check on the girls. They lay beside me in the king-size bed, Kelly in the middle. Both still asleep.

I could hardly believe Erin was here. My mind couldn't quite catch up to all that had happened. How I wished the dreadful events were nothing more than a nightmare.

From the great room I heard the dim chime of the grandfather clock as it struck the hour. I could imagine the sound of its pendulum as it swung. *Tick-tock, tick-tock.* Six hours. The minutes were passing—those critical minutes that, as Detective Chetterling had said, make up the critical seventy-two hours after a homicide. Maybe Dave's return, as hard as it would be for him, was the key to finding Lisa's killer. Dave, more than anyone else, would know who might want something in his office so badly.

I had to get up but couldn't find the energy. Instead I lay staring at the high wooden-beam ceiling of my bedroom. This was where I'd stayed the few times I'd visited my father since the house was built five years ago. That familiarity, and my desire to be close to Kelly, had prompted me to choose this largest guest room instead of the master suite on the main floor. Jenna had taken that for her own, thanking her lucky stars that she, the daughter who didn't even live here full-time, ended up with the fanciest digs.

Oh. A memory popped into my head. *The telephone.*

Because this room had been for guests, it hadn't come equipped with a phone. For some reason every time I went to town, I kept forgetting to buy another handset. I'd promised myself to do that today.

Now it would just have to wait.

I looked at the clock again. Were Jenna and Stephen still asleep? Last night I'd checked to see where Stephen slept, and found him in one of the guest rooms on the other side of the upper floor, above the kitchen. I could imagine the fight it must have taken to get him there. But no way would feisty Jenna have given in. Stephen's bedroom was on the basement level—the easiest place for an intruder to target. The six-thousand-square-foot house was built on a slope, two floors visible from the front, three floors visible in the back. The main level on this home wasn't raised above a hangar and garage, those areas being built off the kitchen. All the rooms on the basement level had large windows facing the back lot, and the rec room had a sliding glass door that stepped out onto a deck.

I pictured Lisa's killer entering—and exiting—through the sliding glass door leading to their back deck. Down those stairs and into the forest, sluicing into the night like some pirate ship in dark seas.

Would we ever again feel safe in this house?

Vic told me I shouldn't move here. As if he had the right to tell me anything.

Vic.

At the thought of him, my built-in projector clicked into action, playing the scene from another bedroom, another time, the film so worn that the picture fuzzed at the edges. He

stands in the bedroom of our home in San Carlos, pulling off his tie with grim intensity at the end of a long workday. The April sun is beginning to set, trailing fingers of light across his profile. Vic's face seems set in stone, his mouth tight and drawn. I sit on the edge of the bed, heart skipping, knowing with a wife's sixth sense that some terrible pronouncement is about to fall from his lips. "It's time I told you," he says, the words matter-of-fact, clipped. Utterly cold. "I'm leaving the marriage." He slips out of the tie and leaves it dangling from his fingers as he has done so many days, months, years, before. "And before you can ask the inevitable question, yes, there's someone else. I'll be moving in with her. I'll see the kids often, of course . . ." The words go on but I don't hear them, don't see my husband, don't even feel. I've turned wooden, hollowed, my thoughts the color of air.

I put a hand over my eyes, then hoisted myself from bed to pad to the bathroom, where the clothes I'd taken off mere hours ago lay. Just before slipping out of the bedroom, I remembered the burglar alarm. I glanced at the keypad on the wall by the bed. The red light was on. Jenna must still be asleep. Once in her room last night, she'd set the alarm to its highest level so no one could walk through the house with-out setting off one of the many sensors. When I arrived home,

I'd turned off the alarm, using the main keypad in the kitchen, then turned it on again in my bedroom.

A bedroom complete with burglar alarm pad but no telephone. I would really have to fix that.

At the keypad I punched in the code. The red light flicked to green.

# # # #

Eight-thirty.

Jenna and I slumped at the kitchen table over mugs of coffee. Even after such a night, my sister managed to look beautiful. Life just isn't fair. Jenna's face is heart-shaped; mine is more like round. Her eyes are large, a stunning velvet brown with long lashes. Mine are . . . I'm not quite sure. Half hazel, half muddy gray. At thirty-three and with perfect skin, Jenna can do without the makeup she usually wears. Unlike yours truly, who needs the full works to appear half attractive.

Well. I have seven years of life on Jenna and much more hard experience.

Through the large front windows I could see cars coming and going from the Willits'. Detective Chetterling had promised not to bother us until Dave Willit returned. We would know when he and Wesley Darrel arrived through their radioed approach. Jenna's scanner sat on the table, tuned to the 122.8 frequency used by Grove Landing flyers.

"Awful quiet out there." I aimed a look at the scanner. The sound of airplane engines was common in our neighborhood.

"Everyone's still in shock." Jenna pushed her thick auburn hair behind her ears. "Besides, the detectives were spreading the word last night for people to stay put as much as possible. They want to question everyone."

"So you're not leaving today?"

She shook her head. "I'll call work. Tell them I may not be in tomorrow either."

"Grove Landing traffic," a muffled voice came over the scanner. Jenna turned it up. "Baron three-nine-two-Hotel-Uniform, five miles to the southeast of runway three-zero. We'll be entering the pattern for full stop. Grove Landing."

"Baron. That's got to be Wesley and Dave." Jenna pushed back her chair.

A flash of movement through the window caught my eye. Another car was stopping at the Willits' house. The door pushed open and Ralph Chetterling got out. His head tipped upward; he must have heard the plane. Such timing the man had.

The detective's final question still rang in my ears. It occurred to me that he probably wished Trent Gerralon's daughters lived anywhere but in his jurisdiction—as if the very blood in our veins could somehow curse his bringing Lisa's killer to justice.

I did not share my thought with Jenna, who would have called it stupid. But then, *she* wasn't the daughter who'd frequented courtroom halls, trying to melt into nothingness when overhearing diatribes of our father's defense tactics. I'd been forced to cover his trials—ironically for me, the most media-watched and therefore the highest in demand for courtroom sketches. I'd drawn my father's face more times than I could count—the Roman nose, square jaw, his trademark salt-and-pepper curls. The flaring nostrils of his indignation, the raised right brow of his cynical disbelief. Few people knew who I was; the members of the media who bought my drawings certainly did not. Vic had given me one lingering gift: his last name. I avoided my father in the courtroom, in the halls, and he avoided me. All for the good of my career, of course. I was glad for the excuse and, although he would claim otherwise, I think my father was, too. I knew too many of his secrets, his betrayals of my mother as Jenna and I were growing up, for him to like me.

Chetterling glanced again at the sky, then headed up the Willits' front steps. Before long he'd be at our door.

I sighed. "Guess I'd better wake Erin up."

Chapter 7

Tick-tock. Eight fifty-five.

I stood on my front walk, watching a very different Dave Willit climb out of Wesley Darrel's car. Dave looked like he'd aged a decade overnight. His back was rounded, clothes rumpled, his blond hair matted. Grief creased his attractive face, his eyes red-rimmed and worn. One look at him and all words of solace melted from my tongue. What could I possibly say to comfort this man?

I hung back as Chetterling introduced himself, Dave's focus wandering like some shocked soul along the crime-scene tape around his house. Erin burst through our door and ran, crying, into her father's arms. Chetterling and I turned away, affording them what privacy we could.

The morning marched on, full of logistical details and people going and coming. Dave and Erin needed to go to the Sheriff Department's North Substation—Dave for questioning and Erin for another try with the Identi-KIT. Gerri Carson arrived as promised to offer help, her chaplain vest looking crisp over a green blouse. The Willits' family members would be arriving—grandparents, sisters, brothers, aunts. All but Dave's sister, who wouldn't be able to leave the hospital. There would be people to pick up at the Redding Airport, all needing places to stay. I offered one guest bedroom for a couple who would be here the next day. Stephen was sleeping in the other guest room, and I could hardly suggest that someone stay downstairs in his regular room when I considered it too dangerous for my own son.

Meanwhile countless people from New Life, the Willits' church in Redding, began showing up. All the food they brought went into my kitchen until the Willits' house could be reopened in a few hours—restored from a crime scene to masquerade as a home. Funeral arrangements had to be made, a casket chosen. Neighbors sought me for details. Hadn't I gone with Erin to the hospital the night before? It seemed I was needed on every side, and my head spun. In the midst of this, Kelly proved clingy and fearful, not wanting me out of her sight. Stephen was no help at all. One look at all the commotion, and he retreated to the lower level to lose himself in computer games.

Tick-tock, tick-tock, nagged the grandfather clock as it ate away at the seventy-two hours. *Please, please,* I prayed to nothing as Chetterling drove Dave and Erin away, *let Dave remember something that will help.*

Obvious frustration slacked the detective's face when the three of them returned a few hours later. As I headed out the front door to greet them, I spotted Gerri Carson coming from the Edinbergers' house. She reached Dave and Erin, speaking to them quietly.

"Do you need a drink?" I offered Chetterling as he climbed out of the car. He flicked a look at the Dave-Gerri-Erin trio and nodded, no doubt seeing through my ploy to pull him aside.

Jenna joined us in the kitchen as I fetched the detective a glass of ice water. "What can you tell us?"

Chetterling placed the thumb and index finger of one hand against his cheeks and pressed. It occurred to me that he probably hadn't slept at all since the murder. "Erin couldn't do the Identi-KIT. She still seems just . . . shut off from it. We're not going to get very far without a composite."

"Do you think she'll be able to do it later?" Jenna asked.

He shrugged. "I've seen people unable to do anything but stare at the wall when they're first questioned. Then in an hour or two they're able to talk. With kids it's different. They can't be pushed, and it becomes a real balancing act, putting their needs first while trying to proceed with the investigation."

"Remember that young girl, Mary Katherine, in Salt Lake City?" Jenna stood at the table, a hand on her hip. "Elizabeth Smart's little sister. Wasn't it some four months after Elizabeth was kidnapped that she finally remembered the face of the man and identified him to police?"

Chetterling gazed into his glass. "That's true. You can't push kids to remember. The detectives in that case told Elizabeth's parents just that." He looked up with a sigh. "But we don't have four months. By that time the killer's trail will be so cold . . ."

"Did Dave have any idea who could have done this?" I asked.

"Not one."

My sister put a finger to her lips. "What evidence did you find in the house?"

I searched Chetterling's face, sensing his hesitation to answer. For the first time I noticed a tiny scar on his left temple. He focused again on his glass.

"Not much. No fingerprints. As your sister may have told you, he had gloves on. We did find some black fibers under

Mrs. Willit's fingernails, most likely from his shirt or the gloves. We've sent them to be analyzed. And we cast a shoe print in the dirt off the back deck. Looked like he was moving pretty fast when he came off the last stair and hit the ground, so that one's not real clear. We also lifted a shoe print on the deck stair, going up—a better one. That's about all I can tell you."

I was right—the killer had come through the Willits' back sliding glass door. "No DNA anywhere? No hair left or a piece of skin?"

He surveyed me for a moment. "We've still got the autopsy."

I felt a chill down my spine. Yes, they still had the autopsy. But they should have had so much more. All night at the Willits' house and the detectives had come up with so little. I could hear the defense's argument against one piece of evidence: "The shoe prints match a brand worn by half the county!"

Unless the bottom was worn enough to have its own distinctive markings . . .

Chetterling placed his glass in the sink and turned to go. The autopsy was scheduled for one o'clock, he said, and he needed to be there.

Before long two large groups of the Willits' friends arrived, bringing more food. They milled in the street, gift bearers barred from their destination, until I coaxed them all to unburden themselves in our kitchen. "Please stay and eat," I encouraged them, seeing how Dave took comfort in their company. "It's time for lunch and everyone's brought so much."

Gerri Carson assumed efficient control of our kitchen, laying out the casseroles and pouring everyone drinks. She seemed to sense that I was overwhelmed, and I felt grateful for her help.

An older woman with a wrinkled face and fingers twisted from arthritis told me the crowd was from Dave's church in Redding. A slim man in his fifties with a jutting chin introduced himself as Pastor Jim Storrel. As they all talked in the kitchen, spilling into the great room, strange comments about God and his grace, and his strength in our weakness, filtered through the air, as foreign to me as fairy dust. How could they believe half of what they said? Where had God's "grace" been when Lisa needed it most?

Dave did not eat. How could he, while ten miles away his wife's body was being cut open, her organs lifted out and weighed? My mind flashed a scene of the coroner

bending over the body, the intermingling smells of blood, steel, and chemicals tainting the air. Instruments clink. The coroner's white-gloved hand scribbles notes . . .

I turned away from the array of casseroles on the counter.

Folks picked at their food, talking in low tones. Erin and Kelly had disappeared upstairs, saying they weren't hungry. Dave sat at the kitchen table, eyes roaming the wood as if clues to this nightmare were imbedded within its grains.

In time a detective came over, pulling him aside. He wanted to escort Dave through the house, he explained. Maybe Dave would see something, perhaps certain papers disturbed in his office, that would trigger a thought of who may have done this.

Dave nodded, his expression patterned with pain. Conversation in the room lulled as all eyes fastened upon him.

The pastor walked over to rest a gentle hand on his shoulder. "You need someone with you?"

Dave looked not at the man but through him. "I can't go over there."

Storrel watched his face. "Want us to pray with you?"

He nodded.

Folks pulled to Dave's side, surrounding him, every one reaching out to touch him. Jenna and I exchanged a nonplused glance, then sidled well out of the way. Gerri stuck with us, as if she realized our discomfort. The pastor prayed aloud, asking God to strengthen Dave as he completed his task. When the pastor's voice fell, others' rose, beseeching God in a way that made my chest both compress in doubt and swell with yearning. Not that I believed a word of the prayers would help. If God existed, he didn't seem to pay us wretched mortals much heed. But those people seemed to think so. And most important, the prayers seemed to matter to Dave. When all petitions ceased, he thanked everyone, tears in his green eyes, then turned to the detective.

"Okay. I'm ready."

The church folk began leaving soon after that, each one taking my hand or Jenna's, hugging us, spilling thank-yous for what we were doing for the Willits. Gerri remained till all had gone, then set about cleaning the kitchen.

"Please don't." I took a plate from her hands. "You've done so much already."

She shrugged. "Glad to do it. I know all this is a lot for you. Oh, before I forget." She pulled a card from her pocket and handed it to Jenna. "Please call anytime if you need me. You've got my cell phone number, but here's my church office number, too."

"You work at this church?" Jenna gazed at the information. "Covenant Chapel?"

Gerri's smile bordered on impish. "Yup. I serve as a part-time assistant pastor for counseling."

"So how did you end up being a chaplain?" Jenna affixed the card to the refrigerator with a magnet in the shape of an airplane. Next to it, under a similar magnet, lay Detective Chetterling's card.

"I wanted to serve the whole community of Redding in some way. I joined the program four years ago."

We talked about the different services she'd provided to help crime victims as well as stressed law enforcement officials. Gerri even had us laughing as she related a story about turning in an illegal weapon at the request of a woman who'd discovered it in her elderly father's apartment. "It folds up," the woman told her. Gerri, knowing nothing about guns, planned to carry it to the police station in a tote bag, thinking it couldn't be more than a foot long.

"Well, the butt of the gun folded up against the barrel," she said, "but the thing was still a good three feet. The gal wrapped it in a towel, but it stuck way too far out of my tote bag. I put it up under my arm, trying to hide it as I slunk out of that apartment building. Imagine if someone had seen me and called the police!"

"Surely you just didn't walk into the station like that." I shook my head.

"Oh, goodness no. I called ahead of time to warn them I'd be bringing the weapon. They told me to leave it in the trunk and fetch a police officer to get it."

"Were you scared?" I asked. "I'd be terrified. I *hate* guns."

Gerri pulled her mouth wide. "Well, there must be something weird in me, 'cause I felt downright excited about carrying all that power. Later that day I got dressed up in my full police chaplain uniform and went back down to the station to have my picture taken with it."

She gave us an irresistible grin.

"That's quite a lady," Jenna commented as Gerri drove away a few moments later.

Tick-tock. The grandfather clock struck 3:45.

"She sure is." Gerri's personality was a unique blend of humility, capability, and humor. I couldn't quite put my finger on why her presence seemed so calming. She had . . . something.

"Okay. Back to work." I headed toward the kitchen to start putting away food, my mind imagining what Dave might discover during his escort through the crime scene.

Chapter 8

Despondency settled over me as I stacked plates and took them to the counter. Lisa had been dead less than sixteen hours, and already the investigation looked bleak. Somehow we were going to have to live with this terror of the unknown.

How I dreaded the night.

"This isn't going to end anytime soon, Jenna."

She clamped a sheet of foil around a casserole dish. "You need to help."

Uh-oh. Her tone held that low thrum, the one that signaled the pronouncement of some formidable action I must take. Something that would rock my world, push me into the slippery unknown like a fledgling skater on ice. She'd sounded like this the first time she warned me to watch my trusted husband a little more closely. And when she told me Stephen looked like he was doing drugs.

My back stiffened. I made no reply.

Jenna leaned against the tile counter. "You're an artist, Annie. And Erin knows and trusts you. You should have a session with her, see if she can give you a description of the guy. *You* draw the composite."

I blinked. "Where on earth did this come from? I draw faces I can *see*, remember? I'm no forensic artist. I have no ability in that field whatsoever."

"Just because you haven't done it doesn't mean you can't."

"Oh, yes it does."

"No, it doesn't."

I tipped back my head and surveyed the ceiling.

"Okay, fine." Jenna was used to arguing with me. She knew all the moves. "Maybe you won't be able to do it. But there's no loss in trying."

"Jenna, Erin couldn't come up with a description even when she had eyes and noses to choose from."

"Maybe the detectives just don't know how to work with her. Maybe showing her face parts is not the way to go."

"That's their *job*. I'd expect them to know what they're doing."

"All right, they know what they're doing. It still hasn't worked."

"And it wouldn't work with me either."

Jenna folded her arms. "You don't know that."

"Yes, I do."

"Oh, for heaven's sake, Annie, you sound like a three-year-old! Would you just listen? You've got an amazing talent. The media in the Bay Area always wanted to use your drawings over other artists'. Now your abilities could possibly help this investigation. And you're refusing to even try."

Refusing to try? That was below the belt. "Jenna, I *can't* help! I can't pull some hidden face out of somebody's mind. Especially a traumatized child's. I've never done anything like that. It takes special training and I don't have it."

"Try it anyway. Under the circumstances, what have you got to lose? What do any of us have to lose?"

"Plenty." I dug my fingers into the roots of my hair. "Look. I'd probably draw a totally wrong face. Then all those detectives would be searching for someone who didn't exist. Talk about hurting the investigation!"

Jenna sighed. "Annie, that's dumb and you know it. If you draw the face wrong, Erin won't recognize it. End of story, and nothing lost for trying. But if you happen to do it right, there's a whole lot gained."

I smacked the faucet on and scrubbed a fork. Why couldn't my sister see that what she was asking was out of the question? The search for Lisa Willit's killer ending up on *my* shoulders? When the detectives themselves hadn't managed to get anywhere? How absurd! So I'd drawn some half-decent pictures in the courtroom. That didn't involve one hundredth of the kind of responsibility she was trying to heap on me now.

Jenna watched me scrub in silence. The fork was long clean. I opened the dishwasher, stuck it inside, then reached for a plate.

"I know what you're thinking, Annie. You're just afraid to fail. You think everything else that's happened to you is all your fault, and you can't bear to add one more piece of guilt."

The accusation pierced. These were feelings too personal—and too on-target—to be spoken. Jenna had uncovered my deepest insecurity, like excavating a mummy from a tomb. She had no right.

The kitchen fell silent. Jenna shook her head and crossed to the table for more dirty plates, exasperation oozing out of her. *Well, let her stew.* Just because she could take on anything. She hadn't been dumped by a husband. She hadn't been the child confidante of our mother, who'd despaired time and again over our dad's infidelities. Everything about life had built Jenna up, up, up. Successful job, one boyfriend after another, beauty. While so much had just beat me down.

Jenna set the plates on the counter, then faced me, a hand
on her hip. I didn't need to look at her to know that two spots
of color sat high on her cheeks. Or that her lips were pressed
yet turned up at the corners. If ever a person could look at
me with a mixture of devotion and pique, it was Jenna.

"You can do this."

I painstakingly rinsed another plate. "Detective Chetterling
won't want me to. After all, I *am* Trent Gerralon's daughter."

"You're right. We're both tainted." The sarcasm in her
voice could be cut with a knife. "So he'll say no. Then you *will*
be off the hook." She gave her head a disgusted shake.

I could find no reply.

"Play Nike for once, Annie, and just do it. If you don't
make the call, I will."

I closed my eyes, wavering. I would hate myself if I did
this. No doubt it would turn out badly. "Jenna, *please.* I won't
be able to help, don't you see? Everyone will count on me,
and then I'll feel so bad that I couldn't do it."

She tilted her head. "Well, Annie, you've finally admitted
the bottom line. Lisa Willit is dead. The entire neighborhood
is terrorized. And here you are, one of the most giving people
I know, holding back something that could help. Why?
Because you're the most important person around here, and
you don't want to look bad."

I froze, struck to the core. The last thing I'd ever think
was that I was more important than anyone else. Is that the
way my fear looked to her? I turned to slide a plate into the
dishwasher, my fingers trembling.

"Well?"

I stared at the white lip of the porcelain sink, searching
for some way to turn back this tide. "Jenna, if I let Dave down,

if I made Erin go through another session like last night's for nothing, I'd never forgive myself."

"So what else is new, Annie? Go ahead, add one more thing to your guilt list." She crossed the kitchen, fetched the phone, and plucked Chetterling's card off the refrigerator. "Call him."

I scraped the bottom of the barrel for argument. "My hands are wet."

She set down the phone and card with infinite patience, ripped a paper towel off the holder, and handed it to me.

I wiped my hands until they'd never been dryer. Then with a deep sigh I picked up the phone and punched in Chetterling's number.

Chapter 9

Tick-tock. Four-thirty.

Now I'd really done it.

As I perched in my father's leather chair behind the desk in his office, strangling my sister was not beyond imagination. The familiar feeling of a sketchpad in my hand only increased my anxiety. The blank and waiting page mocked me, the pencil in my fingers like a scalpel in a faux surgeon's grasp.

I faced a worn and leery Erin, who sat off to my right, slumped on one of two matching chairs pulled out from their usual place against the wall. Dave sat next to her. Every minute or so he would take a deep breath, as if he couldn't fill the cavity in his chest. Detective Chetterling had suggested we meet in my father's office, where Erin would feel more at ease. The room, about twenty feet square, had a fourteen-foot ceiling and plenty of light coming in from the front windows. It was located on the main floor between the master suite and great room. My father had worked here on weekends.

The door was closed so our voices would not filter into the great room.

"Okay, Erin." I gave her a little smile, as if I did this kind of thing every day. "Like Detective Chetterling told your dad, we're trying this because we thought it might be easier than looking at noses and mouths on the computer. If it doesn't work, we'll stop. But it's important that we give it a try. You ready?"

"I guess." Erin obviously wanted to be anywhere but in that chair.

A pained look crossed Dave's face as he gave her leg a squeeze. Chetterling had advised him not to stay. The success of the interview depended upon as little distraction as possible. "I'm going to leave you now and go . . . home."

The word seemed to chill on Dave's lips. The detectives had finished in his house, saying he could return on his own. His tour through the crime scene had yielded no clues, and so, desperate for some answers, for *anything*, he and Detective Chetterling had taken me up on my reluctant offer.

"Just do the best you can, Erin," Dave soothed his daughter. "Maybe by the time you're done, your Uncle Barry and Aunt Sara will be here."

"'Kay."

Thank you, Dave mouthed to me as he left the room. I waited until the door clicked shut.

I hope you'll have something to thank me for.

Nervously I glanced at the soft-leaded pencil in my hand. I would switch to colored pencils if I first managed to get down some of the basic features. Chetterling and I had discussed whether or not to work in color, as was my habit in the courtroom. Most composites were drawn in black and white for various reasons, one being that they were cheaper to copy for distribution. Still, Erin's quickest and strongest memories were of color—yellow-blond hair, bright-blue eyes. Chetterling had thought it wise to make the most of those details.

"All right." *Where to begin?* "Try to picture his face, Erin. Do you remember the basic shape of it?"

Erin focused on her knees. "I don't know how I can explain it. I see it in my head, but . . ."

Heat flushed through me. I hadn't the slightest idea of this interview process. A forensic artist's abilities seemed as incomprehensible to me as the power that created the universe. How did someone gather the nebulae within a victim's mind and shape them into form?

"Maybe if you just close your eyes. . . . Remember him as he stood and looked at you. You saw him well. You even noticed his eye color."

"That was easy. The blue was so bright."

"Okay. Maybe other things will come to you, too."

Erin pinned both hands between her legs and closed her eyes. A slight frown knit her forehead as she concentrated. A minute passed. Her breaths shallowed.

"His face is long. And pudgy around the . . . here." She ran knuckles along her jaw.

I poised the pencil over my drawing paper, still stymied. *Long* and *pudgy* made sense, proportionally speaking, but when you couldn't see the rest of the picture . . .

"Okay." My heart fluttered. I was about to put Erin through these terrible memories again for nothing.

"And, um, his eyes were kind of big. That's how I could see the color, you know?"

I hesitated, then sketched a rough outline of a long face. Added some sag in the jowls. Then outlined large eyes.

Erin's eyes remained closed, her fingers wrapping around the arm of her chair. "There was one thing. He's looking at me." She swallowed. The freckles across her nose seemed to darken, as though to remind me of her fragility and youth. "And his mouth opens just a little, like he's going to talk. But he doesn't."

This was useless information, as far as I could see. But at least Erin was remembering. She shoved her heels together, lifting them off the wooden floor. Set them back down. Her shoulders drew in, as if she wanted to shrink to nothingness.

"Erin? What do his lips look like?"

"I don't know. He's looking at me, and they . . . The corners go down."

I squeezed the pencil. Then made an attempt at a down-turned mouth.

And then I made a terrible mistake. I looked at what I'd drawn. Immediately faces played upon the walls of my memory, like restless ghosts. Faces from my years in the courtroom—defendants, jury members, attorneys, and judges. The beginnings of this face reminded me of a certain policeman from a murder trial last year, or that jury foreman in the burglary trial. Wait, if the eyes were a little smaller, he'd look like the judge in the baby-napping case . . .

I raked my eyes away from the drawing, anxiety pinging through me like the roller in a pinball machine. This was not a problem I'd expected. I would not be able to look at the drawing until it was done, or memories of my previous work would surely taint it. For all I knew, the sketch could end up as a variant of my own father.

Did forensic artists encounter this? How in the world did they control it?

Concentrate! On the individual parts, not the whole.

"All right." I cleared my throat. "What else, hon?"

Tears seeped through Erin's scrunched-up eyes.

Should I stop the session? Might as well fail with minimum damage.

At that moment a serendipitous scene caught my eye. Through the window, out of Erin's sight, I saw a car pulling up to the Willits' house. A man and woman got out. Dave Willit's front door opened and he descended the steps, opening his arms. The woman fell into them, and their bodies shook with sobs. The scene spiraled through me, whisking together bits of resolve like grains of sand in a dust storm. By the time Dave and the woman parted, the landscape within me had been rearranged, blown from unending flatness to small hills I could climb and conquer.

Yes. I closed my eyes, connecting with this new bit of confidence.

I had to do this. For Dave. For Erin. For their extended family.

So I pressed forward, pulling from myself instincts I didn't know existed. Somehow I discovered what to say, how to begin filling in the details of the composite, as Erin's ragged words brought it to life.

"His hair," Erin blurted ten minutes later. "It got messed up when he . . . when they fought, and when he looked at me, it had come down his forehead."

"What do you mean, come down his forehead?"

"It, you know, the whole front part of it covered more of his forehead."

I hesitated. Should I draw the man's hair the way it was before it "got messed up" or the way it looked when she best remembered him? "Was his hair thick or thin?"

"Thick."

"What was it shaped like before it got messed up? Did it have a part in it?"

"A part on the side."

"Which side?"

"Um . . . here." She drew a line with her finger down the right side of her head.

Erin talked next about the eyebrows. She said they were bushy and the same color as his hair. The nose was wide. I prompted her through explanations of eye shape, size of nostrils, skin condition. What was his chin like? His ears? As Erin filled in details, I sketched more rapidly, still focusing on the individual parts. But as time went on, my narrow focus became more and more of a barrier. Without the ability to check one aspect proportionally against another, I had no idea what this face would look like when it was finished. I began to dread viewing the result.

It's going to be so wrong.

Erin's words ran out.

Gripping the pencil, I asked if she could recall anything else. Surely the drawing lacked enough detail—even if it was accurate. I bit the inside of my cheek. Would I taint Erin's memories if I showed her the sketch in this form? What would a real forensic artist do?

What choice did I have? We'd reached a standstill.

I turned the sketchpad over.

"All right, hon." I laid my pencil on the desk. "I'd like to show you what we have so far. Don't worry if it doesn't look very much like what you remember. Because we can talk more and fix it, okay? And I'll add the color later."

Erin straightened her back, as if steeling herself. The air in the room grew heavy, like humid skies awaiting a storm. I attempted a smile. "Are you ready to see it?"

Her gaze drifted to the floor. Some time passed before she gave a brief nod.

"Okay," I said. "How about coming to stand by me."

She pushed to her feet and came to my side, where she stood like a puppet.

"Whenever you're ready, hon."

Erin swallowed, shifted her weight. Then nodded again. I turned the sketchpad over and held up the drawing, not looking at it. She pressed her lips together until they whitened, then lowered her eyes to the picture.

Chapter 10

Erin stared at the drawing, mute.

In the great room the grandfather clock chimed. Forty-five minutes after the hour. Which hour, I could not say. Time was ticking, ticking away.

"Does it look anything like him?"

"Sort of." Her voice sounded tinny, relief mixing with disappointment.

"Can you tell me what parts aren't quite right? Together we can fix them."

She pulled in her shoulders. "I don't know."

Pain for her swept through me. Reaching up, I ran my hand down her cheek. "Do you need to stop, Erin?"

"No. I just . . . don't know if I can do it."

"Well, I don't know if I can, either. But I'm willing to try if you are. It's up to you."

"Okay." She raised her head and inhaled a long, slow breath. "I want to finish it."

Her resolve amazed me. "Then we'll do it," I whispered.

I set the drawing on the desk, facedown, and crossed over to fetch Erin's chair, placing it beside mine. "Sit here at the desk and we'll go over each part."

As she settled into her chair, sudden curiosity pulled my eyes to the sketchpad. Before I could stop myself, I turned it over. Looked at the sketch.

Pinpricks danced across the back of my neck. Even in rough form, there was no denying the evil in those features. And yet . . . they seemed familiar. Once again I fought the fear of drawing someone I'd done before. My courtroom experience was hindering me rather than helping.

Besides, wouldn't Erin's reaction be tainted as well? Her dread of recognition had poised her to react to the drawing even if it was only mildly accurate, as someone creeping down a dark and frightening corridor might gasp at the merest touch.

I was not going to help the investigation at all. I was going to hurt it. Badly.

Sweat dampened my forehead. I wiped it away with the back of my hand.

"Okay. Here goes." I pulled a sheet of drawing paper from the bottom of the pad. "I'm going to hide everything but the part we're working on, Erin." I covered the bottom part of the face with the piece of paper. "First the eyes and eyebrows. Tell me what needs to be changed."

Piece by piece, we worked together, concentrating on details rather than the terrifying whole. The eyes were not quite so big, the eyebrows a little higher, the nose less wide. Too much sag in the jaw. Minutes fused into indiscernible time, our bodies shoulder to shoulder. Erin focused her energy upon that sheet of paper as if taking the most important test of her life. All sound fell away save that of our voices, our breathing, and the scratch of the pencil. The longer we worked, the more we seemed to become one entity, pouring everything we possessed into our task.

We reached the chin. "It's kind of . . . fatter." Erin's voice faltered. I knew she was tiring and could not take much more. I made a few changes. "That better?"

"I . . . don't know." A veil draped over her face. She looked away at nothing. Falling back against my chair, I closed my eyes. Somewhere inside me existed the energy to finish this business.

"Erin? I think we're done with drawing. All I have to do now is add the color. I can do the skin and final touches later, but I want to get the color of his hair and eyes right, because you remembered them so well."

"Uh-huh." Her gaze remained fixed across the room.

"So. Can you just . . . help me do this last thing?"

"Okay."

We leaned toward each other, resting our heads together as we gathered energy.

"All right. Let's do it." I selected a blue pencil.

Covering everything but the eyes, I began adding blue to the irises. Light blue first, then more and more color as Erin insisted they weren't bright enough. When she was satisfied with the shade, the man's eyes were stunning in their intensity. And cold. Like the bluest of lakes layered with ice. Had I seen them before? They seemed to bore a hole right through me, too powerful, too *alive*, to be a drawing. If I were to scramble away from the desk, they would surely follow me.

That personifying thought whirred the movie projector in my head into motion. In vivid color I envisioned a surreal scene from a horror film, the blue, blue eyes

bulging off the page, tugging, pulling with them the rest of the face. Next come the shoulders, torso, waist, legs. In seconds the entire murderous man crouches before us like some half-human beast . . .

My mouth went dry. I slapped my hand over the killer's eyes. Erin turned an anxious expression on me, as if we were two plucked strings on the same harp.

"They're . . . very blue," I managed.

She shivered, and in that movement I caught a glimpse of the terror she must have felt when she gazed into the real thing.

We sat for a moment, pulling in air.

When my fingers would not tremble, I covered all but the forehead of the drawing so we could add color to the hair. As for the skin, I experimented on the forehead with a light tone. Erin said it looked about right.

We were done. With a long exhale, I covered the entire composite and sat back in the chair.

"Okay. I'll do the rest of the skin later. No need to make you sit here any longer. It's time to look at the whole drawing."

She focused on the wall as if she wanted to crawl right through the wood.

"Tell me when you're ready."

"I'm . . . not." She hid her face and began to cry in silent gulps.

My throat locked up. I wrapped my arms around her and pulled her to my chest. "Poor Erin," I crooned into her hair. "I'm sorry. So, so sorry." Tilting my head toward the heavens, I raged against Dave's God, who had allowed this to happen. The evil in this world was too much to bear. Why did this tragedy have to befall the Willits?

Erin cried herself out, leaning against me until her breathing returned to normal. When she pulled away, her cheeks were pallid. She pressed a knuckle into the corner of her eye and rubbed. "I'm ready." Her lips firmed. "To see the picture now."

"Okay."

I reached for the corner of the paper hiding the face of the man who had become our mortal enemy. My heart flopped into an unsteady beat. I hesitated, feeling the miasma of Erin's dread seeping into my own being. She began to tremble. I wasn't sure we could do this.

"All right. Here goes. And just remember, I'll add the final color later if you say this is right."

Holding my breath, I slid the paper away. Our gazes fell to the drawing at the same time.

The face stared back at us.

The face and those bright-blue eyes.

My stomach wrenched into a knot. Those features—

Erin choked into sobs. She pushed back from the desk and swayed to her feet, her cries tumbling through the room. "That's . . . He . . ." The words pinched off. Sickness mottled her face and she wrenched away, then back. Her hands flung out as if to snatch up the drawing and tear it into a dozen pieces.

"No, Erin!" I shoved out of my chair and grabbed her arms. She fought me, her sudden energy a living, writhing thing. "Erin, it's okay, it's okay." Meaningless words spilled from my mouth as I thrust my arms around her and held on.

"I want my daddy!" Her ragged sobs were muffled against my chest.

"Sure, honey, yes. Let's get you home." I pressed her head against myself, away from the hateful picture, and nudged her around the desk. *What have I done, what have I done?* Despite Erin's reaction, I didn't see how the sketch could be right.

We staggered across the room. I fumbled for the door-knob and led her out of the office, into the hall and the great room. Erin's cries filled the twenty-six-foot-ceilinged expanse, bringing a white-faced Jenna and Kelly out of the TV area. Stephen's footsteps pounded up the stairs from the lower level. I caught a glimpse of his brooding face as we headed for the exit.

Erin broke away from me. She yanked open the front door and stumbled toward her violated home. I drew to a halt on the porch and watched, barely breathing, as she sprinted across the street and up her steps, then disappeared into her house.

What have I done, what have I done!

"What happened?" Kelly's voice pulled me back inside. I closed the door and leaned against it.

"Annie?" Jenna took a few steps toward me. "Are you okay?"

No, I wanted to shout, *I'm not okay, I'm not okay at all!* But I could only shake my head. Shake it and shake it. Then my feet set in motion, carrying me across the great room, footfalls echoing. I passed Stephen, who ogled me with the ambivalence of teenage cynicism mixed with fright. A detached part of me noted the expression, realized that his blithe attitude toward all this was only half real.

But I could not think about my son now. As a moth to flame, I returned to the office and stared at the picture my hands had wrought. At the unique set of features that had prompted Erin's fearful outburst.

I could not deny what I knew.

This was a face I'd seen before.

Chapter 11

Mom, what is going *on?*" Stephen frowned at me from the office doorway as if I were some strange zoo animal. Kelly appeared behind him, forehead lined.

Jenna was not far behind. "Go on, you two." She tugged at Stephen's shoulder.

Kelly protested. "But I want—"

"*Go.* We can talk about this later. Just give your mom a minute."

A minute. How about more like a lifetime?

The kids reluctantly moved aside. Jenna slipped into the office and closed the door. I stood behind the desk, half seeing my sister across the room, one of my hands suspended above the sketch as if it could burn me.

"I, uh, take it the drawing worked."

I nodded.

"Wow, Annie, I knew you could do it!"

Her glad expression faded, and she turned her head to look at me from the corner of her eye—the gesture she used in her rare moments of anxiety. "So . . . what's wrong?"

The drawing's hard blue eyes bored into me. With a shiver I flipped the sketchpad over. "I know the face. I've seen it somewhere before."

It. Impersonal. I couldn't say *him.*

"You're kidding. You mean you know who he is?"

My head shook back and forth, back and forth.

"Then what?" Jenna drew closer, pulled by curiosity.

"I've seen the face. But I don't know where."

The implication of my words played across her expression. "Around here, do you think? Somebody in town? Behind a cash register somewhere, or at the gas station?"

"I don't know!" I exhaled my frustration. "You know what it's like when you just know a fact, like someone's name, but it won't come? It's stuck in your brain somewhere. And you think, *If only I could see or hear it, I'd know it.* But without that . . ." I lifted my hands.

Jenna lay a palm against her face. "You've got to tell Detective Chetterling. You've got to get him this picture right away."

"I know, I know." I flopped into the office chair. "But I think it's all wrong. While I was drawing, other faces kept coming to my mind. All the faces I've drawn in courtrooms in the past. I realized I had to look at one feature at a time, because I was afraid I'd end up drawing a face I already knew. And now I *do* know it. So maybe this face isn't right, don't you see? Maybe it's somebody I drew long ago. Maybe even a face I had to practice way back in college."

"But Erin obviously knew it. It scared her to death!"

"Yes, but . . . You weren't here, Jenna." I gestured at the sketchpad. "I can't explain the tension we felt as that drawing came into shape. I covered up all but the part we worked on at the moment. And then when we realized we had to look at the whole thing, it was just . . . terrifying. My heart was beating a mile a minute. I'm sure Erin's was, too." I took a deep breath. "So maybe she was just . . . poised to recognize it."

Jenna nodded. "Maybe. But seeing her reaction, I doubt it."
I sagged in the chair, unable to think. Jenna approached
the desk. "Can I see it?"

"Go ahead."

Faint hope rose as I watched Jenna pick up the sketchpad and study the drawing. Her eyes roamed across every feature. Then she lowered it to the desk, turning it over for my
sake. She shook her head. "Never seen him before."

The hope crumbled away.

She came around the desk and tugged at my hair. "Hey.
Miss I-can't-do-anything-right. It doesn't matter if I've seen
this guy or not. What matters is, you did it. This drawing will
help find the man."

I could not manage even the weakest of smiles. Of course,
I was glad I'd helped—if that was true. But if the face was
right, I was caught in yet another trap. I knew the face . . . and
couldn't identify it. I had to remember.

"Annie. I know what you're thinking." Jenna folded her
arms. "But the whole investigation won't be waiting on just
your memory. If you've seen this man before, others have, too.
Which means when they put up the posters, calls will start
coming in."

I hoped she was right. But some prescient voice warned
me that I'd been taken off the hook—and moved to the noose.

Chapter 12

Detective Chetterling's large frame filled my father's office chair. He rested an elbow on the desk, rubbing his lips as he perused the drawing. The sketch was now in full color. I hung back, holding my elbows, feeling like a schoolgirl awaiting a teacher's pronouncement. At least we were on my turf. Well, my father's turf. Whenever I got the chance to get in here and clean out his things, I intended to make it my own.

"Those eyes are something, aren't they?" Chetterling grunted, then leaned back with a sigh. "Good work." For the first time he gave me a modicum of a smile. "You've got a knack, no question. This drawing is far more detailed than what we're used to. I can't thank you enough. You managed to pull information out of Erin that we couldn't."

"Thanks. Do you recognize it?" *It.* Still not *him.* To endow this face with a body, with legs that could stalk and hands that could kill, remained unthinkable. The eyes alone were enough to haunt me.

"No. But I don't count. The question is, who does?"

He'd unknowingly tossed me my cue, like some mystical ball awaiting my catch. I fiddled with the sleeve of my T-shirt. "Actually, I've . . . seen it before."

Chetterling's gaze cut to me. "You *know* this guy?" There was anticipation in his voice. Here it came—that noose around my neck. I gathered the courage to kick the chair out from under me.

"I don't really know him. I just recognize him from somewhere. But I can't for the life of me remember where."

The detective's keen stare did not betray his thoughts. "Think you've seen him around here? Or in town?"

I shook my head. "I just don't know. I'm sorry. It's been driving me crazy, but I just can't . . ."

"Must have been quite a shock to you."

"It was."

His eyes wandered over the bookshelves, the wooden file cabinet. "First time I've ever had a forensic artist recognize a sketch. But your inability to remember where you've seen the man isn't unusual. We've had lots of calls where the person says, 'I saw the drawing and knew the face, but it took me a while to remember where.'" He looked at me. "It'll come to you. Of course, I don't need to tell you how important that information is."

The comment swung in the air. "I know."

I could not bring myself to tell the detective that the drawing may not even be accurate. Dave Willit had called Chetterling and told him Erin said it was right; that was good enough for the detective. But in his experience, Chetterling must have seen the interview process go haywire. It still seemed very possible that Erin, in her traumatized state, had recognized the drawing in error.

Chetterling pulled the composite from the sketchpad and slipped it into an oversize folder. "We'll get this up around town right away. And to the paper." He checked his watch. "I'll need to hurry to make tomorrow's edition. I warned them it may be coming. Meanwhile we'll start checking it against our own mug shots tonight. I'll take it over to Dave Willit first, though, since some tie to his business seems most likely. It'd be great if he recognized it."

He headed toward the office door in his purposeful, heavy tread. I followed, wishing to know if he'd discovered anything else yet, some piece of evidence that could share the investigative burden now resting so heavily upon the drawing. "Could I ask you what you found at the autopsy?"

The detective turned back, clutching the folder as if it were gold. "She died from a blow to her left temple. She'd been choked but that didn't kill her. The findings fit Erin's story— when she said her mom was thrown aside, into the kitchen. Lisa apparently hit her head on the corner of the counter."

Choked . . . hit her head. I pressed my teeth together, knowing my mental projector would click on. I saw the face in my sketch

drawing his mouth in a rictus of hatred, blue eyes glazed. His hands squeeze Lisa's throat. Gurgling noises erupt from her lips, her eyes widening in disbelief and panic. She fights for her life, clawing at those hands, her skin purpling. The man throws her aside. Her temple crashes into the counter, the sickening sound like meat and bone slapped against a cutting block. She bounces off, crumples into a heap. The Face leans in, narrowing its eyes at Lisa's still body, calculating the next move. Erin freezes before him, then faints, thinking her life is over. The Face watches her hit the floor, its murderous mind deciding whether or not to kill her . . .

My breath stilled. In that instant glimpses of the heinous scene—Lisa's body, Erin, the Face—collided like red-hot pieces of iron to brand its image into my brain. Deep within my being I felt the composite was right.

Which meant I *had* to remember where I'd seen that man.

"Annie?" From a distance I heard the detective's voice. "You think of something?"

I worked to pull my mind back to the present. "I'm sorry, I was just . . . No. I didn't remember anything."

A minute later I stood on the porch, watching Chetterling mount the Willits' steps, folder in hand. Some prophetic knowledge told me that Dave would not recognize the drawing. It seemed an eternity before the detective reappeared. I ventured down the front walk as he made a beeline toward his car. He knew what I waited for.

He shook his head. "No go." Disappointment coated his voice.

I nodded, my eyes drawn to the folder. "You'll get calls tomorrow, once it's in the paper." I hoped I sounded more certain than I felt.

"Yeah, no doubt." Chetterling opened his car door, then considered me over the roof. "You remember anything yet?"

The inevitable question. The words hit my chest like bricks. "No. I'll keep trying."

"You do that. You think of anything, call me right away."

He drove off and I stepped back into the house. *Tick-tock.* The seventy-two crucial hours were counting down.

Who *was* the Face? What cobwebbed corner of my memory must I search to find the answer?

And most important, how long would it take?

Chapter 13

Oh no. We still had casseroles that belonged to the Willits. Four of them stared me in the face when I opened the refrigerator door to start preparing dinner. Dave would need those to feed his gathering family. Reluctantly I put my cooking on hold. I did not want to look Dave in the eye. Did he know I recognized the Face but hadn't a clue as to where I'd seen it? He'd probably want to shake the memory right out of me. Sighing, I took the casseroles out of the refrigerator and slid them into two doubled plastic grocery bags.

Two minutes later I stood at Dave's front door.

"Oh, here, let me help." He took one of the bags from my hand.

I followed him into the kitchen and set my bag on the counter next to his. Dave stood with one hand halfway into the pocket of his khaki slacks. His face looked chiseled, strained. He was so different in coloring than his fair wife and daughter. His skin was tanned, a faint outline from sunglasses running across each temple.

"Do you need help putting these away, Dave?"

"Don't worry, Sara will do it." He took a deep breath. "I was just about to call you. Chetterling said you recognized . . . him."

Him. Embodying the Face when I could not. I felt so small standing before this grieving man. "Yes. But I can't remember where. Believe me, I've been thinking of hardly anything else since. I'm sure it'll come."

He nodded. "You'll remember. I've been praying."

I didn't know how to respond. How could he feel confident that God would care about his prayer? If such a concerned God existed, why hadn't he protected Lisa in the first place?

My mind flitted like a bird over flooded ground, seeking a place to land. "I talked to Detective Chetterling some. He said they don't have much to go on."

Dave's gaze slid to the floor. "The man wore gloves. I suppose you heard that."

"Yes."

"Which means no fingerprints. You'd think in the . . . struggle, a hair would come out. *Something.*" His voice tinged with desperation. "But no. I just keep coming back to one thing, Annie. He was in my office, looking for something. *Why?* If he'd wanted to steal jewelry or something, he wouldn't go there. If he'd come intending to . . . hurt someone, he wouldn't go there. I've gone over and over it. I don't think he came to kill anybody. I think if Lisa hadn't come downstairs at that moment, he'd have found what he wanted and left. She'd still be alive."

The thought was too unbearable to consider. Could mere minutes have meant the difference between life and death?

"And I keep thinking, what did I do to somebody to deserve this? Did I ever cheat anyone? Did I ever raise somebody's rent unfairly? I thought I might recognize your drawing. Then when I didn't, I thought maybe it's someone's relative that I don't know, getting back at me for . . . something. But I can't come up with anything."

"Dave—" my voice thickened—"you can't dwell on this. You can't think that what happened is your fault. It probably has nothing to do with you."

He turned away, blinking rapidly, and it occurred to me how hypocritical I was being—I, who claimed the guilt for everything wrong in my own life.

Dave sucked in a breath. "Thank you again for all your help, Annie."

"Sure."

As I crossed the street, Dave's words echoed through my head. *He was in my office* . . . How I wished that whoever killed Lisa wasn't tied to Dave's business, but that seemed such a foolish hope. Somewhere out there was a man connected to Dave's real estate properties. A man Dave hadn't seen but I had. A man who apparently hadn't had time to find what he was looking for.

A man who, we could all hope, would not come back for a second try.

Chapter 14

Nine p.m.

I trudged across the great room toward the stairs leading to the lower level. Cries of the mangled and dying echoed up the steps. Stephen was playing another computer game.

Only a teenager could do that—choose killing as entertainment when it had capered without conscience across his own street.

Where have I seen the Face?

For the last few hours my mind had chanted the same maddening mantra. *Where have I seen it? Where?* I'd tried envisioning those features in dozens of places around Redding. Those ice blue eyes

meeting mine as the man packs cereal and rice into a plastic bag at the grocery store. He asks me if I'd like help out to the car . . .

No. The Face was not a packer at the store. Nor did he work behind the counter of the gas station I frequented. I hadn't seen him at the nursery when I went to buy plants, at the outlet shopping center outside Redding, or even walking down the street as I drove by.

Where have I seen him?

The computer-generated cries escalated. Stephen was on a roll. I knew he would protest when I called him, and I did not relish the battle. Leaning against the doorjamb, I pressed my eyes shut. They felt like they'd been sprayed with sand.

"You all right?" Jenna's voice came from behind me.

"Just tired." I aimed her a weak smile. She and Kelly sat on the huge couch facing me, Kelly, both legs pulled up on the cushions, leaning against her aunt. Her long brown hair covered half her features. How pretty my daughter was. She took after Jenna, with her heart-shaped face and long eyelashes. How much more beautiful she would become as she grew.

Behind that thought trailed the knowledge of all I had to lose.

I glanced out the wall of windows overlooking the backyard. Night had fallen, pulling a blanket of discomforting blackness over Grove Landing. Those windows, displaying lovely scenery by day, now loomed with the menace of one-way mirrors. I shivered.

For all I knew, the Face could be out there right now, watching us.

At least the alarm was on. I'd activated it a couple hours ago, setting it to level one, which allowed us to move about the house but played sentry against the opening of any doors or downstairs windows.

How different the house felt amid this night of a thousand eyes. After my father died, I was drawn to this house as if by some mystical force. My half of the hefty inheritance made the move possible. The money and stocks left by my father, even with the recent downturn of the market, would keep Jenna, me, and the kids for a lifetime. And the sale of his Hillsborough home netted another three million plus. The

idea that I could afford to flee the Bay Area's traffic and con-
stant motion, the place where memories of my life with Vic
still mocked me, took root, then blossomed. As soon as we
moved, I grew to love the feeling of being surrounded by
woods, by the natural beauty of the neighborhood.

Now I felt only oppression.

Where did I see him?

Enough, Annie.

"Stephen," I called down the staircase, "come out of your
dungeon!"

"Why?" he shouted back over a fatal scream.

"Because we need to talk as a family."

He snorted loudly enough for me to hear. I wasn't quite
sure which he was snorting at—that we were a family or that
he was supposed to care.

"I don't want to talk."

"Too bad. Come anyway; the game'll keep."

Sighing, I made my way to the couch opposite Jenna and
Kelly and fell into it. Kelly shuffled around the glass-topped
coffee table to ease beside me, laying her head on my shoulder. I stroked her hair.

Two minutes ticked by before we heard the slow thud of
Stephen's feet upon the stairs. Two minutes of my mind spin-
ning more scenes of where I could have seen the Face. The water
meter reader who was in the neighborhood two days ago?

No.

Someone pulling up beside me at a traffic light, in a parking lot.

No.

Maybe a mover. One of the men who'd carried in our be-
longings. I focused on the massive stone fireplace, remembering,

imagining the Face plodding through the house, asking where I wanted a certain box . . .

No.

Stephen scuffed to the oversize armchair between the two couches and threw himself into it, sitting low on his spine, legs spread. "Okay, here I am. Let's talk like a *family*."

His sarcastic tone set my teeth on edge. Jenna scowled at him. I could not blame her for disliking him. Sometimes I thought, *If he weren't my son* . . .

I summoned what energy I possessed. "Okay. We need to talk about . . . what's happened here. With so much going on, we haven't had a chance to be with each other."

Stephen rocked his knees back and forth. "What's there to talk about?"

A disgusted tsk emanated from Kelly's mouth. She raised her head and shot her brother a venomous look.

"First, I want to know if you two have questions about the investigation or anything. It's hard enough to go through this, and a bunch of unknowns won't help."

"We already *have* a bunch of unknowns," Stephen countered. "Who killed Erin's mom and why? And where is he now?" He made a point of looking toward the back windows, then tilted his head at me. "And why did Mom move us here in the first place?"

"Stephen, will you knock it off!" Jenna retorted. "We don't need your attitude right now."

His mouth locked tight, his fingers picking at a seam on the chair.

"Is there anything—" I drew out each word as if talking to a belligerent toddler—"that you'd like to ask about the investigation? Or what happens next?"

"No." Stephen's fingers worked with increased force.

"Would you please stop picking at that seam!"

He shot me a look, then jammed his arms over his chest.

"Can Erin come over tomorrow?" Kelly asked.

"It's fine with me." I traced a finger across her forehead. "But they've got a lot of family here now, and she might want to be with them."

"What about the funeral?" Jenna put in. "Have you heard anything?"

"I think Gerri or somebody mentioned Thursday, with a viewing on Wednesday."

Jenna raised her eyebrows, as if surprised that the casket could be open. Apparently, any bruises could be covered. But this was not a conversation I cared to have in front of the kids.

Where have I seen the Face?

"That picture you drew really looked like the guy, didn't it." Stephen jutted his chin at me.

I blinked at him. The kid could read my mind. His tone ran neutral, but did I detect a hint of respect?

"Yes, it did," Jenna replied. "By tomorrow copies of it will be all around town. It will probably play a major part in helping find the guy."

"That's cool." Stephen sniffed, keeping his eyes on his feet. "You oughtta do that more, Mom—draw pictures of criminals. Don't some people do that for a living?"

"I suppose. Okay. Next on the agenda. Until this . . . person is caught, we have to be extra careful. I know the sheriff's detectives are keeping an eye on the neighborhood. But I'm still going to be sure the alarm is set at night. And Stephen, for right now I want you to continue sleeping in the guest bedroom."

He scowled. "Mom—" Abruptly he turned from me to Jenna. "Are you going home tomorrow?"

"Yes, in the afternoon. But I'll come back up Friday after work."

"Not till then?" I couldn't keep the surprise from my tone. "You'll miss the funeral."

"I know, but I'm missing a day at work already."

True, but a funeral was important. Jenna should be there; it was the neighborly thing to do. Of course, I would not say this to Jenna. This was where my sister and I differed—she felt she had the right to help run my life, but I would never run hers.

"Take me with you." Stephen faced Jenna. "I want to go see Nate. I called him today and he said he's not doing anything."

I jumped in. "No." Nate was one of Stephen's friends who didn't seem to be into drugs. Still, the last thing I wanted was for Stephen to be running around the Bay Area again. Besides, I could never tell about any of his friends.

"Come on, Mom, it'll only be for a couple days."

"No."

"Why not?"

"Stephen, you know why not; we've been through this a dozen times."

"So tell me the thirteenth time."

"I do not like your friends in the Bay Area. End of story."

"You said Nate wasn't that bad."

"Yeah, but the rest of your friends are, and what's to stop you from meeting up with them while you're there?"

Stephen glared at me. "So let me get this straight. You'd rather me stay here, where there's some deranged killer running around the neighborhood, than be safe with Nate."

I closed my eyes again, his words bouncing around my head. I didn't have the energy to argue. Besides, he had a point. *Oh. Vic.*

I should call him tomorrow, tell him what happened. The kids hadn't, which spoke of their emotional distance from him. They were supposed to fly to Texas in the middle of August. Maybe they could visit early.

Nudging Kelly off my shoulder, I pushed to my feet. "Come on, it's bedtime." I knew my daughter would be sleeping with me. "Stephen, you're staying here and that's all there is to it."

I mounted the massive staircase, Kelly by my side. We shuffled down the hall, past her room and into mine. Within minutes of climbing into bed, I fell through the trapdoor of sleep. The mantra echoed as my last waking awareness.

Where have I seen that face?

Chapter 15

The day had nearly driven him insane. Handling his business deals, visiting and laughing with his sister, acting normal while his insides churned. Had she noticed anything? He tried so hard to be gentle with her, no matter what. More stress in her life she didn't need. But all the while he wondered what was happening. What were the cops doing? What evidence had he left behind?

Nothing, he told himself. Nothing. Except what he'd gone for in the first place.

No news about the case yet, nothing on any TV channels he could get, anyway. Maybe they wouldn't cover it. Was the woman dead or alive? They would look much harder for him if she was dead. He flexed his hands, remembering, reliving. He closed his eyes and smiled. Savoring.

His eyes popped open. No. He hoped she wasn't dead. That would make things so . . . messy.

Even though she deserved it.

He prowled his living room, smacking knuckles against the palm of his hand. So jittery. So full of energy needing to be spent. Maybe he should go back to the neighborhood tonight, try another strike. How crazy would that be?

Crazy. Plenty crazy.

He'd wait a day. Let things settle.

Pacing some more, he wondered where his cat had gotten to. He wanted something to kick. Something alive.

Maybe he should go tonight. Just finish the thing. Surely this time he'd find what he needed. Tie up those threatening loose ends he left. *Protect* himself.

No.

Better wait.

But everything inside him clamored to go.

He hulked through the expansive kitchen and into his manicured backyard. The pool water shimmered under a rising moon. Idly he scanned the perimeter of his lot for the cat. The beast was nowhere to be seen.

Jingling two coins in his pocket, he considered putting out some food to lure the creature out of hiding. It had to be hungry. He hadn't fed it for a couple days.

Ah, forget the cat.

His thoughts returned to his bungling of the previous night. Anger surged and he turned on his heel, anxious, needing to push it away. To prove to himself he was still In Control. He strode back into the house, down the long hall into the master suite. Opened the bottom drawer of his massive dresser. Stared at the magnificent work of his own hands—the one real skill he'd learned from *normal* employment. A skill so few knew.

A skill that would save his life.

If his own stupid mistakes didn't ruin everything.

He banged the drawer shut. What to do tonight, what to do? He flung himself onto his king-size bed and stared at the ceiling.

Nothing to be done in haste. He was the Man. He was In Control. He would think this whole thing out—and win.

His foot jiggled and jiggled, exuding nervous energy. Like a yanked puppet, he sprang from the bed, then paced into his kitchen and stood staring out the window at the sky, talking to himself.

Thinking.

Calculating . . .

Tuesday, July 22

Chapter 16

The carousel sweeps round and round, its tinkling music off-key. My rigid body is tied to a grotesque animal. Up and down I go, the silver pole slippery under my sweaty palms. My stomach roils, and my head fills with the music and the hideous laugh of some unseen being, like a grave-rotted clown. Colors blur as I spin, running together in reds and white, like bloody rain. The Face waits for me, lunging each time I swing before him. He bares lion claws that snatch at me, closer and closer, until I feel the slash of air. Desperately I lean away, my arms pulling from their sockets. The next time he will have me. The next time . . . the next moment . . . the next second. He circles into view once more, those glazed blue eyes glaring at me, blond hair askew, pudgy jaws open and tense. He swipes at me, claws digging into the tender skin of my scalp. A shriek bursts from my mouth . . .

My throat whirred like rusted machinery. I woke with a start, heart thudding. My eyes would not open. For a moment time cycled me back to the sirens of the previous night. My mind scrambled to remember where I was, what had happened.

In one sickening rush it returned.

I swallowed, tried to smooth my exhaling. Turning my head toward Kelly, I listened for her breaths of sleep. They were barely audible above the whoosh of blood in my own ears. As for me, sleep had fled, a fairy spooked by a demon.

For some time I stared at the high wooden-beamed ceiling, the yellow light from the burglar alarm glowing like the eye of a dying animal. Jenna had apparently set the alarm on its first level, which guarded the doors and downstairs windows but did not activate the inside motion sensors. That made sense. If Stephen needed to use the guest bathroom in the night, he could do so without setting off the alarm.

My thoughts turned to young Erin, awakened at midnight and hearing noises. The unthinkable becoming reality in her own home . . .

Then I heard it. A noise from the great room, a burr followed by a faint squeak, as if someone had bumped into a piece of furniture, scooting its legs over the hardwood floor.

My muscles tightened. Air walled, unmoving, in my chest. I listened.

Silence.

Perhaps I'd imagined it. My overactive mind was alive and well this night, conjuring an experience similar to Erin's. That was all.

Or maybe I'd heard Stephen creeping downstairs from the guest bedroom for something to eat. Maybe Jenna was up. Doing . . . something.

Maybe it was someone else.

I glanced at the yellow light of the keypad on my wall, begging myself to take comfort in it. No one could have gotten into the house without setting off the alarm. If an intruder had managed to disarm the system, the light would not be on. Its very presence signaled all was well.

I pictured Erin lying in bed one night ago, straining to hear. Hadn't she too tried to convince herself not to worry about the sounds?

Jenna slept below me, her bedroom suite down the hall from the great room. If someone had broken into the house, she would be first in line for danger.

That thought jolted me into motion.

I needed to call 911!

Wait. I *couldn't* call. I still didn't have a phone for this bedroom. Why hadn't I bought one when I had the chance? And my cell phone—where was it?

Downstairs in my purse. In the kitchen.

I swallowed hard. No way around it—I had to go down there to make the call.

Folding back the covers, I eased out of bed and tiptoed across the carpet. I reached for my doorknob, imagining the noise it would make when I turned it. A light downstairs would be all I needed to see, telling me that someone in the family was awake. I grasped the knob and turned. When it would turn no more, I hesitated, then pulled to unlatch the door. A little click sounded.

Cold fear washed over me. What if the Face was in the house? He'd have heard it.

I rested my forehead against the wall, forcing myself to get a grip. The Face was *not* here. The alarm was activated.

I pulled back the door.

My eyes stabbed through the hallway, dimly illuminated by a night-light on the wall outside Kelly's room. No light downstairs.

Neither Jenna nor Stephen would be bumping around in the dark.

Fast as lightning, I flicked on the hall light.

A silent breath dragged down my throat. I looked across to the upper level on the other side of the great room. The door to the first guest room was closed. Stephen must be sleeping. If the Face hid downstairs, he'd have seen the light. I pictured myself locking my door, diving back underneath my covers. But the thought of Jenna, alone and unaware, pushed me forward.

Creeping over the carpet, I felt the fibers crush beneath my feet. Every two steps I stopped to listen. I heard nothing save for the tick-tock of the grandfather clock, echoing off the wainscoting below.

Kelly's bedroom approached on my right. The door yawned open like the mouth of a waiting monster. I halted, unwilling to pass it. If the Face hid there, he could spring at my back. Licking my lips, I craned my neck to see what I could of the room. No figure lurked in sight. Gathering my courage, I reached around the door frame to flip a switch.

Light flooded the room. I pulled my gaze over Kelly's rumply bed, her desk and chair, her double dresser, the walls full of posters. On my left ran an entire wall of closets, the doors closed. No way did I possess the courage to check inside.

Kelly's bathroom was on my far right. I peered through its entrance—and turned stone cold.

A figure stared, wild-eyed, back at me.

Electricity sparked from my head to my feet.

Only then did I recognize my own reflection in the mirror above the sink.

I brought a hand to my cheek. For a moment all I could do was breathe.

The bathroom needed to be checked before I went downstairs to the phone and Jenna. The Face could be around the corner or behind the shower curtain. What if he skulked on this floor, where Kelly slept?

Slinking against the wall, I moved toward the bathroom. When I reached the door, I scrunched myself in the corner of its frame, peeking inside and left as far as I could see. Brushes and hair clips and a hand dryer littered the counter between the double sinks. A towel draped across the back of the toilet, haphazardly thrown. Kelly was not the neatest of twelve-year-olds.

Only the edge of the shower curtain was visible, hanging toward the back third of the tub.

I eased through the doorway. The folds of the shower curtain melded into the dimmed corner of the bathroom. I could not see what lay beyond.

My mind's projector clicked on to a scene from some long-ago horror movie. A

dark figure shoots from the shadows, his face a twisted mask. He raises a large gleaming blade in his hand, ready to slash, slash, slash . . .

No, no, no. Stop it, Annie.

I knew the picture was all in my head. But this time maybe it was true. Within seconds I could be stabbed or beaten to a bloody mess. Or the Face would have a gun, maybe with a silencer. Or he'd kill me with his bare hands, like he killed Lisa. I would crumple in a swift, neat death.

Stop it!

I licked my lips. I *would* check that shower curtain.

Now.

Before I could change my mind, I leapt across the bathroom and flung aside the plastic curtain, its rings clanking against the metal pole. I stared at bare tile. No Face. No blue eyes. The sound of the rings reverberated in my ears.

I nearly collapsed into the tub. Then suddenly I had to leave Kelly's room. Now that I'd searched it, I couldn't stand the lingering fog of my own fear. I turned to run over the tile . . .

across the bedroom carpet . . .

into the hallway.

I stopped, puffing.

Peering through the banister about fifteen feet away, I listened. The hall light filtered out over the great room, illuminating the top half of the two massive redwood posts at the entrance to the kitchen. Down below, the kitchen table stood partially visible, and the bottom of the stove island. The wide door to the television room, which shared a wall with the kitchen, was closed.

Hadn't it been open when I went to bed?

That door was never closed when the room was empty. Only when someone wanted to watch television and keep the sound from filtering into the rest of the house would it be shut.

If the Face had slipped into that room when he saw the upstairs hall light come on, would I have heard the door latch?

A chill wrapped itself around my chest.

My bare feet crushed the carpet in cautious steps, and the great room slid into view. To my right I saw the floor near the kitchen, with its twelve-by-fifteen-foot area rug. Then the top of the armchair where Stephen sat last night. The ends of the couches that faced each other. The edge of the coffee table in the center.

I reached the landing area and flipped another switch. Recessed lighting flowed over the stairs, along the railed hall across from me—which ran half the length of the great room—and the wide walkway connecting that side of the upper level with the stairs. The great room now lay before me, darkness chased away. My eyes swept the entire length, back and forth.

Only then did I notice that the armchair facing the fireplace sat askew.

My breath rattled to a stop.

It took no more than a casual bump to move that chair. Wooden legs, even when thick, move easily over a wooden floor. Someone inching through that room in the dark, even a very careful someone, could have misstepped and caused the noise I'd heard.

My thoughts would not gel. I tried to decide what my father would do. What Vic would do. Would they grab something for a makeshift weapon? Nothing in my or Kelly's room came to mind. For the millionth time since Vic abandoned us, anger at my helplessness surged through me. A house full of females and one know-it-all teenage son. How could we defend ourselves?

Heart tripping, I forced my feet to the staircase, then lowered myself down one step at a time, clutching the rail. By the time I reached the bottom, the back of my neck shivered like the skittering of a dozen spiders. I veered for the switch that turned on various table lamps around the room, seeking all the light I could find. The sun wouldn't have been too much for me at that moment.

Nothing else seemed out of place. Nothing but that chair. And the closed door.

These alone, with the sound I'd heard, told me the Face had been here. Was probably still here, balanced on the balls of his feet as he leaned against the wall of the television room, fingers splayed and palms open against the wood paneling. Waiting for me to open the door.

Or he was folded down behind the couch or crouching behind the stove island. Maybe he'd whisked on cat feet through the door in the kitchen that led to the garage and airplane hangar. From there he could use a side exit to escape into the night.

I could not go into that kitchen for the phone. Instead I would wake Jenna. Call 911 from her room.

My head swiveled to the right. The office stood open, the room dark.

The Face had rummaged in the Willits' office.

Farther down the hall, Jenna's bedroom door was closed. Maybe the Face had already trapped my sister. Who knew what I would find behind that door?

My fingers scrabbled for the hall light switch. As it flicked on, I froze, listening for any sound from the office in response. Silence, save for the grandfather clock behind me. Edging forward, I approached the office threshold. Imagining the Face at the Willits', opening office drawers, looking through files. Whatever fetish he carried would follow him here on his second night of terrorizing Grove Landing. In this nightmare the improbable had become all too real. Never mind that his return to the neighborhood so soon would be a stupid move. He'd already broken into one home and killed its owner. How logical a mind could he have?

Something snapped inside me, thrusting me into motion. With a gasp I lunged beyond the office, pounding toward the master bedroom.

Bam!

I rammed into the door with enough noise to wake the dead—and threw it open.

Chapter 17

The door banged against the wall like the blast of a shotgun. I smacked on the light switch. Jenna rose up in bed like some pulled mannequin, squinting in the brightness, one hand thrown before her eyes. "Wh–what? What happened?"

Relief blew over me, then was gone. I thrust the door shut. Locked it. "I think someone's in the house."

Sleep had not yet fully released her. She ogled me, her face paling as the words sank in. "How do you know?"

"I heard someone bump furniture. And the chair in the great room's been moved."

She absorbed my words, her eyes rounding. Her head swiveled to the yellow light of the keypad on her left. "The alarm's still on."

"I know, but I *heard* something."

She licked her lips, trying to think.

"And something else—the door to the TV room is closed. Did you close it?"

"No."

"Maybe he's in there!"

Jenna shoved her fingers into her bangs, elbow hanging in the air. Her eyes darted to the windows, as if she strained to read the truth in the blackness beyond.

"I came to see that you're okay, since you're on this floor. We have to call 911. And then, Jenna, you have to come with me. I didn't check every place." Panic mounted at the realization of what I'd failed to do. A locked door now stood between me and the intruder—and my kids were on his side of it. "I have to get to Kelly and Stephen! What if he's gone upstairs?"

My sister snatched up her bedside phone. "The deputy sheriffs can't be far; they're patrolling the neighborhood."

"I know, but I can't hide in here, just waiting; I *have* to go see the kids."

Jenna punched in three digits. I stood like a zombie. Wanting to sprint upstairs to Kelly. Unable to move.

"This is Jenna Gerralon on Barrister Court out at Grove Landing. Across the street from where Lisa Willit was killed last night. We think somebody's in the house. Please send help." She started to hang up, then pulled the receiver back to her ear. "No, I won't stay on the line. And don't use a siren!" She banged down the phone and jumped from bed. "Okay. What'll we do? *Think,* Jenna!"

She jerked around to stare at the drawer of her nightstand. Then she yanked it open and fumbled inside, withdrawing a small handgun.

"What is *that?*"

"What does it look like?"

"I know, but I mean . . . where'd you get it?"

"I found it on the shelf of the closet when we moved in. Must have been Dad's. After last night I decided to keep it by my bed."

I shrank away from it as she approached. "Is it loaded?"

"No. I didn't find any bullets."

"Then what—"

"Annie, shut *up*, will you? If someone's here, he doesn't have to know it's not loaded. Maybe it'll buy us a minute or two."

She urged me away from the door. I couldn't tear my eyes from the gun, her knuckles whitening around it. I'd always been scared spitless of guns, but not Jenna. A year before, she'd gone with her boyfriend at the time, an ex-marine, to a firing range—and she enjoyed it.

"Okay." She straightened her back. "We'll head right for the front door and open it. A deputy sheriff will be here any minute. They can search the house."

"But Kelly and Stephen!"

"If that guy is here, it's for burglary, not to kill. Just like at the Willits'. He's probably hiding. If he's not fled already, with all your bumping around."

I still couldn't think. "What about the alarm? If we open the front door, it'll go off."

She gave me a look. "Annie, we'll have a full minute to deactivate it. Besides, if it goes off, that means it's still working. And if it's still working, nobody's in the house in the first place."

My eyes slid to the yellow light. It gave me no comfort. I knew what I'd heard.

Jenna squeezed my arm. "Stay right behind me." She eased open the door, the gun up and pointed in her right hand. I clutched the back of her pajama top as she skittered down the hall, not even stopping to check the office. We hit the entrance to the great room. I slowed us both down by looking over my shoulder. If the Face hid in that office, I was the one he'd get to first.

We edged across the great room, not making a sound. Past the built-in stereo cabinets, past the first couch and the armchair. The final couch loomed on our right, the perfect hiding place. Jenna hesitated, then reached back and pushed my fingers off her pajama top. Her muscles gathered. She wound both hands around the gun, then leapt forward, gun pointing to the darkened area behind the couch. I held my breath.

Her shoulders relaxed. "It's okay."

Jenna hurried to the front door, fumbled with the lock and threw it open. A high whine filled the room. "The warning! Go turn off the alarm."

"I can't remember . . . What's the code?"

"Dad's birthday. Go!"

She shoved me and I pivoted toward the kitchen, the high pitch fizzling in my ears. How could anyone think with that noise? What if I couldn't deactivate the system fast enough and the alarm went off and woke the neighbors? They'd be scared to death.

I slapped on the kitchen light and headed for the keypad. In the back of my mind I still couldn't believe the Face wasn't somewhere in the house, hiding. I'd *heard* him. As my fingers touched the keypad, I twisted to glance at the island, half expecting to see him rise, to feel his breath on my neck.

"Annie, turn it off!"

I swiveled back toward the wall, feeling the keypad beneath my fingers. Telling my mind to *think, think!* Dad's birthday. Six digits. Why hadn't I changed the code to something I'd remember better? My thoughts locked up. I stared at the white numbers.

"Annie!"

"Okay!" I scrunched up my face. Thinking, *thinking.* Then punched in the code.

Silence.

I sagged against the wall, unable to move.

"What is going *on?*" Stephen's sleep-husky voice gruffed from the upper floor. Seconds later Kelly's fearful "Mom?" drifted down from the other side. I stumbled into the great room and swiveled my head from one child to the next. Jenna trotted past me into the kitchen, hiding the gun.

"Don't worry," I called up, as if they'd believe the words after one look at my face. "Some detectives are going to check out the house, that's all. You'd better come down."

I heard Jenna yank open a drawer. Standing on the other side of the island, where Kelly could not see, she shoved the gun inside.

Kelly's widened eyes followed the sound, then sprang back to me. "What happened?"

Stephen gave me a disgusted look. "This better be good."

Headlights washed over the kitchen window.

"The deputies are here." Jenna crossed the great room, heading toward the entryway. "You two come down," she commanded Kelly and Stephen with barely a glance. Her terseness was enough to push them into movement. Kelly started down the stairs and Stephen stumped across the walkway to follow her.

"Don't let me forget to get that gun later," Jenna whispered in my ear. "I don't want the kids to find it."

I nodded, gathering my wits. A part of me still could not believe we were safe. The closed door of the TV room loomed on my right. My mind flashed images of the Face, trapped and desperate, behind it.

I hurried to Kelly as she hit the bottom of the steps. She reached for me, looking so vulnerable, her expression solemn and worn. One thin strap of her baby blue pajama top had fallen off her shoulder. I pushed it back up.

Jenna opened the front door. Car doors slammed; feet pounded against the front walk and up the porch steps. Within seconds another patrol car pulled up. Across the street a light flicked on in the Willits' house, soon followed by the one on their front porch. My heart sank. We'd awakened Dave, no doubt nearly stopping his heart. It was the last thing I'd wanted to do.

"I think maybe it's okay," Jenna told the first deputy to arrive. The other three soon gathered, scanning first through the door, then along the perimeter of the house, as they listened to her rapid explanations. "The alarm was activated, so I don't know how anyone could have gotten inside. Still, we heard something."

We. Jenna was sticking by me. Maybe she wasn't going to strangle me quite yet.

Kelly pressed against my side. Stephen's feet thwunked across the great room floor. He leaned against the back of a couch, surveying the deputies as they came through the door, their eyes still darting, as if they were eagles searching for prey. Anxiety flickered across his face, chased away by a nonchalant sniff when he saw that I watched him.

Two of the deputies I recognized from the previous night. Chetterling was not with them.

"You all go outside and wait," a tall and wiry deputy commanded. "We'll check every corner of the house."

We obeyed.

Dave appeared on his front porch, still clad in the khaki pants and shirt he'd worn that day. Had he been to bed at all? He hurried down his steps and across the street, his expression a mixture of exhaustion and dread. I met him at the curb, spilling my apologies, assuring him it was probably nothing.

He looked toward our house, watching as a light flicked on in the office. "Better safe than sorry."

I knew his curt words reflected no anger. He simply did not have the energy to say more. "Is Erin . . ."

"She's still asleep. On the floor of my room."

I drew what comfort I could from that. We huddled outside, waiting for the deputies. "Stephen, did you close the TV room door?" I asked.

He shrugged that he couldn't remember.

"He's the one who probably moved the armchair, though," Jenna offered, "the way he threw himself into it last night when we all were talking."

That made such sense. "Then what did I hear?"

My sister shook her head. "I'm not sure. But you know how sometimes the mechanism of the grandfather clock sort of clunks? Maybe that was it."

"Oh, great, Mom." Stephen wagged his head at me. "You brought four sheriff's deputies here in the middle of the night because of a *clock* noise?"

"Nobody asked you, Stephen." Jenna's black look could have killed.

My son flicked his eyes, lips tightening. Dave looked from him to me, understanding of my motherhood challenges creasing his features.

How would Stephen feel if he lost me like Erin lost her mother? Would he even care?

By the time the deputies returned, my legs shook from standing, although we couldn't have waited more than fifteen minutes. The house was clear.

The deputies milled about, reassuring me when I said the blame was all mine. My conscience wouldn't allow them to include Jenna in their judgment. Too little sleep and too active an imagination, I admitted, adding that next time I'd believe the alarm—if it was activated, we were safe. Deputy Franz, the tall, wiry one, reiterated Dave's words. After what happened, he said with an empathetic nod to Dave, we could not afford to take chances. And the Sheriff's Office wouldn't want us to.

I tried to tell myself Chetterling would not hear of this incident, but knew that was a fool's dream. First my locked-up memory of the Face, now this. He would think me a total idiot.

By the time I crawled back into bed with Kelly, it was nearly three o'clock. Jenna had retrieved the gun from the kitchen drawer and hid it in her nightstand. The mere thought of that killing machine in my house made me shiver.

I could not sleep. My nerves still tingled, and the *Where did I see him?* mantra resumed its chant in my head. Dread grew within me—the sense that this murder investigation was far from over, and that it would suck me further in like a leaf caught in a whirlpool. I tried to tell myself the coming day held promise. Someone, perhaps many, would recognize my drawing.

Please let it be so, I prayed to no one as my limbs weighted and my thoughts turned to sludge. *Please . . . please . . .*

The trapdoor of sleep opened and I tumbled inside.

Chapter 18

I awoke Tuesday morning to memories of the night. They ghosted me like images from a black-and-white horror film. I may have been wrong about what I'd heard, but that didn't lessen the terror I'd felt. Another night in the house, the neighborhood, loomed unfathomable. If I hadn't promised to take in a couple of Dave's relatives, and if I didn't feel I should stay close to Erin, I'd be making plans to pack up the kids and have us all fly out with Jenna.

Tick-tock, tick-tock. Time was slipping away. It was already past nine. I needed another six hours of sleep. Better yet, I'd have liked to crawl under the covers and hide out for the next week. But the clock was ticking, and I would enjoy no more rest now. Some thirty-two hours had passed since Lisa's murder. Almost half of the crucial seventy-two. With each hour the trail grew colder, as surely as the scent of hounds' prey scatters to the wind.

But this morning maybe we'd get a break. The composite should be in the newspaper.

Please, God of Dave Willit, if you're there—let it lead the detectives to a suspect today.

Pulling myself from bed, I headed down to the kitchen. Jenna had already brought the newspaper to the breakfast table.

"Look. It's on the front page. Your first piece of forensic art."

And my last. I wondered at her odd remark as my eyes fell to the composite. The Face stared mockingly at me, sending a jolt through my body. Shuddering, I folded the paper and pushed it away. Someone *had* to recognize this face today. This morning. *Now.* The sooner it happened, the sooner detectives could move in and arrest the man.

"You still don't remember, do you?" Jenna was reading my mind again. She had a knack for doing that.

I shook my head.

"It'll come." She crossed to the coffeemaker. "Out of nowhere, something will trigger it. Or maybe nothing at all. But it'll come." She poured the coffee into mugs, set one before me, and joined me at the table. "Maybe when someone else identifies him, you'll remember."

"Maybe."

I had to hand it to my sister. After the fear I put her through last night—put the whole family through—she'd chosen to reassure me.

"Annie." Jenna leaned over the table and touched my arm. "I'm really proud of what you did. That drawing is amazing. For once I think Stephen's right—maybe you should look into doing forensic art."

I frowned at her. "Hey, enough trying to run my life, okay? Not one day ago you twisted my arm to do this drawing. As if that weren't enough, now you want me to make it a career? Why on earth would I want to put myself in the middle of . . . of . . . *death* all the time?"

"Not all crimes involve murder, Annie. Besides, even for those that do, you wouldn't exactly be in the middle of death. More like . . . on the brink."

"Oh, well, that's comforting."

"All right, all right." She busied herself pouring cream into her coffee. "But eventually you're going to have to find something to do around here. I mean, after you clean out the office and plant flowers and whatever else you've got tucked away in your brain. Making this house yours—"

"Ours."

"Okay, fine. Making it *ours* won't take forever. The summer's going to end, the kids'll go back to school—and what are you going to do out here? You can't even fly the plane, for heaven's sake."

"It's your plane now, and when you're not here, it's with you in the Bay Area, remember? Besides, I have no desire to learn how to fly."

She gave me a look. "You're trying to change the subject."

"I am not! *You* brought up flying."

Leaning back in her chair, she smacked her tongue against her teeth. Summoning her patience. Her eyes met mine and held, heralding the pronouncement of some profound thought. "Last night, after you and Kelly went to bed? I couldn't sleep, so I did something for you."

For me. Coming from Jenna, those were threatening words. "Oh, really."

Jenna ignored my tone. The way she could do that just infuriated me sometimes. "I got on the computer in the office and looked up forensic art—"

"Jenna, come *on.*"

"Wait now, just hear me out. I found this interesting book—like a textbook of all the different kinds of forensic art, everything from drawing a composite to making a sculpture of a face from skull bones."

"Oh, yay. Sounds so appetizing."

"It's written by a woman who's an expert in the field. So I ordered it for you, express delivery."

Air puffed from my mouth. "What did you do that for?"

"Now don't go getting all defensive. I do think it would be an interesting field for you, but that's not why I bought the book. There's a chapter in there about interviewing a witness in order to draw a composite. All the things you should and shouldn't do. After your success yesterday, I thought it would be interesting for you to read, to make you more confident about the drawing. Apparently, you did everything right."

The mere idea of reading the book raised my hackles. I hadn't known what I was doing yesterday at all. I'd stumbled and bumbled around, and it was only pure luck that I'd drawn a face Erin recognized. The last thing I needed was to have an expert point out everything I did wrong.

No way was I going to crack that book.

Jenna sipped her coffee. "Okay, don't thank me. But you should. That book cost me almost a hundred dollars."

"A hundred dollars!"

She shrugged. "We're rich now, remember?"

That we were. It wasn't a concept I'd quite gotten used to. "So quit your job and come here and live with us."

"Annie." Jenna's tone turned impatient. "My life is in the Bay Area. I like all the people, the excitement. I like my job. I like going on dates to fine restaurants."

"Your job is winding down. You could get laid off anytime and you know it. You're without a boyfriend and nobody seems interesting. The traffic is terrible. Your hangar at the San Carlos airport is five minutes' drive away and costs over six hundred dollars a month. Here it's on the other side of that door—" I pointed toward the back of the kitchen—"and it's free."

I wagged my head at her. Why shouldn't I try to run her life for a change? Besides, on this morning, after the last horrible thirty-two hours, it felt downright refreshing to argue about something familiar.

"Well now, aren't you clever." Jenna regarded me with her mixture of affection and pique. "Last I remember, we were talking about *your* life, not mine."

"Yeah, well, I thought we'd try something different." With a sigh I rose from the table. "I need to get dressed. We'll have company sometime today and there's cleaning to do. I suppose you'll be leaving soon."

Jenna had the decency to look apologetic. "In a couple hours."

Before exiting the kitchen, I plucked the newspaper off the table. Doomed by my curiosity, I would read the article in the privacy of my own bedroom—where my daughter still lay in much-envied sleep.

# # # #

Tick-tock. The grandfather clock chimed the minutes away.

The mantra played like a stuck record in my head. *Where have I seen the Face?* I consoled myself that soon my poor memory wouldn't matter; any moment now newspaper readers would be calling tips into the Sheriff's Office.

I dusted the empty guest bedroom and laid out fresh towels. The bathroom needed cleaning after my sloppy son had used it. "Stephen," I warned him, "you're sharing this bathroom for the next couple nights. Don't dump wet towels on the floor."

Shortly after noon our guests arrived—one of Dave's cousins and his wife, Ed and Carol . . . something. They must have told me their last name but I did not retain it. The couple put their things in the guest room, voicing their thanks and extolling the house's beauty. Then they crossed the street toward the Willits', informing me they'd be back only in time to sleep.

The clock ticked and the mantra chanted. And I tried not to think of the coming night.

Where have I seen him?

By two that afternoon I was going crazy. Every moment hung with portent. The memory I sought felt no closer, though numerous times I thought I was almost upon it. Like a cricket in daylight, it mocked me with its song, daring me to creep close and find it. Then as my footsteps drew near, it would fall silent, hunching in the shadows of my mind. Only when I retreated once more, occupying myself with chores about the house, would it creak into song again.

Each time I passed a phone, the receiver would tug at my eyes, inviting me to pick it up, call Detective Chetterling, and beg for information. But I couldn't bring myself to do it. I knew he was busy with the investigation. And besides, I was afraid to talk to him after the stunt I pulled last night.

Out of desperation I called Gerri Carson's cell phone, catching her at her church office.

"Annie, I just heard about last night and was about to call you. How are you and the kids doing?"

"Okay, but Gerri, did you hear about the composite?" My mouth launched into words before I could stop it. "I know I've seen the guy, but I don't know where. I just can't remember. The whole thing's driving me nuts, and the only way I

can keep my sanity is to tell myself somebody else will recognize his face. And then maybe that'll help me remember."
I stopped for a breath. "Do you know anything? Have the
detectives been getting calls?"

A faint squeak sounded, presumably from Gerri's office
chair. I imagined something ancient and wooden. "I did hear
that you recognized your own drawing. I can imagine what a
shock that would be. But I'm sorry to say I don't have any
information for you. I don't keep up minute by minute with
investigations. Tell you what, though—I could ask Detective
Chetterling to call you."

My heart sank. "You couldn't just talk to him for me? Ask
him what's going on?"

"I'm sorry, no. I'm not able to pass on information like
that. But what are you thinking? You sound almost afraid to
talk to him."

Well now, couldn't she see right through me. "Yes,
because I have nothing to tell him! I still can't remember. And
I know the pressure on these guys when they're trying to
catch somebody like this. If I were Chetterling, I'd want to
beat me to a pulp out of pure frustration."

She chuckled. "I really don't think he wants to beat you
to a pulp."

"Okay, half a pulp then."

"Annie. It's okay. Let me ask Detective Chetterling to call
you. I'm sure he'll ease your mind."

I doubted that. But what else could I do but give in?

The clock ticked.

I waited for Chetterling's call.

Jenna was out in the hangar, doing her preflight check on
the plane. The Cessna turbo 210 would get her to the San

Carlos airport in less than an hour. I tried not to think about her leaving me alone. Stephen was back at his computer games on the lower floor. Erin came over for a while, seeking solace in Kelly's company. I held her tightly before sending her upstairs. She clung to me but her eyes were dry.

What to do next? I started some laundry. Wandered into my father's office and heaved myself into the desk chair, remembering how pristine I'd found the room when I rushed here on the day of his death. Nothing was out of place. Now I stared at the large wooden file cabinet, thinking how well it would hold my things. I'd planned to turn the office into a studio, do some painting, which I hadn't done for years.

The phone rang. I steeled myself, then picked up the receiver. "Hello?"

"Annie, it's Detective Chetterling. I hear you had a scare last night."

"Oh." I cringed. "Yes. But we're okay."

"Good. I know it's a hard time for the whole neighborhood. So don't worry about being cautious."

"Okay. Thank you."

"Gerri asked me to call you and let you know what's happening." He hesitated and I sensed his frustration. "We haven't gotten any solid leads yet. But I'm sure they'll come."

"Not *one?*"

"Nothing that's checked out."

Desperation rose within me. "But all those people seeing the paper this morning. *Somebody* has to have seen him."

Somebody had.

Me.

No doubt the detective was thinking the same thing.

"We'll keep hoping. The next call could be the right lead. Meanwhile you keep racking your brain, all right? Call me the second you think of something."

He didn't need to tell me that. "I will. I'm sorry I haven't been any help yet."

"I'd hardly say that. Without you we wouldn't even have a composite."

I hung up the phone and checked the clock on the office wall. Two forty-five. The seventy-two hours were more than half over.

Why hadn't anyone else seen the Face? Why only me?

Maybe Erin's recognition was wrong after all. Maybe her fear got the best of her.

I gazed at my father's bookshelves, trying to imagine what the next few days, weeks, would be like for my family if nothing came of the investigation. My concern for the kids was greatest. Hard to admit but Stephen was proving right. What was the sense of keeping him and Kelly here when danger seemed all around us?

Oh, great. I'd forgotten to call Vic.

Sighing, I aimed an accusing look at the phone, as if the whole situation were its fault. I hated calling Vic. I hated his phone numbers; I hated the sound of the lines ringing. I hated his voice. Our conversations were never just about what they were about. Talking to him was like crossing a rickety swinging bridge above roiling waters.

Vic would be at work, of course. His *amazing opportunity* job that whisked him states away from his children with nary a backward glance. Well, why not? He had Sheryl to make the journey with him.

I picked up the phone and dialed his direct number. He answered on the third ring, sounding pushed for time. Vic always sounded pushed for time.

Might as well jump right in. "Look, Vic, we have a problem, and I'd like to send the kids to you early."

"Annie, what is it?" In the background I heard shuffling papers. "We've already decided on the middle of August, because that's when Sheryl and I have vacation time. You know I can't take them now."

Vic's typical lackadaisical attitude toward his children. Seemed to me, parenthood required a certain amount of flexibility.

"Our neighbor across the street was murdered Sunday night. In her home. The mother of Kelly's best friend here. The neighborhood isn't safe. Sheriff's deputies were here at three o'clock this morning, checking on suspicious noises in the house. The detectives have no idea who committed the murder and probably won't find the guy anytime soon. No doubt *my* well-being doesn't concern you in the least. However, it occurred to me that you, as our children's father, might think that Kelly and Stephen would be safer with you. Vacation time or not."

For the first time in my life I succeeded in making Vic stumble for words.

Then he proceeded to grill me like some marine sergeant. Didn't our house have a burglar alarm? Well, wasn't it on last night? Did the deputies find anything? By the time he said he'd check with Sheryl, Vic had used my reluctant admissions to paint the situation in a far lighter hue. Yes, a murder on the block was a scary thing. But I'd no doubt let my imagination run away with me the previous night. He hoped I wasn't scaring the kids unnecessarily.

I wilted into my father's chair, too worn to defend myself. Vic insisted he needed until the end of the week to decide what to do. By that time, he commented, the murderer would probably be caught anyway.

After the conversation I felt parched from the fire of Vic's words. I shuffled into the kitchen for a drink and had just shoved a glass under the refrigerator spigot when the phone rang.

It was the worst possible timing. My defenses were shot, my nerves jittery, and my body and mind craved sleep. If I'd known who was on the other end of the line, I never would have answered.

Chapter 19

He slumped before the computer in his spacious office, mouth ajar. Fiery ants ran up and down his nerve endings as he read the online news story and stared at the composite.

He could not believe it. How could this have happened? What had he *done*?

He'd been even stupider than he thought.

It was a good thing he hadn't gone back there last night.

The woman was dead.

He considered that. Yeah, well. So be it. He had far worse things to worry about.

He stared at the news story and picture again. Everything was okay, it was okay, he was still In Control. Actually, some of the facts suited him. They'd throw the cops off guard. Way off. Or the sheriff's deputies, that is. According to the newspaper, they were handling the case.

So handle it, whiny little deputies. Chase after your killer. Chase all you want. Examine the evidence you think you have, run all over the county. Just keep busy doing that . . . and I'll do what I need to do.

He stared again at the drawing of the suspect. Such details. And in living color. Fascinating. Utterly fascinating.

But it wouldn't matter.

For once life would hand him a silver lining. He'd have the chance to fix this mess. Make up for what happened. So he'd gotten some things wrong, so what? Everybody made a mistake now and then. Everybody. Even him.

No worries. Even his anger had passed. He was calm once again. Cool. Focused. He knew what he had to do. Better yet, he had time to do it. Time to let things over there settle a bit. Time to wait this out. And plan it right.

He'd just had himself a trial run, that's all.

He glanced at the clock. Soon it would be time to visit his sister. He'd promised her some of her favorite homemade cookies today—his own chocolate chip recipe with the thin fudge glaze.

Pushing back from the computer, he walked down the long hall and into the kitchen. Plucked a chef's apron off its hook in the pantry and slipped it on.

Dough on his white designer shirt would never do.

Chapter 20

Annie Kingston?"

I did not recognize the voice. "Yes."

"This is Adam Bendershil from the *Record Searchlight.*"

The local Redding newspaper. That snapped me to attention. I was in no shape to handle a reporter.

He didn't skip a beat. "Ms. Kingston, I understand you live across the street from the Willits and were one of the first at the scene of the crime."

"Well, I wasn't—"

"Tell me, how did the fact that you knew the victim affect your ability to draw the composite?"

I nearly swallowed my tongue. Afraid I'd drop my glass, I walked to the table to set it down, then stood with the phone pressed to my ear, gazing into the great room, searching for an answer. I should have thought about reporters. I should have been prepared for this.

How much to tell him? My first reaction was to say, "No comment" and bang down the phone. But that response always sounded suspicious. Neither did I want to be unhelpful to the reporter. During my years as a courtroom artist, reporters had been the link to my livelihood. They were the ones who took photos of my drawings for their newspapers

or had their cameramen film them for news shows. I understood their need to "get the story," and I knew what power
the media could wield.

I also knew they could be a royal pain in the neck.

"Ms. Kingston?"

. *How did the fact that you knew the victim . . .*

The urge to defend myself swept through me, as if the
reporter had suggested that my work wasn't competent. But
fear of the unknown stayed my tongue. I still could not
remember where I'd seen the Face. If that composite was
accurate, he was out there somewhere, no doubt watching
the news. Better that he know as little about me as possible.
The reporter must not have heard that I'd recognized my
own drawing. Chetterling, bless him, had kept tight wraps
on that fact. If it were to leak to the press, I would really feel
vulnerable.

"Sorry. Uh, Adam, you said your name was? I will only
say that my . . . friendship with Lisa Willit, the victim, did not
hinder me in any way from doing the task that the Redding
Sheriff's Office requested of me. If you'd like more information about that, you'll have to talk to Detective Chetterling,
as I'm not at liberty to discuss my work."

How stilted the statement sounded. I envisioned the
printed quote, stark black ink on white newsprint, and
cringed.

The reporter tried to extract more from me but I held my
ground. I made an excuse that I had to go and hung up the
phone, trembling.

Within half an hour, a woman reporter from KRCR news,
the local ABC station, called. She got nothing more than

Adam Bendershil had. But I was careful not to sound too brusque. One thing I had learned from being Trent Gerralon's daughter: hounds though they could be, you never knew when you might *need* the media.

And as long as they were running pictures of the Face, whose identity still eluded me, that time was now.

Thursday, July 24

Chapter 21

Twelve-thirty a.m.

I sat alone in the great room, racking my brain for the thousandth time. Everyone else was in bed, including our guests, Ed and Carol Something. Another crucial day had gone, another weary night to pass. But I could not imagine sleeping. *Tick-tock*, sounded the grandfather clock. It had counted down to this—the final of the seventy-two hours.

And still I could not remember.

By late afternoon Wednesday the Sheriff's Office had received only a few tips about who Lisa's killer might be—everything from a previous renter at Shasta Station who blamed the folding of his business on his landlord, Dave, to a new parolee on the streets of Redding. A few more had trickled in about the composite. One woman thought that "if you stretched your mind," it kind of resembled a former neighbor. Another surmised that the features reminded her of a clerk at a twenty-four-hour gas station south of Redding on Interstate 5. None of the leads checked out. Not one.

I slumped on a couch, eyes closed, forcing my mind over faces, locations, events. But the harder I tried to remember where I'd seen the Face, the more elusive the memory became.

The clock's hands moved. Twelve-thirty five. About this moment three days ago, Lisa Willit was murdered.

This afternoon would be her funeral. I dreaded being surrounded by all those mourners. How difficult the day would be for Dave and Erin. And the heartrending sight would only make me feel more responsible that justice for Lisa was slipping away.

I stared through the front windows into the darkness.

Tick-tock. Twelve-forty. Around this time Erin would have awakened on the floor. She would find her mother in the kitchen, call 911. The countdown would start.

Seventy-two hours ago.

Our time was up.

Chapter 22

The New Life Church sanctuary was packed for Lisa's funeral. The service was unlike anything I'd expected and very different from my father's. The gathering to memorialize Trent Gerralon had been a dignified, cold event. A pastor hired for the service—one we did not know, since we never attended church—said all the right things and recited words from the Bible. But those biblical promises of a blissful hereafter seemed as untouchable to me as the moon. How could those verses have anything to do with my father? I'd never known him to care one whit for God. In fact, it seemed to me he did everything to spit in God's face. He was a womanizer, a liar; he was hardhearted and arrogant and power-hungry. Now, upon his death, he was to be transported to a heaven where God is worshiped for eternity?

At Lisa's funeral people still appeared shocked, and the sight of the flower-laden open casket seemed unbearable. Yet the service proved both grief-stricken lament and victorious send-off. Family members and friend after friend took the podium to speak of Lisa's faith in Christ. How her life had been a living testament to "her Lord." The Bible verses read— some of them the very same as at my father's funeral—did not fall as words spoken into a chasm but seemed to soar like birds on the wind. What amazed me most were the two emotions underlying every story: a deep inner joy despite the pain of the current circumstances . . . and hope. They permeated the sanctuary as tangibly as droplets of dew in chilled morning air.

Even my nonchalant and self-absorbed son appeared to notice. Numerous times I glanced at Stephen to see that he soaked in every word, although puzzlement filtered across his face. I understood his ambivalence. I too wanted to believe all I heard. I wanted to dwell in the claims that Christ as God's Son died to redeem all mankind and that he now lives again, offering each of us a personal relationship with him on this earth and a future with him for eternity.

"Though we mourn Lisa Willit, as she has passed on from this life," Pastor Jim Storrel declared, "we can rest assured that she still lives—now a new and joyous life in the very presence of Christ. As John 5:24 says, 'I tell you the truth, whoever hears my word and believes him who sent me has eternal life and will not be condemned; he has crossed over from death to life.'"

At these words from the New Life pastor, I scanned the congregation, taking in the clutched tissues and pinched faces—and the nods of agreement, the whispered amens, the tears that mixed joy and pain. They *knew* what this man was talking about, knew it deep within their beings.

My father had always sneered at Christianity. "Religion's for the weak," he would say. I never made the conscious decision to agree with him, but his attitude did affect me. Over the years his acidic comments burned their way into my being. I hadn't become an open cynic like him. Rather I did not think of Christ at all. Perhaps God floated in the ether somewhere, but I couldn't imagine he cared about what happened on earth. If he did, he'd make it a more comforting place.

If he did, Lisa Willit would still be alive.

As Pastor Storrel spoke, I found myself wondering if a path existed between the person I was to the kind of people who now surrounded me. Most likely not. They must have been born from different stock, somehow destined to have this intimate communication with God.

The service was drawing to an end. Kelly started to cry. I pressed a tissue into her hand and she leaned against my shoulder. Ten rows in front of us Dave and Erin sat stolidly, for the moment out of tears. Pastor Storrel announced he would close in prayer. "Dear Lord Jesus," he began . . .

But I heard no more.

Two unexpected things occurred in rapid succession.

First, the surprising effect of those three words, particularly in light of what I'd just been feeling. They knifed me like a poisoned stiletto. My vague desires to know God as those around me knew him seeped away. In their place mounted a cold anger. *Wait just a minute. Why should Jesus demand that these people call him "Dear Lord" when he let Lisa Willit be attacked? When he let her die?* I should not covet their blind devotion. The more I thought about it, the more it sickened me. All that Dave believed, all that these New Life people believed, couldn't *possibly* be right.

My jaw hardened. I stared at my lap, unwilling to close my eyes, wanting nothing more than to snatch my children out of that sanctuary and run home. I focused on the black fabric of my dress, staring through it until it blurred. Trying to shut my ears and block all other thought. I glared at the weave of that cloth until it seemed to wriggle alive.

Then the second thing happened.

My staring at the fabric hurled my thoughts to the total black that Lisa Willit's killer had worn. And with that prompting, my internal movie projector ground into motion, flashing vivid stills of Lisa's murder like a horror film under strobe lights.

Flash—

his hands at her throat, her mouth open, eyes bulging

Flash—

her claw-fingers latched onto his

Flash—

ice blue eyes narrowed in hatred and resolve

Flash—

the same blue eyes squinting in sudden daylight.

The Willits' hallway has dissolved into a familiar street in Redwood City, one block from the San Mateo county courthouse. I stand at my car, portfolio in one hand, keys in the other, surprised by the voice that has caused me to turn . . .

I gasped. Kelly slipped her fingers into mine, thinking I had choked back a sob. My eyes squeezed shut and I couldn't breathe. I sat still, as if the smallest movement might cause the memory to poof away.

Think, think!

Three months after my father's death—that's when it happened. I'd been in court all day, covering the trial of Walter Best, who'd allegedly robbed half a dozen Bay Area banks. I'd walked to my car after court adjourned. My key was in the car door . . .

"Hey, you draw some great pictures," says a male voice behind me.

I turn, expecting to see a face I recognize. A stranger stands on the sidewalk, hands in his pockets. Squinting into the setting sun. Bright-blue eyes. Blond hair—unusually so, given the man's apparent age of around fifty. A long face. Saggy jowls. His lips turn down at the corners, hidden in skin folds, so that even as he smiles, he doesn't look friendly.

My artist's eye records all this within a split second. "Thank you." Normally I would ask how he knows who I am. But something about this man is unnerving. Turning back to the car, I unlock the door, hoping to end the encounter.

"Sorry, should have introduced myself. The name's—" He tells me the name but I fail to listen, focused as I am on getting in my car, on leaving. His voice, droning on, pulls me back. ". . . work around here as a courier. Most of the legal eagles have used me to ferry documents back and forth. Your dad used me numerous times, just recently on the Edgar Sybee case."

I flinch. Sybee's case was the last my father handled. "Oh." My lips draw into a weak smile. "Well. Nice to meet you." I pull open my car door.

"I was very sorry to hear about your father. He was a great attorney. I miss him."

At this I can only nod.

The man turns as if to continue down the sidewalk. Then swivels back. "Hey, I'm just curious. Even though the trial's over and everything. There was a file on the Sybee case that Sid Haynes wanted. But it never turned up, as far as I know. Something having to do with a conversation between your father and Sybee. Haynes asked me if I'd ever seen it. It occurs to me now that maybe your father had it with him in that other house of his—the one up near Redding. Apparently, that's where he was when he had the heart attack. You happen to come across that file?"

I twist to face the man once again. "I have no idea what you're talking about."

He stares at me a second too long. Then shrugs.

"Not that I've cleaned out the office up there."

Now why did I bother to say that? If Sid Haynes wants some old files of my father's, I'll make sure he gets them, but that is not this man's affair. What difference will files of the Sybee case make now, anyway? Edgar Sybee was acquitted, and even fresh evidence will never put him in jail for the crime he committed.

"When I do—" I turn away, dismissing him—"I'll see that Mr. Haynes gets everything he should."

Before the man can say more, I slide into my sun-warmed car and shut the door. The man raises his pudgy chin at me in a gesture of farewell and moves on down the sidewalk. I pull out of my parking place and drive in the opposite direction . . .

I sat frozen in the New Life sanctuary, Kelly pressed against my side, the scene playing and replaying in my head. Four days and three nights of begging my mind for the memory—and it springs forth like a taunting jack-in-the-box.

How could I not have remembered this until now?

My eyes would not open; my brain reeled as it tried to logic through the memory and its implications.

I had never seen that man again. Nor had I thought of him until this moment. What a terrible, tragic mistake. Perhaps I would have, if my life hadn't been so embroiled in changes. Jenna and I had been in the midst of selling Dad's Hillsborough house. My move to Grove Landing was only days away, and I was packing and dealing with resistance from the kids. Especially Stephen, who was sulky and rebellious, sneaking out with his friends at night, getting into trouble at school. If I hadn't felt so overwhelmed, maybe I would have considered the man's odd request and his claims. A file courier? Maybe, but it didn't make sense between two partners in the same law firm.

That other house of his—the one up near Redding.

The man's words faded into Dave's grief-stricken voice: *He was in my office, looking for something. Why?*

The house up near Redding.

My father's house, at the end of Barrister Court.

Across the street from the Willits'.

An eel slimed its way through my gut. Far, far away Pastor Sorrel droned his prayer to the living God, the protecting God, the one who now sheltered Lisa in heaven. But the words could not reach me. Far away Kelly laid her head on my shoulder. But I had whisked away to some other plane, frozen and desolate—and inescapable.

That man in Redwood City was Lisa's killer.

But he went to the wrong house.

He'd meant to break into my father's house. Into *my* house. Find some file in attorney Trent Gerralon's office and flee with it into the night.

The knowledge stuck to me like burning oil.

This funeral, the droning prayer, was not supposed to exist. Lisa was the victim of a *mistake*, a wrong turn under the veil of night. She should not be dead. *I* should. My body lying in that casket, my hands folded across my chest. My son and daughter, motherless.

A sob rose in my chest. Kelly squeezed my hand. "Mom, come on. It's time to go."

Go? How can I even move?

Somehow I managed to pull myself from my seat. To hold Kelly's hand and slide out of the pew, walk up the aisle and out the door of that church. People moved around me, talking in low tones, but I couldn't hear their words above the noise in my head. A new mantra had hummed into existence within me, chanting, chanting.

The wrong house.

The killer had gotten the wrong house.

Chapter 23

I barely remember going to the gravesite, hearing the final words over the closed casket. Driving home woodenly, fear and guilt rendering me silent. I do remember thinking the kids could not know. This was my private nightmare.

When we arrived home, I hastily changed out of my black dress into shorts and a T-shirt. "I'm going to work in the office," I informed Kelly and Stephen. "Lots of your grandfather's stuff to clean out in there."

Stephen eyed me with the knowing look of a teenager proud of his perception. Clearly, he thought I was upset over the funeral and now sought to dispel my grief through tackling some new project.

If he only knew.

Scuttling into my father's office, I closed the door and leaned against it, as if to keep some pursuing demon at bay.

My eyes cruised the office, right to left. Starting with plaques and framed prints of private airplanes in flight on the wall, moving to a leather couch with small glass tables and lamps on either side. The ottoman at one end of the couch. Across a few feet of bare floor to the edge of the area rug. On to the front windows, starting at knee height and reaching all the way up to the fourteen-foot ceiling, and in front of the windows, the desk and chair. My gaze moved left, over the edge of the rug and onto bare hardwood floor, then to the matching chairs upon which Dave and Erin had sat four days ago. Bookcases lined the wall from those chairs to the front corner of the office. And to my far left, against the wall that sheltered the door frame, sat the massive oak file cabinet—wide enough to contain legal documents. Four drawers with brass handles.

My father had been incredibly neat. When I first viewed this office on the day we were called to Redding due to his heart attack, not one file was out of place. His massive oak desk was cleaned off, his computer and printer and stacked in-boxes and penholder and telephone all dusted. I came in from the hospital that evening and sat, shell-shocked, in his leather chair. Looking at the singular perfection of his office and wondering how such a powerful man could be struck down by mere centimeters of arterial plaque.

Life was so fragile, it was frightening.

I had not liked my father. But I had loved him. On some deep level I wanted him to reach out to me, to *see* me. To tell me, as fathers are supposed to do, that he loved me for who I was and what I'd accomplished. But, being his child—and female at that—I was to him another feather in his cap, something *he* had created, and therefore someone who owed him. Just as Jenna owed him, and my mother owed him, and any mistress he'd chosen to bask in his affections owed him.

Stunned at his death, I'd sat in his chair caught in the gunfire of dueling emotions—a bitter disappointment that what I'd longed for would never come true, and a nauseating relief that I no longer needed to fool myself into thinking it might. I'd opened the drawers of his desk one by one. Marveling at the neatness of the long middle drawer—pens, stamps, small notepads of paper, clips, scissors—everything in its place. In the top right drawer, I recalled seeing a ream of typing paper, plus stationery and envelopes bearing the Gerralon & Haynes maroon-and-gray logo. The second drawer held manila envelopes, legal-size folders, an expandable file.

A hanging rack, full of files, filled the bottom drawer.

Remembering all this, I now moved toward the desk and lowered myself into my father's chair. With a deep breath I opened the bottom drawer.

Even as my eyes sought the file names through their clear plastic tabs, I tried to tell myself that I would find nothing; I had imagined it all. My memory of the Face was real, all right. And he had mentioned a file. But to think that the Face needed some papers from the Sybee trial so desperately that he would stage a chance encounter with me as I reached my car that day . . . To think that he would want this file in the first place—when the trial was over and done. That he would take the chance of showing his face to me. That he would drive all the way up here to Grove Landing, intent on breaking into the house, and end up on the wrong side of the street . . .

My fingers flicked through the closest tabs. These were not even related to my father's work. There were files about the house mortgage, the landscape and outside light systems, repairs to the airplane, magazine articles related to flying. Beyond these lay bills, stock market information, media clippings of my father's trials. More folders on the airplane. Another of pilot maps.

Not one file from Gerralon & Haynes.

I flopped back against the chair. For a moment I basked in relief. This drawer would have been the most likely place for such a file. The wooden cabinet surely contained papers of old cases, information Sid Haynes hadn't asked for to this day.

In the distance I registered the drone of a private plane. One of the Grove Landing residents was about to land. How I wished it was Jenna.

I crossed the office toward the cabinet. Pulled out the top drawer.

Dozens more files hung in their green sheaths. One by one I slid them forward, reading their titles and dates. They held papers relating to cases going back four or five years— around the time my father had built the house. None was more recent than three years ago.

My hands reached the back of the drawer. One down. I pushed it closed and pulled out the second, which held more of the same.

The third drawer slid out. No files here. Only an array of airplane paraphernalia. Joysticks for the computer and simulation software for flying by instruments. Extra cannulas for the Cessna 210 that my father had passed to Jenna. The craft was capable of flying at over twenty thousand feet, but the cabin wasn't pressurized. The oxygen tanks and breathing tubes were necessary for the higher cruising altitudes.

Next I saw books on airports, folded maps, a couple headsets, and a handheld GPS unit. Did Jenna know all this stuff was here?

In the bottom drawer lay my father's briefcase.

I drew back, sudden tears biting my eyes. How many times had I seen that case dangling from my father's hand? Those times it was stuffed to the gills with paper. Now it lay almost collapsed upon itself.

Sitting on my haunches, I stared at it, unwilling to pick it up. My gaze took in the brass clasp, the supple reddish-brown leather, the matching stitches around its frame and handle, various nicks it had sustained over the years of use.

What was the briefcase doing here, anyway?

True, my father had been a neatnik, but putting this away in a drawer? Maybe Jenna had done it. She and I and the kids drove up together when we got the call from a doctor at the hospital in Redding. By the time we arrived at the hospital, my father was already gone. Frowning, I tried my best to remember seeing the briefcase when we came into the house that Saturday night. I didn't think I had. The heart attack struck early Saturday morning—apparently before he had the chance to so much as enter his office. He'd probably placed the briefcase in this drawer the night before, upon his arrival from the Bay Area.

I shifted my position to sit cross-legged on the floor. Reached into the drawer and pulled out the case. Laid it on my legs. Then I stared at it once more, caught in the predicament of weighing the unknown against the possible known. For a moment I considered dumping it back inside, shoving the drawer closed, walking away.

I pulled open the covering flap. Inside, the briefcase had two compartments. I slid my hand into the back one. Nothing. In the front compartment I touched a thin file folder. After a moment's hesitation I pulled it out.

An ordinary brown folder with a raised tab. No heading. Opening the file, I discovered two pages of lined yellow paper, like pieces pulled from a letter-sized writing tablet. The top page was titled "Sybee Interview, 3/14." A stream of air escaped my mouth.

Sybee.

What was that date?

March 14. The day before my father died—the Friday he flew here to the house. Whatever was in this file represented the last task of his career.

Chapter 24

My father's handwriting left a lot to be desired, I thought as I sat in his desk chair. Letters ran together, part of them cut off. What he had written was not in complete sentences. Still, they gave detailed descriptions through key words. The first paragraph consisted of one sentence: *Crime accding to S.*

S had to mean *Sybee.*

Two months after my father's death, the Sybee trial began. It had been scheduled for the end of March, but that being two weeks after my father's unexpected death, Haynes had asked the court for an extension. I covered the case for local media, pouring every ounce of concentration I possessed into studying those faces, drawing those pictures. Especially the pictures of the defense attorney.

Concentrate on Sid's square face, I'd told myself, *the high forehead, the bald pate with wisps of brown hair. Don't think that the results of your fingers should have yielded a much different face—one that now lay cold and silent in the grave.*

Even with the artistic concentration, I had absorbed the details of the case—the evidence, the testimony of a grieving widow, the theatrics and prodding questions of both prosecution and defense. I heard enough about Edgar Sybee to detest him. He was thirty-one, the mewling, spoiled dope-fiend son of Matt Sybee, wealthy owner of over half a dozen foreign car dealerships in the Bay Area. Edgar married when he was twenty-eight, promising his young bride, Crystal, that he'd slip out of his drug habits as he slipped on his wedding ring. He had not kept his promise. A year later Crystal had a son. The Sybees lived in an expensive house in Atherton, an upscale area just south of Redwood City.

Edgar Sybee worked—if that's what you could call it— as a salesman at his father's dealership in San Mateo. In that capacity he rubbed shoulders with plenty of other well-to-do folk who came in to look at cars. These people were often of a different caliber than Edgar's other business associates— those who sold him drugs, and those who bought drugs from him. Edgar was a firm believer in the saying "Never too rich." As far as he was concerned, his commissions from Daddy's business could not support his intended lifestyle. Selling drugs, on the other hand—now *that* was big business.

One of the car dealership customers Edgar served was Barry Draye, an insurance broker in his mid-thirties who, along with his wife, nurtured a secret taste for cocaine. Reportedly, Barry and Edgar got to talking one day, their conversation continuing after the dealership closed for the night. Edgar did not walk away from that discussion with a hefty car sale. But he did walk away with an order for four ounces of cocaine—and the promise of plenty more purchases to come.

Barry Draye's wife, Lynn, wasn't at their Redwood City home when Edgar showed up to sell him the drugs on the night of September 16. According to Lynn's testimony, Barry had sent her off on an errand, saying he'd promised Edgar she would not be home during the transaction. Apparently, Edgar had told Barry that his ever suspicious supplier insisted on coming along to check Barry out, and this man chose to show his face to as few clients as possible. Lynn was uneasy about the request—and would later regret not paying more attention to her sense. When she came home around ten p.m., she found Barry sprawled on the family room floor, dead from a single stab wound to the chest. There were no defense wounds—bruises or cuts—that would indicate he'd fought his assailant. He must have been surprised by the attack. The knife was never found.

Nearly hysterical, Lynn wailed to the 911 dispatcher the story about the intended drug purchase from Edgar Sybee. Sybee's name was not new to police—he'd been arrested once before on drug possession. Due to the vast number of drug possessors arrested daily, the California penal system works to keep first-time offenders out of jail. Sybee paid a fine, then was placed on probation and allowed to continue his life.

When police arrived the night of Draye's murder with a warrant to search Sybee's house, he appeared nervous, his answers evasive. They pulled a crisp one hundred dollar bill from his wallet, but the rest of the money Draye had allegedly paid Sybee was nowhere to be found. Police also discovered two ounces of cocaine inside a small vase pushed far back in a kitchen drawer—perhaps Sybee's personal stash.

Meanwhile, at the crime scene someone had left a smeared bloody print on an end table in the Drayes' family room. This fingerprint proved to be highly contended in court, the prosecution's expert witness saying the print matched Sybee's, and the defense's expert saying that because it was smeared, it was at best inconclusive.

To the prosecution's disappointment, Lynn's claim that Sybee came to sell drugs could not be proved, and no charges on the matter were filed. There were no drugs in the Draye home and Sybee wouldn't cop to pushing dope. He'd just wanted to pay a visit to a friend, he repeated again and again to the police, but this "drug supplier" who'd come with him had evidently formed plans of his own to sell drugs—and ended up stabbing Barry Draye in self defense. In a myopic view common to the courtroom, the prosecution accepted half of Sybee's tale and discarded the rest. There was no second man, the deputy D.A. told the jury. However, Draye's murder *was* the result of a drug deal gone bad—a drug deal that Sybee, and Sybee alone, had aimed to carry out. And the murder certainly had *not* been in self defense.

There remained the inconvenient matter that Sybee's story of a second man did fit with Lynn's statement to police that she'd been asked to leave the house. Still, police and prosecution discarded the claim. Sybee's request to Lynn was a mere ruse to assure that Barry would be alone in the first place, they said. Besides, they insisted, there was no evidence that anyone had arrived with Sybee, and what little forensic evidence they'd identified—namely, the smeared fingerprint—pointed to Sybee. Most telling, throughout the trial neither Sybee nor his defense ever produced the name of this supposed second man. The reason was clear, the prosecution declared in final arguments.

He didn't exist.

Sybee did not take the stand. But Haynes, no doubt following through with the defense my father had established, combined Lynn Draye's statement to police about the second man with some fancy footwork—literally. A shoe print had been lifted from the tiled entryway in the Draye home— one that did not belong to either of the Drayes or Edgar

Sybee. And a dark-brown human hair—also unknown in origin—was found on the carpet of the family room. Surely, Haynes argued, these pieces of evidence didn't belong to some friendly visitor in the Draye home, as the prosecution had suggested. No, these pieces of evidence belonged to the real killer. What's more, Edgar had repeatedly told police during his videotaped interview that this other man—whose name he would not divulge, "or his family would die"—had stabbed Barry Draye. Anyone, claimed Haynes, could see that Edgar Sybee had no motive whatsoever to kill his friend.

Public opinion ran strong for the prosecution. Sybee was a slimy, lying, rich-kid druggie, and the holes in his story couldn't be plugged with a truckload of redwood logs. All the same, the twelve upstanding citizens of the jury fell under the spell of Haynes's defense tactics.

Sybee was acquitted.

The Bay Area was stunned.

Post-trial interviews with jurors yielded the same general statement: as much as they'd wanted to find Edgar Sybee guilty, the prosecution had not offered sufficient evidence to prove that another person hadn't been present at the time of Barry Draye's death, and in fact hadn't been responsible for it.

Art Springer, the deputy D.A. who'd handled the case, scuttled through the courthouse halls for the next month with the fire of self-defensiveness in his eyes. He'd lost in front of his colleagues and the public, and his ego drove him to lash out against the firm of Gerralon & Haynes (which hadn't changed its name yet) to any reporter who would listen—and there were plenty. He hated Sid Haynes. And he hated my father, who he knew had put the case together, although out of public deference to the dead he did not speak my father's name. Springer's meager solace was that Sybee would be awarded six months in the county jail for possession of cocaine—his second drug offense.

As I sat at my father's desk, I skimmed the first paragraph of his notes, and my heart kicked up my throat. For some reason, two weeks before the trial Sybee had decided to talk. Maybe my father convinced him their defense was iffy at best, that Sybee had a choice between serving a long jail term and presenting a name that could be connected to the footprint and hair.

Taking a deep breath, I began to read, the movie projector in my head whirring into motion. The scene began with Edgar Sybee

answering a call on the personal business line in his home from "Tip," his drug supplier. Sybee sees Tip as unpredictable, volatile, and paranoid. One minute the guy's calm, cool; the next minute his temper is flaring. He's incessantly careful about getting caught by police. Tip's calls are the only way Edgar can talk to him. The man has never given Edgar his number, and the digits are blocked from appearing on caller ID. Edgar does not even know his real name.

Now Edgar tells Tip he wants eight ounces of cocaine.

"Eight?" Tip's voice turns suspicious. "Why so much on one day?"

"No reason." Edgar waits for Tip to speak but the silence draws out. "What do you care?"

Tip's voice ices over. "You are asking me why I care?"

This is enough to scare Edgar. "Okay, okay. I found a new client."

For the next two minutes Tip rants and raves. Edgar is an idiot who wouldn't know a jump rope from a rattler. He's a rich man's son trying to play tough in the streets, and one day it just might get him killed. Or worse, it just might get him caught by the police. And then where would ol' Tip be, huh? Turned in, that's where. The big fish named to authorities while the little fish cops a deal.

But Edgar would never do that, would he. Not as long as he enjoys the health of his wife and son . . .

Edgar chills to the bone. He hates this man. He wishes he'd never met this man.

He needs this man.

Tip forces Barry Draye's name from Edgar. The remaining details bounce from Edgar like popcorn on cement—their agreement to meet at Barry's home the next night, the promises of business deals to follow. With a stream of curses, Tip tells Edgar what he thinks of "his little plan." Upstanding insurance man Barry is probably an informant. He'll be wired. Sell him the coke and police will be waiting on the front porch.

Too late now, though, Tip says. Now he's got to clean up Edgar's mess. Tip insists on going with Edgar to Barry's house. If the man's wearing a wire, he'll know it. "Make sure," he adds, "that the guy's alone."

Not until the following night, when they are greeted on Barry's unlit front porch, does Edgar think, wait a minute, if Tip thinks this guy's hooked to cops, why are we here? Tip is high and wound up tighter than a coiled spring. He's wearing a designer nylon jacket. He keeps his hands in his pockets as Barry leads them into the house.

In Barry's family room Tip takes charge, like the turf is his own. He's not quite six feet but he's muscular as all get-out. And his expression can blacken like the mask of death. Tip gets all up in Barry's face, pushing his finger into the man's chest, saying he'd better not be tight with any cops. Roughly he searches Barry's body. Barry turns ghost pale as he insists he's on the level. Edgar can tell Tip's enjoying himself, liking the fear he inflicts. Then Tip goes off on a real tangent, talking about the people he's killed and how he'll cut Barry up and put him in a dozen trash cans if Barry ever so much as mentions to anybody what's gone down here. Barry tries to keep his cool. Tells Tip, okay, let me just pay you and you can give me the stuff, then be on your way. Tip says, "Give Edgar the money." Barry takes out his wallet and passes Edgar a small stack of one hundred dollar bills. Tip waits until Edgar counts it.

Barry replaces the wallet in his back pocket. "Okay, now your turn."

Tip tells him he'll get the stuff when Tip's good and ready to give it. And for good measure he punches Barry in the chest. Barry stumbles back and falls like a sack of potatoes. His head misses an end table by inches. Edgar backs away, trying to make himself small. He wants to tell Tip, hey, take it easy, Barry's okay. But he can't speak.

And then Barry surprises the daylights out of Edgar. He scrambles to his knees, pulls open the single drawer of the coffee table, and yanks out a gun.

No, no, no, no, no, Edgar thinks, and words start spilling from his lips. His mouth turns motor. He begs Barry to put the gun down and Tip to stop and says this is not the way to do business, guys, what are you, both crazy? Know what would happen to my car sales if I tried to sell a sport coupe this way? This is just a nice little deal, and we can all be nice little friends. Tip, let's just make the connect and get out of here; Barry, put the gun away.

Tip makes a noise in his throat like an infuriated bear and kicks the gun from Barry's hand. The gun flips in the air and lands a few feet behind Barry. The man yells and holds his fingers. "Get the gun, Edgar," Tip demands, and Edgar does what he's told, because what else can he do?

Tip pulls a knife from the pocket of his jacket.

That scares Edgar bad. Real bad. All he can do is tell himself everything will be okay. Just get the gun, do what Tip says. And if I turn away from that knife, concentrate on picking up the gun, it won't even exist.

His motor mouth runs on—okay, okay, I am picking up the gun. See? Not a threat anymore. See, Tip, now it's in my hand, and I'm gonna turn and give it to you . . .

Barry makes some weird cry that pinches off. Edgar whirls to see Tip's knife buried in his chest. Barry topples over on his side, right next to Edgar. No, no, no, Edgar says aloud, and the next thing he knows, Tip's pulled out the bloody knife and is wiping it on Barry's shirt. Edgar's legs get all weak and he sinks to one knee, nearly dropping the gun. His right hand flings out to catch himself, his forefinger swishing across Barry's bloodied chest. "Come on, come on," Tip urges, and Edgar grabs the end table to help pull himself to his feet. Tip puts the knife back in his jacket pocket and zips it up.

Then they are out the front door, Tip turning the knob by sticking his right hand underneath his jacket so he won't leave prints. And they're climbing into Edgar's car and driving away. "Go slow, go slow," Tip warns, "like there's nothin' wrong." Tip takes the gun from Edgar and says he'll keep it as a souvenir. Edgar shakes the whole way to the back parking lot of the grocery store where Tip's luxury car awaits. And the entire trip is filled with all sorts of creative ideas from Tip about how Edgar and his family can die if he ever tells . . .

By the time I read the last sentence, my heart fluttered like a trapped butterfly. I could hardly take it all in.

How could this story be connected to Lisa's murder?

I set the file on the desk. Then swiveled in the chair to stare at the Willits' house.

Think, Annie, think.

Okay, facts. First, the composite. The man in my drawing was the same man who stopped me on the Redwood City street. The man who wanted the file I just read.

Did the discovery of this file prove my composite was right?

I pondered that. Maybe the man in Redwood City had been telling the truth. He *was* a courier for Gerralon & Haynes, and he *did* wonder about a missing file. And okay, so the file existed. I still could have conjured him from my subconscious when drawing the composite. In that case the only coincidence here was that I drew him by mistake.

But Erin recognized the drawing.

True, but Erin was a highly traumatized twelve-year-old.

Traumatized or not, when she first described her mother's killer, she told of his bright-blue eyes, his blond hair.

I sighed. I could go around and around with this. But bottom line, what could I or the detectives do but believe Erin when she said the drawing was on target?

Second, the file. If that man on the street lied to me, if he wasn't who he claimed to be, who was he? Evidently, he'd cared enough about recovering this file to seek out Grove

Landing and the house he believed to be my father's and break into it. He'd cared enough about not getting caught that he'd attacked Lisa so she couldn't call the police. And maybe the only reason he let Erin live was because she'd fainted. All these thoughts brought me to the question, who else would care about this file so much other than Tip, whom it implicated?

One more niggling thought clamored. If Lisa Willit's killer indeed broke into the wrong house, he must have realized his mistake. The papers on Dave's desk would be all wrong, plus Lisa didn't look a thing like me. Even if he didn't get a close look at the papers, and if he knew enough about my family to think Lisa was my sister (and there *was* a twelve-year-old girl in the house), surely by now he realized his mistake. The media had covered the crime. The victim's name wouldn't fit.

Now he would know the truth. And given that he so badly wanted this file . . . what was to keep him from coming back?

Chapter 25

My fingers shook as I dialed the offices of Gerralon & Haynes. No. Now Haynes & Asher. One man's death meant another man's promotion.

It was already nearing five. I *had* to get through to Sid—a man so busy that I imagined his wife even screened his home calls. Even as I dialed the number, myriad responsibilities bombarded me. I would have to tell Detective Chetterling all I'd discovered. And Dave Willit. I should admit to him the horrible truth: if he lived anywhere but across the street from *me*, his wife would be alive.

And the kids. I had to protect them. The more certain I became that the Sybee file had led to Lisa's death, the more I knew I could not take chances with my children. They would have to get out of this house, go to their father's. Surely even Vic wouldn't fight me on this one.

But first I had to gather all the knowledge I could about the papers. I still could not let go of the hope that the Redwood City man was who he claimed to be and not some paranoid drug dealer called Tip.

By providence Sid Haynes picked up his own phone.

Where to start?

"Sid, it's Annie. I'm in trouble."

His hesitation lasted a fraction of a second. I knew he paused not because of the words, which he'd heard hundreds of times from clients, but because they came from me.

"Tell me about it."

That was Sid. Terse. Ever efficient. I pictured him reaching for a white pad of paper and pen to take notes, envisioned the starched cuff on his right sleeve, the fine gray fabric of his suit.

The story rushed from me in a torrent. Lisa's murder, my composite, the Face, my remembering. Sid made no more sound than an occasional grunt. When I was done, I stopped to catch my breath.

"Well," he said slowly. "What do you know."

I knew Sid would not tell me the inner workings of his "other man" defense for Edgar Sybee—that is, how it had been built. I could only assume he'd picked up what my father had already put into place, based upon the evidence at the crime scene, and continued with it. It occurred to me now that he may be quite surprised to hear how close to the truth his defense turned out to be.

But Sid's surprise wasn't my concern. I jumped to my most pressing question. "Do you know the guy I saw on the street? Does his description sound familiar?"

Please tell me he's for real!

Sid inhaled. "Annie—" his concerned tone told me I was about to receive answers I didn't want to hear—"there is no such person who works for us. As a courier or anything else. And even if there were, I wouldn't need him to get me a file from someone in my own office."

My eyes fell to the pages, looking through them, as if the truth were hidden somewhere within the weaving of that paper. "Did you know about this file?"

Brandilyn Collins

"No."

"Do you think it's real?"

"Evidently, it was real enough to get somebody killed."

Lisa's face flashed before me. I pressed my knuckles against my chin.

"Ironic thing, it couldn't be used against the guy in court, because it would fall under hearsay."

"Oh." The legality of the file hadn't even occurred to me.

"But the file's being used in court isn't the issue. The point is, if this story got into the authorities' hands, it would give them good reason to find this man Tip and question him. That could lead to a whole new investigation."

That made sense. *Paranoid*, Sybee had called Tip. *Incessantly careful about being caught by police.*

"But why wouldn't you know about the file? You took over Sybee's defense. If he needed this story at trial, surely he'd have told it to you."

"He didn't need it, as you know. Not all the details, anyway." Sid fell silent for a moment. I heard the faint tapping of fingertip against wood, and an uncomfortable twinge that he was not being completely forthcoming skittered across my nerves. "Apparently, sometime between his telling your father all this and my taking over the case, he changed his mind."

It dawned on me then. Even if Sid did know about the file, he couldn't tell me everything. The trial was over but attorney-client privilege remained. I bit my lip. I didn't want to go to Detective Chetterling with half a story. I wasn't sure he'd listen to me, especially after I cried wolf about an intruder Monday night.

Although with what I knew now, I couldn't help but wonder if I was right and the Face *was* here . . .

187

"Okay. I realize you can't tell me everything about the case. But would you just answer a few more questions?"

"Annie, I am telling you everything I know about that file, which is nothing. But one thing is clear. You're playing with fire. One woman's already been killed. You don't need to be the second. Get that file out of your house—today. Call the detective in charge of the investigation and tell him everything you've told me."

"Of course, I'll do that. But it's not just the location of this file, Sid. It wasn't in the Willits' house and Lisa was killed anyway. What matters is that it's *supposed* to be here."

"What matters is that someone out there wants it very much. And if it's Tip, which sounds quite plausible, you really could be in danger. Drug suppliers are the worst, Annie; I've been around criminals long enough to know that. They're power-hungry and greedy, and most of the time they do not care who lives or dies."

I still wanted a reason not to believe all this. There must be *something*, some plausible explanation, that we had overlooked. "It just seems so crazy that the man would take such chances to get the file. Why would he want it that much?"

"Annie, think about it. He'd counted on a guilty verdict. Then he'd have been home free. But Sybee was acquitted. And you remember how angry the D.A.'s office and the cops were about that? All those articles in the newspapers down here, people upset with the jurors and with me? In fact, as I recall, things heated up just about the time you say that man talked to you on the street. But it doesn't matter how much anyone rants and raves, including the wife of the victim. Thanks to the double jeopardy law, Sybee will never be convicted of that murder. Which means, those same cops still have an unsolved case on their hands. Now, after their very public arguments that Sybee was the murderer, the detectives and the D.A. might not want to admit they were wrong. But you'd hope they would do the right thing. If they saw a strong indication that a second man, the possible killer, was with Sybee that night, it would be incumbent upon them to check it out. No wonder Tip is worried."

I pressed my fingers against the yellow pages on the desk—pages that should have been red for the blood they'd caused to be spilled. "Sid, how would Tip have learned about the file?"

"I have no idea."

"Please don't pull attorney-client privilege on me now! If you know anything, *tell* me. I need to know."

"Annie, I will say it one more time. I don't know anything about the file. Except that it's dangerous and you need to take it to the authorities now."

"Would anyone else in your firm know about it? I mean, maybe my dad told Gary about it so he could start looking into the identity of Tip." Gary Wallinger was an investigator in the Gerralon & Haynes office.

"If Gary knew about it, he'd have told me." Sid paused. I could almost hear his lawyer brain turning its gears. "You know . . . the last time I saw your dad was that Friday. He was leaving the office about three o'clock. I remember him sticking his head in my door, saying he was checking out for the weekend—that he'd be flying up to Grove Landing. I made some comment about his taking off so early. He said he had a meeting at the jail with Sybee. He obviously had that meeting, then flew out for the weekend."

I stared at the bottom cabinet drawer, still yawning open, my father's briefcase beside it. Lisa Willit had paid for the contents of that drawer with her life. "Then no one knew about the file except my father and Edgar Sybee. And my dad did nothing with it, just left it in his briefcase." Which, in my mind, left one possible conclusion. For whatever reason, Sybee told someone about it. Maybe he talked too much to the wrong person in jail. And the news got to Tip.

"I can imagine how frightening all this must be for you." Sid's voice was the kindest I'd ever heard it. "Look, just in case, I'll ask Gary about this guy you've described and get back to you. I've got the number to the house there, but do you have a cell phone? And meanwhile, you *will* call the Sheriff's Office as soon as we hang up, right?"

"Yes, I will." I told him my cell number. "Thanks, Sid. You've been a big help."

I hung up the phone and cradled my head in my hands. A cold wind picked up in my mind, buffeting my thoughts like feathers. So much to do. Jenna would be arriving in an hour or so. I would have to tell her everything. That was the easy part. In fact, that was the only *good* part. I needed my sister's strength right now. Jenna could help me think this through.

But first I had to call Detective Chetterling.

I stared at the phone, unwilling to pick it up again. When it rang, I nearly jumped out of my skin.

Déjà vu? I braced myself. This had better not be another reporter.

"Hello?"

"Annie—"

Jenna's voice caught as she said my name. An icicle slid down my spine. So rarely had I known my sister to cry. But she was crying now.

Chapter 26

Jenna, what's wrong?"

"They laid me off." The words came hard, bitter. "Can you believe it? My supervisor called me into her office today— you're done, just like that. Take your things and don't let the door hit you on the way out." A sob escaped her.

"Oh, Jenna."

"It wasn't just me, not that it makes me feel any better. They laid off a whole slew of people today, twenty-four altogether. Not one of us knew it was coming. I mean, we all knew the company hasn't been doing well, but we didn't expect *this*. They could have warned us. But no. They had to steal up on us like a thief in the night."

Of course they did. Wasn't this the way our lives were going right now? I pushed out of my father's chair and began to pace. My sister's job. Not that she needed it financially anymore, but it was her world. I understood what it meant to lose a world.

"Oh, Jenna, I am so sorry."

She made no reply. I could hear her sniffling.

I stopped pacing, lowered myself to the thick area rug. Then stretched out flat on my back. My elbow hung a few inches off the carpet as I held the phone to my ear.

"Why don't you fly on up tonight. No point in hanging around there by yourself."

"I know. I thought I might as well come, especially with all you're facing there. But I didn't want to wait to tell you. I just . . . wanted to hear your voice now."

I gazed at the office ceiling, so far away. I could just as easily jump to touch it from my supine position as find the strength to deal with this one more thing. I'd been looking forward to Jenna's return so she could support me. Now I needed to help her.

"Sure, I understand. Listen. Bring a lot of clothes. Just come up and stay awhile. We'll be together and . . . figure everything out."

She expelled air. "Everything, huh."

"Yeah. The universe, even."

We were silent for a moment. Then I chanted soothing platitudes—that she would find a better job, one more exciting. That this would all work out, she would see. I even scraped the bottom of the barrel, encouraging her to "think good thoughts"—the old, empty words of our mother. Jenna listened and thanked me, not for any wisdom in my words, for there was none, but for my concern.

She changed the subject. "How was the funeral?"

Wasn't that a loaded question. I couldn't begin to explain on the phone everything that had happened.

"It was very nice."

I glanced at my watch. Past five-thirty. Anxiety seized me. Darkness was less than four hours away and there was much to be done. I could picture my sister moping around her town house, taking her time. She would call friends who'd been laid off, coworkers, maybe even an ex-boyfriend or two, seeking commiseration. "Jenna, listen to me." I didn't try to keep the urgency from my voice. "Hurry and get up here, okay? I hate to put this on you now, but some things have happened and we've got to decide what to do."

Jenna drew in air. "Did you have another scare last night in the house?"

"No."

"Do they think they've caught the guy?"

"Oh, how I wish."

"Annie. You remembered."

"Yes."

My sister knew me too well. She could hear from my tone that the result was anything but positive.

"Tell me!"

I would not, even though she continued to press for details. For once, I did not cave in to her demands. I just could not imagine telling the whole story over the phone while the sun moved toward the horizon, dragging our fate into darkness. What's more, I knew that if I did not tell, Jenna's innate curiosity would get the best of her—and jump-start her on the way to the plane. "Just get here and I'll explain everything."

We started to hang up but I pulled the receiver back, my mouth forming words I could not have imagined saying even an hour ago.

"One thing before you come, Jenna, but do it quickly. Buy some bullets for that gun."

Chapter 27

Beep-beep, beep-beep, came the faint tone from the timer in the kitchen.

He grabbed the stack of printed pages from his office desk and headed down the hall. Tossing the papers on the kitchen table, he crossed the room to pull his tenderized leg of lamb from the convection oven. Laying the pan on the granite counter, he sniffed and smiled. Baked to perfection, and the herbs smelled heavenly. In careful array he served himself on a large plate. Leg of lamb toward the bottom, jasmine rice to the left, mixed vegetables to the right. A slice of his own baked wheat bread on a side plate. He took his meal to the table, fetched some silverware, a napkin, and a glass of red wine, and sat to enjoy his culinary abilities as he read the newspaper articles once more.

He spread out the various pieces of paper in order. Online articles from the Redding paper for Tuesday, Wednesday, and today. He'd read them a dozen times.

Wednesday's article had caused his jaw to drop. Annie Kingston drew the composite. Annie Kingston!

He thrust a bite of meat into his mouth, savoring its flavor. He'd gone around and around, thinking about Annie. Considering the possible fallout of her involvement. After seeing today's article, he'd convinced himself he was safe. Reporters were a nosy bunch. If there had been information to turn up, they'd most likely have done it, just like pigs turning up the ground with their snouts.

But he'd seen nothing.

He grunted at that and thrust his fork under the mound of rice.

According to yesterday's news, the funeral had been this afternoon. There'd be mourners about the neighborhood, grieving relatives staying overnight. Too many people coming and going.

But things would die down after that. No matter what happened in life, people had a way of getting back to normal.

So many times he'd counted on that. People got lazy when things became normal.

He wiped his mouth, then sipped the wine.

When the time to go back was right, he'd know it. He'd feel it. Until then he was safe. Bunch of stupid sheriff's deputies out there, thinking they knew everything. Thinking they'd catch their suspect. He chuckled. They'd never catch him. He was the Man.

He was In Control.

Just one little thing kept bothering him. One little voice in the back of his head. Little Ms. Annie Kingston could get to thinking too much.

He narrowed his eyes.

So what? She obviously didn't know everything.

Still. She could open up . . . things.

She could make his plans go Out of Control. And that was something he could never allow.

He cut another bite of lamb and laid it upon his tongue. Cut one bite of meat at a time, that's what his mother had taught him. It never paid to lack manners.

He took a breath and chewed with satisfaction.

Annie Kingston had better watch herself.

Chapter 28

As I hung up the phone from Jenna's call, the doorbell rang. Though the door to the office was closed, I heard Kelly's footsteps reverberating through the great room, the sound of voices. I recognized Erin's.

Irrational panic seized me. For a second all I could do was stare at the telltale yellow papers. Erin should not be allowed to see them—these pages that had caused her mother's death.

Slapping the file closed, I shoved it into the middle drawer of the desk, scattering my father's perfectly arranged pens and paper clips. The dull thud of the drawer's closing rocketed me back to the night of the murder, listening to Erin's description of the sounds she heard in her home. For no reason at all my heart slammed into a rapid beat. I could not let Erin see me here—at the office desk, guilt on my face. Hiding what her mother's killer was looking for.

I moved around the desk and across the office to the file cabinet. I tossed my father's briefcase back into the open drawer and rolled it shut, then headed for the door. There I paused, working to pull myself together. Willing myself not to think of how Erin would see me, see this entire household, when she heard the truth.

Erin's presence brought other problems as well. I needed to call Detective Chetterling right away. But how would I explain his arrival, and our low-voiced discussion behind closed doors, to Erin? Dave should not have to hear rumors through his daughter.

Dave.

His anguished question of three days ago—*Why?*—resounded in my ears. And his words about the killer: *He was in my office, looking for something.* When he heard the truth, he would not have to blame himself any longer. He could turn his anger instead on me. Pain shot through me at the thought, both for myself and for our daughters. They were friends, and I didn't want them to suffer any more than they already were.

But I couldn't think of that now. I opened the door and left the office.

Across the great room I saw Kelly and Erin standing before the refrigerator, surveying its contents. I couldn't help but smile. There stood Erin, a twelve-year-old on the day of her mother's funeral, searching out a snack.

The world did go on.

"Erin, honey, it's so good to see you." I entered the kitchen and pulled her into a hug. "Is all your family still at your house? Looks like a lot of cars over there."

Our own guests, Ed and Carol, would be leaving tomorrow. They had told me they would return to Dave's house following the funeral.

"Yeah. Most of 'em go tomorrow." She pulled away with a small attempt at a smile.

I ran my hand down her silky hair, searching for something else to say and finding nothing.

"What are we having for dinner, Mom?" Kelly asked.

Dinner. I hadn't even thought of it. "Uh, I don't know."

"Erin's tired of casseroles." Kelly made a face. "It's all she's eaten for the last three days."

I nodded. "Shall we order pizza?"

"Yes!" Erin and Kelly answered as one.

We hadn't found a take-out place in Redding that would deliver to Grove Landing. I'd have to go pick it up. At the thought my way grew clear before me. Ordering a pizza would give me a reason to drive to the city—where I could meet with Detective Chetterling in his office.

"Tell you what. I have to run some errands anyway. I'll order the pizza when I get into town."

I peeled Chetterling's card off the refrigerator. My eyes fell on Gerri's card, and something inside me leapt at the sight of her name. On impulse I took it as well.

On the way back to the office, I detoured to stand at the top of the stairs leading into Stephen's cave, yelling down to ask him what he wanted on the pizza. He spent far too much time down there at the computer. But what else was he to do? Summer vacation, and I'd moved him out to the sticks, where he had not one friend. I did feel sorry for him, even though I knew I'd made the right choice.

Sausage and pepperoni, he yelled back.

I reentered my father's office and shut the door. Crossing to the desk, I picked up the phone, looking at the two business cards in my hand. I fully intended to call Detective Chetterling. But somehow I ended up dialing Gerri Carson instead.

Before I knew it, I was rattling off the entire story about the file and the Face. Gerri's soothing manner pulled it from me and wound it around the spool of her stability, as one might wind a tangled mass of thread. She uttered words of support and comfort, as if she understood my every emotion. Then I told her everything else—my concern for what to do with the kids, and Jenna's losing her job, and that I planned to come into town, see Detective Chetterling, and pick up a pizza.

"That's good. You're bringing the kids with you, I assume?"

Her words hit me like a sledgehammer. I blinked, my answer sticking in my throat. No, I hadn't planned on bringing the kids. In fact, I'd wanted to leave them home so they wouldn't know what was going on. Home—alone. What had I been thinking? At fifteen and twelve, the kids under normal circumstances could be home alone, but after the past few days we weren't exactly living under normal circumstances. There I was, the fretting mother worried over my children's safety, and at the very same time I was planning a move that was anything but safe.

Selfish gratitude for Jenna's lost job burst through me. I was going to need my sister's help through this. I needed her beside me, talking things through, protecting me from doing something stupid. At the very least I needed her to stay with the kids if I was forced to go into town.

"Gerri, can you believe this? I wasn't planning on bringing them! I just . . . wasn't thinking straight." My throat pinched closed. I lowered my head and rested it against my fist. "All of a sudden I don't know what to do."

"Sounds like you're feeling overwhelmed at the moment." Her voice was gentle. "How about if I come over right now? In the meantime you could make two phone calls. First to Detective Chetterling, telling him you've remembered where you saw the suspect and asking him to come over right away.

And second, if you'll call in your pizza order, I'll pick it up and bring it to you."

I could not see my way any further than the path Gerri had laid before me. Two phone calls—that I could do. "Okay. To everything you just said." I told her what restaurant I'd be ordering the pizza from.

"And Annie, one more thing. I'm going to be praying for you, starting right now until I reach your door. I'm going to pray that God eases your mind, gives you clarity of thought. He is the God of peace, you know, and he can bring you calmness—even in the midst of a storm like this."

"Thank you," I managed, even though I felt not the least trust in her prayers.

I hung up the phone and dialed the number of the restaurant.

Chapter 29

Something strange happened inside me after I ordered our pizza. It wasn't sudden or strong. It was more of a quieting, like the slow settling of whipped winds into a gentle breeze. Somehow my fears lulled, my thoughts stilled, became more clear. When I gathered the nerve to call Detective Chetterling, I was able to talk to him calmly, while conveying that I needed to see him right away.

This reining in of my fears transcended any power I had within me. I'd never experienced anything like it before and didn't quite know what to make of it. To attribute it to Gerri's prayers would be as foreign to me as reading Chinese. To attribute it to mere coincidence, when I believed Gerri *was* praying for me, seemed . . . ungrateful. As if I were belittling her sincere faith.

It was probably just the result of the power of suggestion.

I hung up the phone from talking with Detective Chetterling and leaned my head back against the chair. From a distance I heard a plane engine. This was the time of day when those Grove Landing residents who commuted to work by air would be returning home. Already two planes had chutchutted their way to our street. I was so used to the sounds by now that I hardly registered them. Soon Jenna would be taxiing up the street, and I would run to open the hangar door. She'd turn the plane perpendicular to the house and shut off the engine. Knowing my sister, she'd be pumping me for details even as the powered tow bar pushed the plane into the hangar.

The office door opened. Kelly appeared, disapproval wrinkling her forehead. "I thought you were going to get the pizza. We're starved!"

"It's already on its way. Gerri Carson's bringing it."

"Why?"

How to answer that? "I just happened to call her, and she was on her way here, so she said she'd bring it."

Kelly looked at me with suspicion. "Why was she on her way here?"

"She just wanted to talk to me, that's all." I heard the rising frustration in my tone and fought to push it down. Kelly was sensitive enough. I did not need to give her reason to think something was wrong. "Listen, Kelly. Detective Chetterling is going to come over to talk to me, too. No big deal, it's just about the composite I drew. And, you know, they're still trying to find the man who . . . broke into Erin's house."

Kelly absorbed the words. Then she eased inside the office and shut the door. "Do they know something?"

"No."

"Then why come to you just to talk? Why aren't they talking to Erin's dad? She told me they promised her they'd tell him everything they found out."

My daughter's smooth young cheek firmed. Apparently, she and Erin had talked in detail, and she felt protective of her friend.

"I'm sure they will, Kelly. Does Erin have any reason to think they *haven't* been telling everything?"

She hesitated. "No."

"Then why the third degree? I'm just trying to get you a pizza." I gave her a wan smile.

"Okay." Mollified, she moved to leave.

"Kelly. Let's not make a big deal to Erin about these visits, okay? I don't want to upset her."

She regarded me with a slight frown, then nodded. As she slipped through the door, pulling it closed, I wasn't sure she fully believed me.

I checked my watch, my thoughts skidding back to the unknowns this evening would present. It was almost seven o'clock. Jenna would be here within the hour. Maybe she'd arrive while Gerri and the detective were here. How awkward that would be—trying to explain to her what was going on in the midst of dealing with them. If only she were here already. Darkness crept toward Grove Landing like some giant tarantula, and there was still so much left to decide. The kids . . . telling Dave . . . should we flee the house tonight or take the chance and stay?

We *had* to stay. Dave's relatives weren't leaving until tomorrow.

My chest tightened at the thought of facing the night here, and the inexplicable calm I'd felt trickled away. I tried to fight the rising fear, reminding myself that Gerri was praying for me. Maybe somewhere within the cosmos, prayer *did* register in the ears of God.

Think good thoughts, think good thoughts.

I shifted in the chair, my eyes falling to my father's combination printer-scanner-copier on the desk. And like a bolt of lightning a thought jagged through my head.

Make a copy of the file.

Whoa, wait a minute. Why on earth would I do that?

The idea was crazy. I needed to get *rid* of the file. Its mere presence in this office had caused Lisa's death. And because of that I never wanted to lay eyes on it again. Still, a part of me resisted handing it over to Detective Chetterling. Even if it couldn't be used in a court of law, that file was proof. That file meant power. That file could draw out our elusive killer.

Which is why I didn't want it in my possession.

I stared at the printer. Sounds from the television filtered across the great room and through the office door. The girls were watching music videos. Stephen, no doubt, still perched in front of the computer downstairs, either chatting with friends online or playing video games. Such kid things to do, in the midst of chaos.

My children trusted me. Whether they admitted it or not, particularly Stephen, they looked to me for safety. No sane mother would keep a copy of this file in her home. Detective Chetterling would take care of this. He would know what to do with my father's notes.

But what if Chetterling and the other detectives failed to find the Face? How could we sleep here night after night, wondering? At what point would the Face decide to leave us be?

Still, if Chetterling couldn't find the truth through this file, what on earth made me think *I* would?

I couldn't answer that. All the same, my fingers found the handle of the drawer in which I'd shoved the file. I pushed back my chair, giving myself room to pull it out. There lay the beige folder, as lethal as a ticking bomb. I picked it up. Set it on the desk without opening it.

What would my sister do?

Easy answer. Jenna would copy it.

I opened the folder and gazed at the handwritten pages. Then before I lost my nerve, I switched on the printer. While it warmed up, I busied myself with placing the first page of the file just so on the copying surface. Making sure all the edges were straight, as if one skewed move at this moment would lead us all down a crooked path to destruction.

The printer's green light blinked on. I hit the copy button and waited while the machine whirred out a grayed replica of the original. New arguments crowded into my mind like malignant cells, but I pushed them aside. I copied the second page, then slid the original file back into the desk drawer.

Where in the world should I hide the copy?

A car door slammed. I turned to look through the window and spotted Gerri heading for our front walk, two large pizzas in hand.

Bolting out of the office, I hurried up the staircase, calling for the girls to answer the door. The pages fluttered as I trotted down the hall and into my bedroom. Flinging to my knees in front of the bed, I lifted the covers and mattress and smacked the pages down on the box springs. When I was sure they lay flat and safe, I arranged everything back in order. I smoothed the bedspread like a child hiding a possession that meant certain punishment if discovered.

From the great room I heard the sound of the front door opening, voices mingling. With a deep breath I turned to go downstairs and face Gerri—and soon the detective—hoping my expression would not betray the deed I had just done.

Chapter 30

Detective Chetterling sat rock solid in my father's chair, his meaty hands on the desk, fingers spread, reading Sybee's version of Barry Draye's murder. I'd already filled him in on the details—how I'd remembered the Face, my encounter with the man on the Redwood City street, where I'd found the file. Chetterling knew the basic facts of the Sybee case, the trial having made local Redding news. No doubt the main point he remembered was that Edgar Sybee had gotten away with murder. The same thing I once thought. Now, watching him read the file, an unusual defensiveness of my father stole over me. If the detective believed those words, he'd have to admit that the acquittal was justified.

Gerri and I had pulled the matching chairs toward the desk. Gerri's presence didn't seem to bother the detective, particularly after I insisted that she stay. Meanwhile the pizza had distracted the kids. The girls were eating their pieces in front of the TV, and Stephen had emerged from his cave long enough to fill his plate.

Chetterling finished reading. He leaned back with an audible exhale and surveyed the ceiling, tongue stuck under his upper lip. One thumb tapped the top yellow paper. My eyes wandered over his wide shoulders, the square chisel of his jaw. The large office seemed filled with his presence, which exuded a mixture of street smarts, experience, and reliability. I tried to soothe myself with that, guessing at the number of cases he'd solved, from minor crimes to homicide. Dozens. Maybe hundreds.

Gerri broke the silence. "Well, what do you think?"

Chetterling dropped his narrowed eyes to the file. I sensed that what he'd read excited him more than he wanted to show. He hunched forward, eyes darting over the page as if it reflected his bouncing thoughts.

"Normally, I wouldn't give this kind of thing a second look. Suspects lie like dogs. You get them in jail, up for something as bad as murder, they'll squeal any kind of story to get off. Especially to their attorney, who's dying to hear something he can use in court, whether he believes it or not. But I can't deny the tie here to our own case. Somebody must want this file very badly." He rifled the edges of the two pages, then slapped a palm down on the desk. Swiveling the chair, he looked at me. "In the end, I don't care much about the Sybee case. I've got my own to worry about, and this is the best lead we've had. This and your composite. Which, by the way, we obviously have to distribute in the Bay Area. No wonder it wasn't bringing in any decent leads up here."

"What should I do?" I clasped my arms, hugging myself. "Tip has to know his mistake. He could come back to search this house. He probably *will* come back."

"Well, we don't know that for sure. He made a fatal mistake once, and now he's got to know we're patrolling the area. But just in case, you can know that we'll be watching your house. If you want to leave for a while, that wouldn't be a bad idea. But you can't go far. If we can find this guy, we need you to be able to get here quickly for a lineup."

"We've got guests for one more night. Some of Dave's relatives. My sister's flying in and should be here anytime. Tomorrow we could go back to her town home in the Bay Area. I'm trying to send my kids off to their father in Texas. But I'll stay at Jenna's, and if you need me, she can fly me back here in a hurry."

The detective nodded.

"Seems ironic to go to the Bay Area," Gerri noted. "You'd be moving closer to the suspect, not farther away."

"Yes, but it's not us he wants. It's the file. And he's going to think it's still here."

"I have to go down to the Bay Area and check all this out," Chetterling said. "If Tip has his ear to the ground, he'll hear I'm asking questions."

I thought about that. "So he'll know I've found the file."

"It might come to that." Chetterling ran his hand along the edge of the desk. "Then again, he might not know we're on to him. From your perspective, it wouldn't be a bad thing if he did. If he knows we have the file, he won't come back here looking for it. But from my perspective, it may drive him even farther underground. We'll just have to hope we can wind this thing up quickly."

No kidding.

But thank goodness Chetterling's going to let us leave. I'd been afraid he wouldn't want to let me go. I understood the need to be in contact with the Sheriff's Department; in fact, I *wanted* that. I didn't want to think of leaving and not being told what was going on. I pictured the kids gone to Texas, and Jenna and me waiting, waiting, for a good word. I wouldn't feel safe coming back to Grove Landing until the Face was captured. But Vic probably wouldn't keep the kids for more than a week, and what if the Face wasn't caught by then?

The movie projector in my head clicked into gear to flash scenes of fighting with Vic over keeping the kids; sitting on Jenna's couch hour after hour, waiting for the phone to ring. My relief vanished like a phantom at dawn. What if there was no way out of this? We could be caught in a nightmare with no end, either trapped in our own purgatory at Jenna's or never feeling safe again in our new home.

I closed my eyes and sagged against the back of my chair.

"Are you all right?" Gerri asked.

No answer would come. Any control I'd had over my life seemed to be slipping away. I wished I could *do something*. I wished that I wore a sheriff's badge, that I could pursue this evil man who had turned so many lives upside down.

Gerri's fingers pressed my arm. Somehow I sensed that she silently prayed for me. I grasped for that surreal peace again, knowing I would need it in the coming days.

"Annie." Chetterling leaned toward me, hands linked between his knees. "We *will* find this guy. Your family's going to be all right; we'll make sure of that. You're doing the right thing, leaving for a while and trying to get your kids out of here."

"How will we know what's happening?" I blurted. "Please promise me you'll tell me everything. I want to know what you're going to do—the minute you leave this house, and tonight, and tomorrow. I can't just be left in the dark!"

"Okay, all right, that's fair. I can tell you some things right now. We'll distribute your composite in the Bay Area, like I said. I'll head down there myself tomorrow. I'll work from there, and the other detectives on this case will work from here, contacting the Police and Sheriff's Departments in the

Bay Area to see who's handling drug cases. We'll talk to them, try to track down Tip. For all we know, they're looking for him already. But we hope they'll let us have first dibs on him. When we find him, we'll haul him in for questioning and a lineup, hoping you and Erin can identify him. If he doesn't cooperate in the interview, we'll wave this file in front of him, threaten that he'll also wind up on trial for Draye's mur—"

"He'll see right through that. The story can't be used in court. My dad's partner, Sid Haynes, told me."

"I doubt Tip realizes that. If he did, he wouldn't have gone to such trouble to find it. At any rate, we're not bound by law to tell the truth when questioning someone."

My shoulders sagged at his words. Had mere mistakes and skewed thinking cost Lisa her life? A burglar in the wrong house, after a supposed lethal file that couldn't even hurt him?

Stupid, *stupid* man.

"We'll do our best to find him quickly, Annie. I promise you that. If things go according to plan, we could have him in custody within a couple days."

I looked at my father's handwriting on the yellow pages. From my well of intuition rose a bubble of knowledge that all would not go according to plan. Why should I believe they would? What had gone right for me so far? My marriage to Vic? My move into this house? Lisa's death?

Hardly.

Another thing I knew for certain: I *had* to do everything possible to help. I could not run and cower in Jenna's town house, waiting for word to return for a suspect lineup. I owed Dave and Erin more than I could ever repay. I couldn't bring Lisa back, but if I could do anything more to help track down her killer, I would.

Not that I had the slightest inkling of what I could do.

"And if you can't find him?" I asked. "What then?"

The detective nodded with the surety of having justice on his side. "We'll find him. And I wouldn't ordinarily tell you this, but I want to put your mind at ease. We've got some good evidence to use to convict him, too. The print we lifted from the Willits' deck was perfect, and we now know the size and make of the shoe he wore. Plus we've got enough unique markings from wear to enable us to match it to an exact shoe, if we can locate it. Same thing with the black fibers, if we can pick up the gloves and shirt he was wearing that night. These pieces of forensic evidence, Annie, plus your and Erin's ability to pick the guy out in a lineup—that'll do it."

A memory thrust itself into my head. "What about the flashlight?"

"Never found it. He must have thought to pick it up."

"So things aren't totally bleak, Annie," Gerri put in. "I have no doubt that they'll find this guy."

I looked Chetterling in the eye. "And you will keep in touch with me, right? I'll give you my cell phone number and Jenna's number. I want to know what's happening." My voice flattened. "If you don't call me, I promise I will call you every fifteen minutes. I just *have* to know."

He couldn't repress a little smile. "I don't doubt you will. You're a strong lady, Annie; I admire you for that. I know this isn't easy for you."

For a moment I thought he merely spoke kind words to encourage me. But sincerity rested in his eyes. I gawked at him. Me, strong? I was the weakest woman on the planet.

"Thank you. Um. One more thing I wanted to ask. What should we do about telling Dave? Seems to me, he deserves to know the truth."

"Well, yes, he should know. But he doesn't need to know right now. He's just come from the funeral today; he's got lots of family still here. After everyone goes home, he'll have plenty of time to turn his thoughts back to the investigation."

"I doubt he's turned his thoughts away from it."

Chetterling patted his hand against the desk. "Look. Let me handle that part, okay? I don't want you running over there tonight and telling him why you're flying out in the morning. Just let him think you're visiting your sister and friends in the Bay Area. The most I may tell him for now is that we're working on some leads that involve another case. The less people who know about this file—" he indicated the pages with a tilt of his chin—"the better."

A plane droned overhead. I turned toward the window, although I knew I couldn't see the aircraft. Most likely it was Jenna. Remembering the purchase I'd asked her to make, I almost asked Chetterling a question about gun possession but held my tongue. My sister had a secret hidden in her room and I had one hidden in mine.

And that's the way it would remain.

# # # #

Exhausted, I toyed that night with the idea of taking a sleeping pill but decided against it. Sleep seemed almost fearsome to me. Our guests were in their room, blissfully unknowing of the vulnerability of their quarters. All doors and windows were locked and double-checked. The alarm was activated, and outside, a deputy sheriff would watch our house until dawn. Even so, I worried about Tip's somehow getting inside.

I'd had a brief conversation with Vic in the evening—*I* had to call—about sending the kids to him immediately. He responded that he and Sheryl hadn't "talked it out yet" and that he'd call in the morning before we left for the Bay Area.

After I had a chance to inform Jenna of all the developments, we had sat down with the kids to tell them we were flying out the next morning. Stephen was overjoyed and embarked on a merciless mission to convince me he should stay at Nate's. When I told him and Kelly that I hoped to ship them to their father's, he turned sullen.

"No way, I don't want to go! I don't like Sheryl anyway. She's a—"

I held up a hand. "Enough, Stephen."

"Let me go to Nate's!"

"Look. One thing at a time. For right now let's just . . . get to the Bay Area."

"What about Erin?" Kelly wrinkled her forehead. "I don't want to leave her."

"Honey, I'm sorry. But you're going to have to."

"*Why?*"

"Because I'd just . . . rather have you gone right now until this man is found. Erin has other friends here, and her dad. She'll be all right and you won't be gone that long."

God, let that be true.

Tears glistened in Kelly's eyes. "I can't leave without telling her. I at least have to call her."

I hesitated. "Of course. But tell her we probably won't go until the afternoon."

The hostess part of me hadn't wanted to make our guests feel they had to be up and out early to accommodate us. In truth, I'd have liked nothing better, for once I'd decided upon leaving, I couldn't wait to go. But after the last few days, Ed and Carol deserved to stay as long as they needed to.

After the kids and our guests went to bed, Jenna and I had sat in the TV room, talking quietly. Behind drawn blinds that shut out the tyranny of the black night, we shared our fears, our sorrows, and the world's injustices. We were both jumpy. The gun now sat loaded in the drawer of Jenna's nightstand.

I told her about copying the file. She gave me a sly smile of surprise and admiration, but she couldn't fathom any more than I could what we would do with it.

"Make sure to bring it with you," she told me. "Just in case."

I said I would.

By twelve-thirty I'd lain in bed over an hour, staring at the ceiling. *Tick-tock.* It was now four days since Lisa's death. Ninety-six hours.

Please, let it not be too late.

My scene-a-second mind wouldn't leave me alone. It flashed through myriad imaginings of

the Face hunched in the darkness, picking the lock on the sliding glass door off the lower deck . . .

Kelly scrunched into a dim corner, hiding, trembling . . .

Jenna's double-fisted hands pressed around the handle of the gun . . .

At the bottom of the bed, I could have sworn I felt a rise in the mattress, as if the copied file were growing, swelling in proportion to the havoc it could wreak.

My last waking thought was of Dave alone in his bed, trying to sleep on the night of his wife's funeral.

Friday, July 25

Chapter 31

The book on forensic art arrived in the mail Friday morning. *Book* was an understatement. It weighed in more like a college text. I opened the package without a clue as to its contents, my conversation with Jenna about her purchase temporarily forgotten. Pulling it out, I blinked at the cover. *The World of Forensic Art* by Diana Worling. A series of photos spread across the front—from a composite to drawings of a person at different ages to a clay model of a skull.

Jenna crowed. "Oh great, perfect timing! You can bring it with you and read it."

"Sure, probably finish it in twenty minutes." I sat at the kitchen table and flipped through some pages. "Just look at this thing."

"No, *you* look at it." Jenna pulled eggs and bacon from the refrigerator. Our guests would soon be down for breakfast. "Therein lies your future."

"Thanks, dear sister, for your words of wisdom."

Not for the world would I have admitted it, but an uncanny sensation stole over me as I paged through that book, as if I'd discovered something vastly significant that I didn't even know I'd sought. In particular, the chapters on drawing composites called to me, even as apprehension made my nerves tingle. What would the author say about conducting the interview with the victim? Had I done the right things with Erin? Or would I find that every choice I made was wrong—so wrong that the results could not possibly be right?

I pushed that fear aside. I *knew* the composite was right. So did Erin. And I had an encounter on a Redwood City street to prove it.

Jenna and I served Ed and Carol breakfast and lingered with them over coffee, listening with bitter empathy to their reminiscences of Lisa. The entire time, a vague unsettling about that book's contents worried at the back of my mind.

Once we were in the airplane, I would read the chapters on composites.

Stephen shuffled into the kitchen. "Hey, Mom, when are we getting out of here?"

My son, the wonderful host. I was certain he'd posed the question for our guests' benefit. One of Stephen's cheeks was red, as if he'd slept on that side and just pulled himself from bed. He wore a black T-shirt with questionable graphics on the back, and his typical drag-on-the-floor baggy jeans. When I'd first seen the shirt, which he told me a friend had given him, I thought the vaguely drawn outline surrounded in smoke stood for some kind of pot smoking through a pipe, but Stephen had assured me it was just pop art. Looking at it now as he rummaged in the refrigerator, I wondered anew.

"How about saying good morning to our guests, Stephen." My tight tone betrayed my embarrassment at his manner.

"Morning," he mumbled without turning around.

Ed and I exchanged a glance. Although the man said nothing, I sensed that if Stephen were his son, a serious verbal exchange would have followed. I lowered my eyes as a pang of all-too-familiar guilt shot through me—that I was not raising my son strictly enough, that I was losing control. A part of me wanted to defend myself. Say something about how hard it was to raise a son when his father had abandoned him. But of course I would not.

Carol rescued me. "Did you want to leave this morning?" Remorse creased her face. "Here we are, just sitting around."

"Oh no, no." I threw a narrow-eyed look at Stephen as he pulled out the milk. "It's not a problem. We're just going to the Bay Area for a few days. This afternoon is plenty of time for us to head out."

All the same, and over my continued protests, they packed their suitcases after breakfast and vacated the room. I hoped my son's behavior hadn't run them out, even as I knew it had. "This way you can leave when you want." Carol smiled. "We'd just planned to be at Dave's anyway until we go."

They both hugged me and Jenna, thanking us again and again as we walked them out on the porch. "You've done so much for Dave and Erin." Carol put her arms around me. "That's meant more to us than anything."

When we pulled apart, I saw the tears in her eyes. Her words, supposed to soothe, chafed my heart. How would she feel when they heard the truth behind Lisa's murder?

How would any of the Willits' family feel?

We waved a final goodbye as they walked across the street toward Dave's; then I slipped back into the house with Jenna and closed the door. My sister stood with hands on her hips, mouth pressed. "Annie. *Don't.*"

"How can I help it? None of this would have—"

"Well, it *has*, so that's that. We can't look back, Annie; that's the problem—you're always looking back. And picking up guilt along the way when it isn't even yours."

The words stung. "Come on, Jenna, don't lecture me now. I've got enough to deal with."

Her expression softened and she squeezed my wrist. "I know, I'm sorry. I'm just . . . being Jenna. All this is getting to me, too." She smiled with one side of her mouth. Sunlight from the front windows cast a sheen on her hair, making her look beautiful and plaintive and vulnerable all at the same time—a rare combination for Jenna. My heart swelled with love for her. She was right; things were difficult for her, too. I needed to remember that. *I* wasn't the one who'd just lost my job.

"It's okay." I shook my head and sighed. "Let's just . . . get our work done and get out of here."

I climbed the stairs to gather the sheets and towels from the guest room and throw them over the balcony onto the great room floor. From there I hauled them into the laundry room off the kitchen to wash when we got back. As I returned to the kitchen, I realized I'd better call Vic, since he wasn't expecting us to leave until the afternoon.

Oh, great. He'd think I was being pushy, not waiting for him to call. Tired as I was, and in my present frame of mind, the conversation could be particularly unpleasant.

So be it.

I picked up the receiver and dialed Vic's office. At least I didn't have to call him at home, where Sheryl could answer. The only thing worse than talking to Vic was talking to Sheryl.

"Hi, Vic, it's me."

He wouldn't even grant me a hello. "I told you I would call." He sounded irritated.

I tried to keep my voice level. "Sorry, but we're about to leave early and it couldn't wait. When can I send the kids to you?"

"Not for a couple weeks, like we planned."

"What? That's impossible. I need to send them now! I've told you everything that's going on, and we have to get out of this house!"

"You *are* getting out—to the Bay Area. Jenna's got a place there, so what's the problem?"

"I can think of a couple right off the bat. First, that she's got a two-bedroom condo and we're four people. More important, the Bay Area's the last place I want Stephen to be, thanks to all his skuzzy friends. If you'll remember, that's why I moved *away* from there."

"Yeah, and look where it's gotten you." Vic always knew how to hit below the belt.

I pressed my teeth together. "Look, Vic, could we stay on the subject for once? I need to send the kids to you."

"What you need, Annie, is to not run away from your problems. Watch Stephen while he's in the Bay Area, that's all. Don't let him see his friends."

"Do you know how hard that's going to be? Stephen in Jenna's town house all day, and doing what?"

"Motherhood isn't always easy, Annie."

Anger shot up my spine. "No thanks to *you*." I breathed hard into the phone. "Tell me why you can't take them."

"Because we don't have vacation now. And Sheryl doesn't trust them in the house alone."

That really fried me. Deceptive, husband-stealing Sheryl didn't trust *my kids*? I couldn't find my tongue for a worthy response.

But the anger was good, *good*. Better than the self-deprecation Vic usually made me feel. I latched onto it, piling it up within me like kindling for a fire.

"The loving father, putting his children first." My words seethed. "As he always does."

Vic made a disgusted sound in his throat. "I thought you wanted to stay on the subject."

"I *am* staying on the subject. The problem is that the subject never changes!"

"Annie—"

"Never mind, Vic! Just never mind. I don't want to hear anything else you have to say. And in fact I don't *want* to send my children to you. They don't like you very much, anyway, since you chose to walk out on them. And in case you didn't know it, they *really* don't like Sheryl!"

Mouth twisting, I punched off the line. Wishing the receiver was the kind that could be banged down for good measure.

"Whoa." Jenna's voice came over my shoulder. "That was good. I'll give you a seven."

I puffed out air. "Seven? What would I have to do for a ten?"

She shook her head. "To that creep? You don't want to know."

I leaned against the kitchen table, my wrath turning into quiet desperation. "What are we going to do now, Jenna? We're stuck with the kids."

My sister shrugged. "We'll handle it, that's all."

"Stephen's going to drive us crazy."

"Yeah, I know. But we'll . . . cross that bridge when we come to it. For now let's just head out."

By noon the four of us were loaded in the Cessna, head-phones on and ready to go. My book on forensic art lay at my feet, leaning against the side of the plane, waiting to be read once we were in the air. The hangar door was closed, the house locked, and the alarm set at the highest level. I couldn't help gazing at the Willits' house as Jenna prepared to fire up the engine. The only car left out front belonged to Ed and Carol.

"Clear!" Jenna yelled out her window, then started the engine. The airplane tail rose from the force created by the churning propeller; dust in the street whisked away on the hot wind. A July noon in the Redding area meant sunny skies and high temperature. We were all sweating. Rising to a cooler altitude would be pleasant indeed.

We reached the run-up area just off the runway, where all systems of a plane are checked before takeoff. That done, Jenna turned the Cessna in a complete three-sixty for a sky check—an extra precaution taught by her flight instructor some seven years ago. Declaring over the radio that she was "taking the active," Jenna closed her window, pulled onto the runway, and gunned the engine. Seconds later we rose effort-lessly into the air despite the heat outside, which could reduce the lifting ability of a lesser plane.

The airstrip beneath us fell away, bouncing up into a package of green forest ribboned with rural roads leading toward Interstate 5. From the air, the dividing line that is Redding is even more pronounced than on the ground. To the city's south lie miles of boring flatness. To the north, the inter-state crosses beautiful Lake Shasta, then begins a long, ardu-ous climb through verdant hills.

Jenna's ability to fly never ceased to amaze me. Our father had been a private pilot for so long that I hadn't thought much about it. But when Jenna began ground school, then flying lessons, I was amazed. She'd spout to me what she learned about the various instruments and how to read the navigational maps, which seemed incomprehensible to me. They still do.

Had we been raised in the same household?

The plane turned south. As if a ghostly hand had plucked at its spine, the forensic art book fell over, landing on my feet. I picked it up. The book lay in my hands, a weighty tome filled with information that could threaten what I knew about Lisa's killer. As frightening as my discoveries of the Face had been, it would be even more frightening to have them all taken away, to be pushed back to complete ignorance of who he might be or what he looked like.

Jenna glanced at me and raised her eyebrows. Her support gave me the courage I needed.

I opened the book.

Chapter 32

The beginning chapters looked safe enough. Putting off the inevitable, I decided to skim them before immersing myself in the pages about interviewing.

First came an introduction to forensic art, followed by a chapter on its history. The drone of the airplane engine and voices of other pilots in my headset faded as I found myself pulled into the book. I was fascinated by various composites next to photos of the apprehended suspects. Some composites were more detailed than others. Some looked exactly like the suspects; others were not as good. But all had led to the arrest of the person in question. How amazing that artists could play such an important part in law enforcement.

The skin on my arms tingled. In my own little and amateurish way, I'd linked myself with true professionals—heroes—in the field.

Okay. Get on with it, Annie. I told myself I really should skip to the chapters on composites.

But not yet.

Shouldn't I at least skim the chapter on capturing the face—everything from features to facial proportions to drawing materials? Lighting. Profiles. Accessories. Disguises. I stared at the now famous composite of the Unabomber, with his large sunglasses and hood. Although the eerie drawing had been plastered all across America, it was a tip from the Unabomber's brother, and not the composite, that had led to his arrest.

My fingers turned pages. Before I was ready, I faced the chapter on interviewing. The temptation to skip over it, read something else—*anything* else—surged through me. I closed my eyes, took a deep breath, and plunged in.

Certain information jumped out at me right away.

First, that trauma can badly affect memory, depending upon how involved the witness was as a victim in the crime.

Erin had certainly been "involved."

Second, that sleep can help such a person recall events.

Take that, Chetterling. I'm the one who begged you to let her rest.

That victims sometimes fall into unconscious transference, in which a face they see in some other context becomes blurred with the face of the criminal. That younger children and the elderly usually make less accurate witnesses than young adults, while teenagers often seem to notice details that others miss.

What did that mean for Erin? She was no longer a young child and not yet a teen, although close to it. Did that place her in the "more reliable" category?

In spite of my anxiety, I couldn't help but be fascinated by a section on victims who lie. According to the author, sometimes composite artists could pick up on these lies, noting inconsistencies in a witness's descriptions. The forensic artist who had interviewed Susan Smith, the young mother who was later convicted of killing her two sons, had sensed that something was amiss. Later he was proven right. The kidnapper of her children did not exist.

Did not exist.

For some reason those words taunted me. I pushed them from my mind.

My heart tapped an extra beat as I began reading about the composite-specific interview, which was based on cognitive methods for retrieving memory from a victim's mind. "The forensic artist should take time to establish rapport with the victim," wrote the author. The artist should not view pictures of suspects ahead of time, nor should there be pictures of faces on the walls where the interview takes place. And the interview should occur in a comfortable environment.

So far, so good.

I raised my head for a moment, glancing out the window. We were approaching the edge of the richly soiled Napa Valley. Vineyards stretched before us, running up hills and striding over flatlands, parting around the magnificent homes of wineries. Although my brain registered the luscious landscape, I barely noticed.

Maybe buying this book would prove to be the best thing Jenna could have done for me. Maybe its words would validate everything I'd done, secure my knowledge of the Face with the strength of a dead bolt in a lock.

My eyes returned to the book. I pressed the knuckles of my right hand against my chin and continued reading.

The next boldfaced sentences clanged through me like a warning bell.

An artist should not face the interviewee, the book said, but the two should sit side by side. And they should not make eye contact at all. Looking at the artist's face, the victim could inadvertently recall similar features. My breath pooled in my lungs. Erin had been facing me until I first showed her the picture. I closed my eyes, reviewing each feature of the Face. Were there any that even remotely resembled mine? If not individual features, did the proportions?

No, not at all. And even if Erin had faced me, she hadn't really looked at me, had she? Hadn't she looked down, away, squeezed her eyes shut?

The book turned worse from there. Oh, there were numerous things I had done right, but I couldn't note them for all those I hadn't. I should have listened to a complete run-through of the man's description before I started drawing. I should have majored more on proportions of the face, rather than worrying first about its separate components. Once Erin looked at the drawing and we needed to fine-tune individual features, I should have shown her pictures of faces, using perhaps mug shots or the *FBI Facial Identification Catalog*, neither of which I'd possessed.

I sank my thumb into the paper. Detective Chetterling must know about this catalog. Why hadn't he told me I should use something like it? Why had he set me up without help—*me*, with no experience and a heart too close to the victim?

I read on.

The pictures were to be shown judiciously, the book said, and not too many of them. The artist shouldn't overwhelm the victim with too many features to choose from.

Well, I can't exactly be faulted for that mistake.

But I had pushed Erin in her exhausted state—another thing that should not be attempted—to clarify each feature from her memory. And during her tiredness, instead of only allowing her short viewings of the drawing, I let her see individual features for long stretches at a time while I worked.

For long stretches at a time.

Blazing each feature into her memory.

Her exhausted memory.

Her child's . . . traumatized . . . susceptible memory.

Wait. What was that part about unconscious transference?

I turned back and reread the passage. Victims indeed could remember the wrong face. The book noted that composites have even been known to end up being the face of a policeman at the scene of the crime, or someone else who'd stopped to help.

What about the artist? I flipped pages. Had artists ever been known to unconsciously transfer a face they'd seen to the drawing before them? I skimmed more pages, then checked the list of contents in the front. Nothing on the artists. Nothing.

Terrific.

No doubt I'd be the first. A real case study. Wouldn't the author of this book be fascinated to hear the havoc I'd wreaked.

Breath caught in my throat. The plane felt claustrophobic. If only we were in a car, where I could open a window and get some air.

I smacked the book closed and tossed it onto the floor. Jenna glanced at me and started to speak, but I turned toward the window. I could not handle talking at the moment; my mind was too busy wresting through all the information.

Maybe I *had* unconsciously transferred the Face. And then tainted Erin's memory by allowing her to study the various features for so long that by the time she saw the whole drawing . . .

I stared out the window, trying to think, *think*. We were over the Bay. On the radio, the Norcal controller was handing Jenna off to the tower at Oakland Airport so we could fly through its air space. In the distance I could see San Francisco, draped in a shawl of fog and shimmering like the mysterious city of Oz. I thought of the Cowardly Lion, cowering before the great Wizard, asking for courage. Courage was what I needed right now—in major quantities. Courage and conviction. But I felt little of either. What amounts I'd possessed were slipping away from me with each passing second, as surely as the hills and freeways of Oakland now slipped beneath our wings.

What if I was leading us all down a false trail? I'd convinced myself that the Face on that Redwood City street was Lisa's killer. But then, I'd also convinced myself he was in our house four nights ago—a paranoid notion that was proven entirely false. Now we were fleeing to the Bay Area, and far worse, Detective Chetterling was headed there as well, pursuing a lead that may be equally false. Meanwhile Lisa's killer could be roaming the streets of Redding or even Grove Landing.

And no one would have the slightest idea what he looked like.

The Oakland runways stretched at an angle below. Jenna stayed at two thousand feet, as I'd vaguely heard the controller instruct. The westernmost finger of the Bay rolled beneath us as our flight following was routinely canceled and Jenna listened to San Carlos weather, then contacted the airport tower. Before us lay the Peninsula—the Bay Area cities between San Francisco and San Jose that melded together into one huge machine of humanity.

From the corner of my eye I saw movement. I looked over my shoulder to see Stephen pumping a victory fist in the air at sight of the Peninsula cities. The movie projector in my head turned on, flicking through pictures of his various shady friends, all with beckoning fingers and smirking grins. I shivered.

What had I done?

Jenna followed the controller's instructions for altitude over the San Mateo Bridge, informing him when we glided past the cement plant landmark at the edge of the Bay. Easing into the pattern established for air traffic, we were cleared to land.

Back in the Bay Area.

I focused on my lap, exhaustion kneading its knuckles against the back of my neck. Stephen would wear me down, then waste no time hooking up with his druggie friends. Kelly was separated from Erin. Jenna would mourn anew the loss of her job. And I would wait every anxious moment for the Phone Call from Detective Chetterling—hoping against hope that they'd caught Tip, the Face, and that he looked just like my composite.

The phone call I now doubted would ever come.

Chapter 33

Jenna and I spoke little as we put the plane away in the hangar, hauled our bags to her Toyota Camry, and drove to her town house in Redwood Shores. One look at my face and she knew something was wrong. It would take little insight for her to know that my anxiety arose from what I read in *The World of Forensics*. Kelly shot me a couple of questioning looks, and for her sake I feigned a smile. She was not fooled.

"All *right!*" Stephen crowed as we pulled onto the freeway for our short jaunt to the next exit. "Civilization!" He bobbed around, thumping the backseat with his thumb as if listening to a private radio station in his head. "Mom, I want to call Nate as soon as we get to Aunt Jenna's. I told him I would. You can take me right over there."

Here we go again.

On top of all my other worries, the thought of dealing with Stephen and his attitudes made me slump. Already I found myself rationalizing that of Stephen's friends, Nate was the least worrisome. Why couldn't I let my son go there? Just get him out of my way for a while, let me try to sort out the ambivalence in my head.

"I want to call Emily first," Kelly insisted, speaking of her best friend in the Bay Area. "'Cause her mom said I could come over there."

"Stop arguing, you two. I don't need that right now."

I didn't mind Kelly's staying with a friend. And as for Stephen, if by some remote chance the Face heard we were in the Bay Area and chose to come after me, shouldn't both my children be off somewhere? Hadn't I wanted them to be with their father?

Really, this was all Vic's fault.

My cell phone! I'd turned it off while we were in the plane. Detective Chetterling could call at any time. Pulling it out of my purse, I turned it back on.

Jenna's town house is a two-story beige stucco affair, with the main bedroom upstairs and the second, which was set up as an office, off the entryway on the first level. The couch in the office could transform into a decent bed for me. I placed my bags on the blue carpet, beside Jenna's desk and computer. Jenna lugged the soft suitcase she'd just packed for Grove Landing the night before back up to her room. The kids threw down their things in the hall and headed for the kitchen—and the nearest telephone.

I sank onto the office couch and stared at the telltale rectangular bulge in the top zipper section of my suitcase. The forensic art book mocked me. Within the space of an hour it had managed to chop my darkling forest of knowledge about Lisa's killer into kindling and sawdust.

"Steph*ennn!*" Kelly's protest bled into my thoughts.

"Too bad, I got it first!"

I heard the sound of an impatient finger punching digits into the phone. Distantly I watched my son veer out of the kitchen with the receiver stuck to his ear. His quick footsteps took him down the tiled hall and onto the hushed carpet of the living room. I heard the tone of his voice, if not the words, as he talked to Nate—that "hey dawg what's up" chugging-engine tenor that signaled his intent to cruise down roads of which I would not approve.

Wearily I hauled myself from the couch and out the office door. "You can't go anywhere until I talk to his mom, Stephen," I called.

Kelly stood with her arms folded, leaning against the threshold of the kitchen. Waiting none too patiently. "He's just gonna end up with T. J. and Jack and all of them." Sunlight oozed through the leaded glass in the front door, coating one half of her firm-jawed face. I could not tell if her disdain was really due to my letting Stephen go or if she was just mad that he'd gotten to the phone first. I nodded, searching for a response and finding none. All I could do was walk over and hug her. Hug my beautiful daughter and tell her I loved her. She'd been through too much in the last few days.

Stephen brayed for me to "come talk to Nate's mom!" Rationalizing all the way, I left Kelly and headed toward the living room.

In a little over an hour I'd borrowed Jenna's car and hauled Stephen to Nate's house in Redwood City, and Kelly to Emily's in Menlo Park. As I drove Kelly down El Camino through Atherton, I couldn't help but think of Edgar Sybee's expensive house, just one block east. The address had seen quite a media parade during Sybee's trial. Even I had been curious enough to drive by the house when I was in the area. Crystal Sybee had to feel mighty lonely now, knocking about such a large home with only her son.

My heart went out to her. True, she made a bad mistake in marrying the wrong man. But then, so did I. And I knew what loneliness was all about.

Jenna and I still had found no way to talk, agreeing in silent communication that we would do so upon my return. I drove back to the town house, relief and guilt doing a dance in my stomach. If Stephen got into trouble in the next few days, I didn't think I would be able to handle it.

As I stepped through the door of the town house, my cell phone rang.

Chetterling.

The sound burned through me like a smoldering brand. I jammed my hand into my purse in search of the phone and knocked the bag to the floor. A second ring. Collapsing into a kneel, I grabbed the purse and snatched up the phone. "Hello?"

Jenna emerged from the office, the forensic art book in her hands. Had she read anything? If so, she now understood the source of my fear.

"Annie, this is Detective Chetterling."

"Oh. Yes. Hi," I panted, feeling so exposed, as if he could look into my head and see the unraveling threads in our cloak of logic. I slow-pivoted off my knees to sit on the entryway tile.

"Where are you?"

"At Jenna's house in Redwood Shores. We just got here a little while ago." My sister raised her eyebrows at me. I gave her a little nod. "Where are *you?*"

He sighed and my heart plummeted. It could only mean he hadn't found one policeman who recognized the faxed composite of the Face. I locked gazes with Jenna, seeking calm in her eyes, and was dismayed to see a reflection of my own worry.

"Sitting in my car outside the Redwood City Police Station."

"You're already here?"

"Yup. Been here since ten. I left Redding around six. Had to get moving on this thing." He paused. "Look, I don't have any real good news to tell you so far. I met with the detectives who handled the Draye murder, plus two others who're working in tandem with police from nearby jurisdictions on trying to bust a Peninsula-wide drug ring. The detectives on the drug case suspect there's a higher-up who's the main supplier for a lot of little guys like Sybee, but they haven't gotten anyone to point the finger at him yet. They're watching numerous suspects. But I have to tell you, neither of them has seen anyone looking like the composite. While I was in their office, they faxed the sketch around to a few other officers they're working with. Of course, not everyone was in their office and could respond. But those that could—nada. And nobody's heard the name Tip."

"I see." That's all I could say. The movie projector in my head turned half comic on me, choosing black-and-white footage. Out spat jerky frames of an

Old West sheriff with a cowboy hat and day-old beard, puckering his jaw over a grainy composite and shaking his head. "Ain't seen nobody lookin' like that in these here parts, Mister . . ."

"As for the homicide detectives—" Chetterling's voice pulled me back—"they didn't recognize the composite. And they assured me that Sybee was the only murderer in the Draye house that night. I let them read Sybee's story and they laughed the whole thing down. Said it sounded like a suspect's last-ditch effort to save his skin. If I was in their shoes, I'd be inclined to agree."

Even with my own uncertainty, the notion of detectives laughing at Chetterling galled me. "Did you tell them about how I saw the guy on the street and how he wanted the file? They shouldn't just blow that off."

"I know. And they couldn't explain it. Except to say that whoever the guy is, they still don't think he has any significance to their case."

I dug my fingers into the top of my hair. "Okay. So now what?"

"Well, I'm hardly giving up. I'm making sure copies of the composite are posted around the area. It's going into the *San Jose Mercury* tomorrow, and some of the local city papers. Someone has to know who the guy is; after all, he talked to you on a Redwood City street. I do think that in the next day or two leads will start coming in."

"So are you done here already? Are you going back to Redding to wait for those calls?"

"I don't want to go back too soon. When leads start coming in, I want to be here to run them down. As for the rest of today, I've got a stop to make. In fact, I'm headed there now."

"Where?"

"To meet with the deputy D.A. from the Sybee case."

"Art Springer."

"You know him?"

"Sort of. I saw him every day in court. I covered the Sybee trial, remember. Art would recognize me if he saw me."

"Oh yeah."

"So." I shifted my position on Jenna's floor. The tile was feeling harder by the second. My sister remained at the office threshold, watching me intently. "You're going to show Springer the Sybee file, too, see if he thinks there's any merit to it. See if he's got any idea who Tip might be."

"You've got it." Chetterling's voice betrayed his doubts.

"Does Springer know you're coming—and why?"

"Basically."

"I'll bet he's thrilled."

Chetterling grunted.

I could picture Art Springer pulling at the collar around his goose-thin neck, his protruding eyes flicking at the ceiling as he talked to Chetterling. One of the deputy D.A.'s eyebrows always seemed to be higher than the other, and this feature, combined with the rest, gave him the appearance of a suspicious praying mantis. As for Springer's defeat at the Sybee trial, it had not set well with him—or the entire D.A.'s office, for that matter. The last thing he'd want is to revisit the case. Some out-of-jurisdiction detective positing the "second man" theory would be about as well received as whale blubber at a Greenpeace convention.

"Well, I need to get going." Chetterling's voice turned all business. In the background I heard his car engine start. I envisioned him pulling out of the parking lot at the Police Station and heading for the courthouse, formally called the Hall of Justice and Records, in downtown Redwood City—a drive of only a few minutes. My head then flashed a close-up sequence of

Art Springer as Sybee's verdict is read. His buggy eyes widen, a flush rises to his cheeks, followed by the poker-faced hardening of his narrow jaw. He stares straight ahead as if looking through

the courtroom wall, through some hazy scrim dividing this world from the next, searching for a logical reason for a decision that looms so illogical in his mind . . .

The scene was so vivid, I could almost feel the colored pencils in my hand, hear the faint scratch of point against paper as I captured Springer's expression. To think that while I blithely drew this picture and others of Sybee's trial, the bricks were being laid in the path to Lisa Willit's destruction . . .

Before I could stop myself, I opened my mouth. "Let me go with you to see Springer."

Chetterling's hesitation spoke volumes. His gut reaction to deny my request was no doubt tempered only by his promise to keep me informed. "Why?"

"Because *I* found the file, in my house. None of this was supposed to happen. So now I have to help. And I think I can with Springer. He's not going to like talking about the Sybee case, which he lost, with someone who wasn't even at the trial. At least I was there, and he'll remember me. Maybe I can be sort of a . . . buffer."

I cringed at the last word. Surely the last thing Chetterling thought he needed from anyone, much less me, was some form of protection.

"I appreciate your willingness," he said rather formally, "but I'm not sure what you could accomplish."

"What I can accomplish is continuing to help in this investigation. I did draw the composite for you." I blinked at the force of my reply but could not back down now. "Please. I promise you, if I can't say anything helpful, I'll stay quiet. But it won't hurt to have me there, and you never know what might come up."

Silence.

"I'm not that much farther from the courthouse than you. If you'll wait five minutes, I'll be there."

Chetterling exhaled into the phone. My own breath stilled. "All right. I'll meet you outside. Don't take long."

He clicked off the line.

I pulled the phone away from my ear and stared at it.

"What'd he say, what'd he say?"

I looked at Jenna, stymied. "He said okay."

"Well then, go!" She strode over to help me off the floor.

Not until I was driving down the freeway did I allow myself to think of what I hadn't told Chetterling. True, Art Springer would remember me as a courtroom artist at the trial. But like everyone else in that courtroom, other than Sid Haynes, he didn't know whose daughter I was. That would have to be revealed as Chetterling and I explained our story.

Knowing how much Springer hated the law firm previously known as Gerralon & Haynes, I could only hope he wouldn't throw both of us out of his office.

Chapter 34

By the time I pulled into the covered parking lot near the Hall of Justice and Records, doubts blew through my mind like an ill-begotten wind. Everything seemed wrong, down to the khaki pants and short-sleeved blouse I'd flung on before dashing out of Jenna's town house. They were better than the sweaty T-shirt and shorts I'd worn in the plane, but I'd had no time to iron them. My thrown-together appearance mirrored how I felt on the inside.

I pulled myself out of the car, slinging my purse over my shoulder. Musty air swirled through the open sides of the parking area, sending a balled-up piece of trash skittering across my foot. For a second I stared at it, drawn to its wayward journey across the oil-stained cement.

I'm just as buffeted as that ball of paper.

Hurrying along the sidewalk toward the courthouse, I felt anything but the professional I'd once been in these surroundings. The familiarity of this walk, the building, the wide steps leading up to the entrance, pulled at me in ways I couldn't fully comprehend. Edgar Sybee's trial seemed eons ago.

I spotted Chetterling waiting for me near the door, out of the sun. Compared with his clothes, mine looked well ironed. His sport coat hung from slumped shoulders, and his pants bore the scars of his road trip to the Bay Area. The man had barely slept during the past five days. Chetterling's huge hand cupped the spine of a blue notebook. Something about the hunch of his shoulders, the way he bounced the notebook off his thigh, spoke of impatience. No doubt it rose from regret for allowing me to come.

My hand lifted in a brief wave. Why had I done this? I should have stayed at Jenna's. Art Springer would not welcome me—the daughter of the man who defeated him, even from the grave. All of Springer's defensiveness would rise to the top like clotted cream in rancid milk. And Chetterling would be royally ticked at me. He wouldn't want me to have anything to do with the rest of the investigation. Maybe wouldn't even tell me what was happening.

Chetterling returned my wave, unsmiling.

Please, please, somebody up there, let something good happen here today.

The prayer made me blink. I hadn't thought about God as much in my entire lifetime as I had in the past few days.

My brain flashed sequences of Lisa's funeral and my conversations with Gerri Carson. Pastor Storrel's words drifted through my mind. I pictured Dave and his friends praying in my kitchen, sincere in their belief that God was listening. As the memories flicked by, once again a desire to know a God like that surged through me. To know a God who would really listen. Whom you could take with you wherever you went, to whom you could talk—and who would answer.

Would you answer the kind of prayer I just prayed, God? Something that must be so insignificant to you?

Breathlessly I trotted up the steps to join Chetterling. He nodded at me.

"That was pretty quick."

"I told you I'd hurry."

I passed through security as an ordinary citizen while Chetterling flashed his badge. A long escalator straight ahead led to the second level, where Sybee's trial took place. I glanced upward, thinking of the trial . . . of Sid Haynes . . . my father. Chetterling looked at me, a knowing expression on his face.

"Memories?"

"Yeah."

He inclined his head. "Springer said his office is on the fourth floor."

"Okay. Let's take the elevator." I pointed the way.

Chetterling eyed me as the elevator rose. "Let me do the talking unless I ask you, all right?" His words were a statement, not a question. I nodded.

The courthouse air smelled dust-covered and old, a testament to the miasma of anxiety and dashed hopes. Art Springer's small office was crowded with cabinets and stacked boxes of files from various trials. His well-used desk was oak, chipped and scarred, the varnish of its corners long worn. Sunlight filtering through dusty blinds on the room's one window did little to lift the oppressive aura. I couldn't help comparing this with my father's office at Gerralon & Haynes, where ebony furniture shone and luscious ferns graced the corners of designer-painted walls. Such was the difference between successful defense attorneys and government-paid prosecutors. This dichotomy had carried over into the courtroom during Sybee's trial, albeit in other forms. There it was the "justice-minded" prosecutor against the hired "big gun." The "protector of the people" versus the "fast-talking" defense lawyer.

And in the end, the loser facing the winner.

Judging from Springer's stiffened movement as he rose to greet us, that outcome was not far from his mind. I'd judged him correctly—he was not happy to revisit the Sybee case on this fine summer day.

Springer was dressed in his inevitable brown suit and striped tie, the collar of his shirt too big for his scrawny neck. He stood behind his desk, shaking Chetterling's hand and casting a dubious look at me.

"You were at the trial. One of the courtroom artists."

"Yes, Annie Kingston." I held out my hand and he shook it limply. Chetterling glanced at me, as if surprised that Springer had not mentioned my relationship to Trent Gerralon. *Oh boy, here we go.*

"I didn't expect to bring Ms. Kingston along when I talked to you," Chetterling explained as we took our seats across from Springer's desk. The detective's chair creaked as he settled himself. "But it occurred to me she may be of some help. So I hope you don't mind."

"No, no, of course not." Springer's tight smile creased his sallow cheeks. The gesture looked almost mechanical, as though pulleys on either side of his mouth jerked taut, then relaxed. Not a charming sight by any means.

Chetterling set his notebook on the desk, seemingly unaware of Springer's demeanor. How could he miss it?

Then again, Chetterling rarely missed anything.

"Thanks for your time," he began. "As I mentioned on the phone, I'm investigating a homicide outside of Redding that may have ties to Edgar Sybee's trial. Information leads us to believe that the suspect could have been involved in Barry Draye's murder."

One of Springer's eyebrows rose. That cynical-praying-mantis expression of his.

Detective Chetterling opened the notebook. In a pocket on the inside of the cover lay a copy of the composite. He slid it out and laid it before Springer. "Recognize this guy?"

Springer bent forward, peering at it. I watched his eyes wander from the top of the drawing to the bottom and back again. Then he leaned back in his chair with a shake of his head. "Never seen him before."

I let out a breath. But then, hadn't I guessed this? Somehow I knew that the Face, from the beginning to the very end, would continue to remain elusive. Almost as if he were taunting me.

"Who is he?" Springer looked up.

"We don't know, but we think he's from this area." Chetterling left the drawing in front of the deputy D.A. "This composite was drawn after interviewing the one witness—the victim's daughter."

Springer perused the sketch once more. "Quite detailed. This daughter gave you an awful lot of information." He looked at Chetterling through the tops of his eyeballs. "She says the drawing looks good?"

"She swears by it."

"How old's this girl?"

"Twelve."

Springer pursed his mouth. "She saw the murder? She was traumatized?"

My lips pressed together. If Springer knew I'd drawn the composite with not one iota of training in forensic art, he'd probably be outright sneering.

"Yes, she was. It took us a while to let her calm down and be ready for an interview. The first two attempts didn't work at all."

Springer studied the drawing, a wince at one side of his mouth. "The eyes are so blue, they don't look real."

Chetterling glanced at me, as if he felt my frustration. "We believe in the veracity of the composite as far as it concerns our homicide. It will be printed in local papers here tomorrow, and we expect to get some leads. In the meantime we'd like to get a jump on this guy."

"Okay." Springer leaned back in his chair. "So how can I help you?"

His tone signaled anything but a willingness to help. As before, Chetterling seemed to pay the man's demeanor no heed. But he used his posture to communicate plenty, hunching forward, his hands clasped and elbows resting on the arms of his chair. As if puffing out his frame to appear even larger than normal. Comparing the body language of the two men in our small quarters, I'd say Springer appeared to have retreated as far as he was able.

The detective got right to the point. "We believe that when this man—" he indicated the drawing—"committed the homicide, he was seeking a file on an interview between Sybee and his original attorney, Trent Gerralon. In that interview, Sybee tells Gerralon how Draye's murder went down— that a drug dealer did it. A man he names. We think that drug dealer and the man in this composite are the same. Evidently, he got scared once the case was left open and wanted to purge the file."

Left open. Chetterling was reading Springer, all right. Playing the politic, he'd refrained from saying the word *acquittal.*

Springer was doing his best to keep a poker face, but even as his mouth remained closed, his jaw hung askew, and that telltale eyebrow had crept upward again. His lips parted then as he seemed to ponder which question to ask first.

"Sybee's a lying druggie and a killer. Why on earth should you believe him?"

Chetterling shrugged. "If the story's a lie, why would this guy come all the way to the Redding area and break into a house just to get the file?"

The deputy D.A.'s nostrils flared with a long intake of air. "I'm clearly not getting the whole story here. Maybe you'd better start from the beginning."

That would be my cue. Chetterling turned to me with a slight nod. "The story starts with Ms. Kingston."

Pinpricks danced across my shoulders. Worried as I was about Springer's reaction to my filial ties, even stronger rose my desire to not let Chetterling know I was concerned—and hadn't prepared him.

"You know me as an artist at the Sybee trial—" I forced myself to look Springer in the eye—"you may not be aware that Trent Gerralon was my father."

Springer hooked a stare at me as he processed the words. I dared not look at Chetterling. No doubt the deputy D.A.'s reaction was not lost on him. A low-slung cloud seemed to form around Springer's shoulders, sullen and thick with the dust of resentment. My thigh muscles tensed, preparing for a quick rise when he ordered us out of his office.

"Go on," Springer said tightly.

I hesitated. Slowly it dawned on me that Springer would save face in front of Chetterling. To display ill will against my late father would show that his loss in the Sybee trial continued to sting. I plunged into my story. By the time I finished, my palms were sweaty. Springer had barely moved. Not so Chetterling, who'd shifted in his chair as though we were engaged in casual conversation.

As my words fell away, Springer gave a slow blink, as if searching the back of his eyelids for an answer to this conundrum. "Well." He raised his chin. "I agree you have a fascinating tale there. And of course—" he looked to Chetterling—"I understand your need to apprehend your suspect. I don't know what the correlation is between your case and mine. I can't explain the coincidences. But I'm sure that's all they are."

He pinched his lips together and stared at me. "One thing. You seem to have numerous secrets, Ms. Kingston. Just as I wasn't aware of your relation to Trent Gerralon, neither was I aware that you, a courtroom artist, are trained in forensic work."

Springer's snide remark sank through my chest like a rock. I was willing to bet he already knew the truth. "Actually, I—"

"She was available," Chetterling stated, "and she could calm the witness. As it turned out, Ms. Kingston's interview yielded a detailed composite."

I could have hugged Chetterling—until I realized he was defending himself and his investigation more than he was defending me.

"Yes, isn't it, though." Springer lowered critical eyes to the drawing. "So . . . *very* detailed."

No one said anything for a moment. Springer's cynicism hung in the air. Chetterling slid the composite across the desk as if it were gold and slipped it into his notebook.

"No need to keep you any longer," he declared with measured politeness. "I'd just like to ask once more, now that you've heard the entire story, if there's anyone you can think of—perhaps some vague suspect whose face you have not seen—that could have been involved in the Draye murder."

Springer held the detective's gaze before gifting us with his precise and disdained answer. "Absolutely no one."

Chetterling nodded curtly. "Thanks for your time."

Defeated, we left.

Chapter 35

Why didn't you tell me he didn't know you're Trent Gerralon's daughter?" We stood on the sidewalk outside the courthouse, Chetterling's jaw set and eyes narrowed. "And don't tell me you didn't think about how hostile he'd be when he found out."

"I did . . . but only when I was on the way here. And then I just . . ."

"Didn't want me to say you couldn't go in."

"N–no. Well . . . yes."

Chetterling shook his head, looking across the street toward the county jail. "Some buffer you are."

"It wouldn't have mattered anyway. Whether I was there or not, you'd have had to tell him about me, about my part in this whole thing. He'd have acted the same. Springer just can't get over that he lost the case."

The detective opened his mouth, then snapped it shut. He bounced the notebook against his leg. "Maybe so. It was a long shot and I knew it." He fixed his eyes on me. "All the same, I don't need surprises, okay?"

"Okay," I said, my voice small.

He pulled in a long breath. He had to feel beaten down, frustrated, and bone tired. With no rest in sight.

"All right. Thank you for coming." It was an exit line if I'd ever heard one. "I'll call you if anything else comes up. Like I promised."

I gathered my courage. "Where are you going now?"

Not that I had any right to ask.

"Annie. Just leave me to my business, all right?"

His business. Irritation flared within me. Like it or not, it was my business, too. "You're going to see Edgar Sybee, aren't you? If anybody can identify the composite, it's him."

He gave me a wary look and said nothing.

"Let me go with you."

"No." He stretched out the word, like a parent denying a meddlesome child.

I sighed up at him. "Please."

"Annie, look. You've done all you can for this case. You've done a lot. Now let it be. Let me do my job."

"I *can't*, don't you see?" Desperation tinged my voice. "What am I supposed to do, just sit in my sister's town house and wait? My whole life's on hold! It's not safe in Grove Landing because a murder happened there. A murder that should have happened in *my* house."

Chetterling's lips parted but I cut him off.

"And it's not safe here, either. Not so much for me but for my son."

He frowned. "What's the matter with your son?"

Oh great, why had I brought that up?

"He tends to hang out with the wrong kids here. Kids who do drugs. It's a big reason why I moved to Grove Landing."

"You'd best get home and keep an eye on him then. Drugs aren't something you want your son messing around with."

As if he had to tell me that. "It doesn't matter if I 'get home,' because he's not there anyway." The defensiveness in my tone could not be stayed.

"Where is he?"

I half turned away, lowering my gaze to the sidewalk. "He's staying with a friend."

"One of *those* friends?"

"I don't think so. I don't know. Maybe."

Suddenly my purse weighted my shoulder like a ton of bricks. I looked at Chetterling, feeling both enervation and defiance march across my face. For the first time since I met him, he looked nonplused.

"Never mind, you wouldn't understand." My voice veered off pitch. "You don't know what it's like to try to raise kids alone. I'm just . . . tired, that's all. Even in this situation, my ex wouldn't take the kids, so I had to bring them here." I lifted my hands and let them flop back to my sides. "And I can't watch Stephen every minute."

Chetterling's expression stilled, as though something I said had cut through his competent exterior. For that brief moment I saw not Detective Chetterling of the Redding Sheriff's Department but Ralph Chetterling, the man.

"I know what it's like to raise a kid alone."

The words pulsed with experience. I had no idea what to say. "I'm so sorry. I didn't know."

He shifted his weight, tapping a thumb against the notebook. Then cleared his throat. "Look. I'm doing all I can to solve this case quickly. I'll do all I can to get you and your kids back to Grove Landing soon—a *safe* Grove Landing. And let me just say that I think it's a good thing you've done for your son, moving there. If you have problems with him in the future, Annie, I want you to know you can come to me." He shrugged. "Kids tend not to listen to their own parents. Maybe I can talk some sense into him." He gave me a half smile. "Or maybe I can play sheriff's detective and scare some sense into him."

I nodded. "Thank you. So much. I'm . . . sorry I went off on you."

He raised a hand. "Don't worry about it."

Suddenly the conversation felt awkward. Too touchy, too . . . personal. I still couldn't fathom why I brought up the subject of Stephen, particularly in the middle of an argument about this case and its latest dead end.

I straightened. "Well. Thank you again for your understanding. Didn't mean to bring up my own problems at a time like this." I fastened a gaze on him, hoping to look a lot more courageous than I felt. "Anyway, we'd best get moving. Something tells me Edgar Sybee's our man. We're going to find out something important from him."

Exasperation played across Chetterling's features. Almost as if he were unsure whether I'd manipulated the entire conversation just to soften him up. Not that I'd stoop that low. But I couldn't find a way to deny it. Doing so would lend the idea a certain . . . credence.

"I know you don't want me to go. But I can't do any harm this time. Really. Sybee won't care whose daughter I am. In fact, he's got every reason to like me for it. So please don't make me go back and just . . . wait. I have to do something. I *have* to."

He tilted his head to regard the sky. I held my breath.

"All right, Annie. You can go. But let *me* do the talking." He spun on his heel and headed for the jail.

Yes!

I launched after him, hurrying to keep up with his long strides. As we crossed the street, my recent prayer flashed into my head. *Let something good happen here today.* I meant the courthouse, Springer's office. But maybe this was the good part? That God was letting me continue to help with the investigation?

Oh boy, I was really going nuts now—rationalizing that prayer was working.

As we entered the county jail, I couldn't help but pray one more time. Surely it would be my last.

Please, God, let Sybee tell us something.

Please.

Chapter 36

A jail is not the friendliest of places.

The atmosphere of lost dreams and vengeful schemes threatened to choke me as soon as we were seated. We'd been allowed one of the rooms that attorneys use, with a pass-through for documents in the separation glass and a speaker that would allow us to hear the inmate without using phones. The tiny room smelled of dust and sweat. One minute of waiting and already I couldn't wait for this to be over.

Sybee shuffled into his area on the other side of the glass. He looked at me, then Chetterling. Back at me. Vague recognition washed his hazel eyes. With a purposeful sniff he slumped into his chair. Tipped it back and crossed his arms.

As I'd drawn Edgar Sybee's face at the trial, I was reminded of a pudgy boy in middle school. His features were as rounded off at the edges as Springer's were sharp, even though he was only mildly overweight. Sybee's jawline sort of smudged into his neck, his circular ears lying close to his head. Now, just as at trial, he did his best to display nonchalance, but his darting eyes gave him away. That and the odd tic that jerked his lips to one side.

"So." He lifted his shoulders. "What's up?"

Detective Chetterling introduced himself and me. Sybee's eyes bounced back and forth between us.

"Yeah, they told me who you were." He looked to me. "And I remember you from the trial. You drew pictures."

"Yes, I did. But I'm also—"

"She's also related to someone important to your case," Chetterling jumped in. "Ms. Kingston is the daughter of Trent Gerralon."

That got me the once-over from Sybee. Then his gaze fell for the first time to the notebook in Chetterling's lap. A veil of distrust draped over his face, as if he sensed this would be a revisitation of the case he'd put behind him—the charge of which he'd been acquitted.

"Yeah, well, that whole thing's over and done with, isn't it."

Chetterling refused to be baited. Opening his notebook, he slid out the composite. As he placed it in the pass-through, my eyes were riveted to Sybee's face. I held my breath. If only Sybee recognized the drawing. If he'd just cooperate, police could be hunting down the killer within the hour . . .

Sybee leaned forward and took the drawing. Held it up and looked at it.

No reaction on his features.

None.

This was not my imagination. I watched every inch of Sybee's face, waiting for a sign, the smallest flicker of recognition. Sybee was not as smart as he'd like to think. Even if he wanted to hide what he knew, some bit of body language, however subtle, would give him away.

But his face remained blank.

He pulled in a breath and shrugged. Tossed the sketch back into the pass-through. "Never seen him before." His eyes moved from me to Chetterling. He must have noted the intensity on our faces, because he pulled back his head a little, frowning. "So who is he? And what's he supposed to do with me? I don't get why you guys are here."

"We're here," Chetterling said quietly, "because we believe this is the man who killed Barry Draye."

Sybee's mouth spread in disdainful surprise. "*This* guy? You're crazy."

Chetterling kept his cool. "Edgar, he's killed again. A mother, right in front of her young daughter. Think of it; you've got a wife and kid yourself. And the man's likely to keep doing it until he gets what he wants. In fact, knowing what you do, isn't he a threat to your own family? If you help us, we can stop him."

"I tell you, I don't know the guy. Never seen him before in my life!"

Chetterling processed the answer. "Then who killed Barry Draye?"

Sybee's expression folded over on itself. "Well, I sure didn't. I was acquitted."

"I know that. There was another person with you that night at Draye's house, wasn't there. Tip, he calls himself. Volatile, unpredictable Tip. He insisted on going with you. And when you got there, he pulled out a knife and stabbed Draye."

Sybee's cheeks paled. "Who told you that? I never told anybody that!"

"But you did, Edgar. You told your attorney, Trent Gerralon. On the last night you ever saw him. He took notes."

Sybee's neck swiveled from Chetterling to me. "I don't know anything about this story. I don't know anything about any notes."

For a moment I dared to hope. He'd shown no recognition of the Face, but now he was blatantly lying about the file. Maybe his blank reaction to the composite had been faked after all.

"It's okay to talk to us," Chetterling soothed. "I've seen the notes from Trent Gerralon's files on the case."

Sybee shoved back in his chair, pulse beating in his neck. Chetterling and I waited in silence. Anxiety quivered across Sybee's face, then an abrupt relaxing, as if he'd just realized some point of major significance. His gaze fell to the floor, and when his eyes met the detective's again, they were full of puzzlement.

"Wait a minute." He interlocked his fingers. "Tell me again what that drawing has to do with Draye?"

There it was again—that anesthetized expression of ignorance. This was no masquerade. This was real.

Chetterling sensed it, too. Although he did not move, I could feel the swell of doubt around his wide shoulders.

"Tell me something, Sybee. How much longer you got in here?"

A shrug. "About three months."

The detective nodded. "And with Tip on the streets, do you believe your family will be safe during those three months?"

Sybee's lips parted. His tongue found his top row of teeth and slid from one side to the other. "I think you'd better stop threatening me."

"I'm not threatening you at all, Edgar. I'm just reminding you of the danger that could exist. Now, I understand why you're afraid to talk. Like you told your attorney, Tip's threatened to hurt your family if you say anything. But the guy's unpredictable, Edgar. And if you point us in the right direction, we can pick him up before he can do anyone harm."

Sybee locked eyes with the detective. "I *don't know* the guy." His face slipped into a sneer and he pushed to his feet. "Forget this, I'm out of here."

He banged on the door with his fist, head turned away as he waited to be let out. There was not one thing more we could say.

The door opened. Edgar Sybee strode through it without so much as a backward glance.

Chapter 37

Chetterling and I trudged across the street in silence. Fears and defenses sizzle-danced through my head like water droplets on a hot griddle. I couldn't deny the truth that spat at me.

"Where are you parked?" Chetterling asked as we hit the curb.

"In the garage over there." I gestured with my chin.

"I'm up the street at a meter, so I guess we'll part here."

The detective looked spent, as if the interview with Sybee had eaten up his last spark of energy. He shifted his weight and passed the notebook from one hand to the other.

"He was telling the truth, wasn't he? Not about the murder but about the composite."

Chetterling's eyes closed. "Either that or he deserves an Academy Award."

I worried my lip between my teeth and stared at a large stain on the pavement. Distractedly I scuffed at it with the toe of my shoe. "Which means I made a mistake." The words came out flat.

Chetterling gazed into the distance, saying nothing.

"I don't know how it happened." The words spilled from me. "But when I was drawing the composite, I kept remembering all the faces I sketched in the past. And I think maybe . . .

maybe I sort of unconsciously remembered that particular face and drew it. And then when Erin saw it, she was just so upset and scared, expecting to recognize it, that she *did* . . ."

The detective rubbed his jaw with a knuckle. For the first time, I noticed he did not wear a wedding ring. "But the man you drew . . . he did have reason to break into your house. That file on the Draye murder *was* in your dad's office."

"But he didn't come to my house; he went to the Willits'. I don't know, maybe he really did want something from Dave's house. Maybe this has nothing to do with me at all!" I swallowed hard. My gaze fell again to the stained cement beneath my feet. "Nothing, that is, except that I've made a terrible mistake. Cost you and the other detectives a good four days in your investigation—the most important four days."

Chetterling's shoulders rose with a deep intake of air. "Annie, I am too tired right now to think through all this. Can't think through much of anything except to get to my hotel room and into bed. My head'll be clearer tomorrow." He ran a hand across his eyes. "We can't do anything else right now anyway. The composite is set to go into papers tomorrow. Let's see what kind of leads that generates. In spite of what Sybee insists, we *know* that this guy—" he gestured at the notebook—"is in the area, because you saw him here. Somebody's bound to lead us to him, and then we can see if he's got anything to do with our case or not."

Our case. I couldn't help but latch onto that word. It had slipped from Chetterling's mouth without his awareness.

"Okay. You're right. We just have to wait." I started to head for my car, then turned back. "You'll phone me tomorrow, won't you? When the calls start coming in? I promise I won't insist on going everywhere with you, but I just . . . have to know."

He nodded. "I'll do it."

When I'd walked a few steps away from him, he called my name. I looked over my shoulder.

"When you get back to your sister's place, check up on that boy of yours."

I hesitated, not sure if his words were a veiled chastisement—or empathy. "Don't worry, I will."

Ten minutes later I dragged myself through Jenna's door, and she immediately beset me for all the details. Tired and defeated, I told her what had transpired.

"I'm going to read some more of that forensic art book tonight." I forced determination into my tone. "Maybe there's some kind of clue in it. At the very least I'll know more about where I went wrong."

One more thing I had to do—check up on Stephen. And it had better be a good report. Reluctantly I dialed Nate's house.

"They were doing fine here," Nate's mom assured me. "They're out right now."

Out. What was that supposed to mean? I worked to keep my tone steady. "Did you drive them somewhere?"

"A friend came by and picked them up. I haven't seem them since. But they're supposed to be back for dinner." She sounded not the least bit worried. What if Nate was not the harmless friend I'd thought him to be? With a single mother who was not watching over him . . .

My conversation with Chetterling rang in my head.

Like you, Annie, not watching over your own son. She's no worse than you.

"Well, as soon as they get back, please tell him to call me."

"Sure. That shouldn't be too long."

I hung up the phone and wandered back into the living room, where I dropped onto Jenna's beige leather couch. She was slumped in the matching love seat. We exchanged silent, grim looks.

"Tomorrow." She nodded firmly. "Tomorrow's going to break this case. I just feel it."

"Yeah, right. If it doesn't kill me first."

Later I would remember her words.

And mine.

Chapter 38

His cell phone rang. Driving with one hand, he snatched the phone off his car's center console. "Yes."

Cars whizzed by him on the freeway. Everybody was always in such a hurry. He always chose the slow lane. Easy does it, nice and methodical, that was his motto. Other people, idiots all of them, were likely to get themselves killed. But not him. He was always careful.

No getting killed.

No getting caught.

He was In Control.

The male voice spoke in his ear. He knew this voice. Whiny, obsequious. (He liked to use that word: *obsequious.* Only superior people used such words.) The voice never failed to grate on his nerves. But the man was a necessary evil. Kept an eye on a certain person. A person who needed to be watched.

A person who, in time, would be dead.

His teeth clamped together as he listened to the jailhouse snitch. Once again Sybee had been visited—by someone other than his pretty young wife. This was not good—oh, no, no, no. Look at the mess the idiot had caused the last time he saw that Gerralon attorney alive. Gotten all soft and talkative. How quickly he'd forgotten the penalties he'd pay if he started spouting.

But he'd been reminded, hadn't he. A few pictures of his wife and kid outside on their lawn, sent to his home address, had reminded him just fine. No message. Just . . . pictures.

How he wished he could have seen Sybee's face when his puzzled wife took those pictures to the jail.

"So who were the visitors?" he growled into the phone.

"He didn't give names. Some detective from Redding, and get this—a woman who's the daughter of his lawyer. The one that died."

Acid and ice slid down his spine. For a moment he couldn't form words. He could only press the phone to his ear, grip the steering wheel, as sinuous thoughts like twisted seaweed floated through the brine in his head.

"What did they want?"

"Some weird thing about whether he recognized a drawing of some guy. And they wanted him to tell them how the Draye thing went down."

"Why?"

"They claimed to know something about that night. Stuff he told his attorney. I don't know what, but . . . maybe it goes back to that other time I told you about before the trial."

The words knifed him in the gut. His thoughts lurched and he nearly hit the car in front of him. He needed to exit the freeway. Needed to pull over and just think, think, *think*. This was bad news, *terrible* news. They'd traced him here.

They were putting the pieces together.

Thoughts of his sister left alone in the world crowded into his brain. He flung them aside.

Keep calm, man, keep calm.

"What'd he tell 'em?"

"Nothin'."

"How do you know?"

"He said he didn't, man, and I believe him. He acted all ticked that they'd bothered him. Like he didn't get what the deal was."

That would be Sybee. Not smart enough to understand much of anything. Not smart enough to put it all together.

Still, the guy could get cocky. He could be just dumb enough to forget the lessons Tip had taught him. Start thinking he should be done with Tip once and for all. Start thinking the Sybee family could hide behind the law's protection . . .

"All right, man, thanks a lot."

"Yeah. Don't forget what you owe me now."

The guy made him sick. "Don't worry. You'll have plenty of goodies waiting when you get out."

He smacked off the phone and threw it on the seat. The seaweed slimed in his head.

Annie Kingston had found the file.

She'd taken it to those Redding sheriff's deputies.

She found it because he *missed* it. By a mile.

He let loose a stream of curses. The words bounced around the car, taunting him like the long-ago, hoarse voice of his father.

The Whipple exit stretched out ahead. He turned onto it and headed east, toward the flatlands butting up to the Bay and the San Carlos airport. Jerking his car to a stop, he nearly hit a dog that was bounding about, waiting for its master to take it running on the trail. Still cursing, he turned off the engine and banged the side of his head once, twice, against the window.

He *was* In Control. It wasn't his fault he'd gotten into the wrong house. Hadn't found the file. It wasn't his fault that woman came downstairs and caught him. And it certainly wasn't his fault she was dead. He hadn't even *tried* to kill her— just to stall her enough so he could run.

Nothing was his fault. He was the Man. A leader. Cunning. Taking payback out of a world that had knocked him down since the day he was born.

Take it easy now, man. Think, think, think!

He raised his head from the window, leaned it back against the seat. His fingers flexed against his meaty thighs. He stared across the flats, absently watching the runners and walkers and dogs. Watching a private plane descend for a landing at the airport. Slowly his breathing returned to normal.

Okay. So there'd been a few setbacks.

No more.

First, he'd see to it that Sybee didn't talk. Give the man a ... gentle reminder. He ground out a chuckle.

Then there was Annie Kingston. She'd gotten too sneaky for her own good. Someday she just might open her mouth in a courtroom and chatter like a jaybird.

That could never happen.

He worked things, that's what he did. Changed events. Caused certain ... upsets.

The composite drawing of that Willit woman's killer was the perfect example.

He tapped a manicured nail on the steering wheel.

Tap ... tap ... tap.

Thinking about what needed to be done.

Tap ... tap ... tap.

Nice and slow, like a metronome beating out a death march.

Saturday, July 26

Chapter 39

The Face stared at me from the pages of the *Mercury News*, complete with an article about the murder. Chetterling had been cunning in what he told the reporter. Just enough for a good story. Enough to warn the public that a killer was at large. But he'd given away no more than he had to. People with information about the man in the drawing were asked to call the Shasta County Sheriff's Department.

Which in turn, I knew, would immediately contact Chetterling if any leads came in.

No. *When* the leads came in. Like Chetterling said, someone had to recognize this man, even if he had nothing to do with Lisa's murder. I'd seen him on a Redwood City street; I knew he existed.

For a quirky moment I imagined the Face

punching in the number for the Redding Sheriff's Department. "What is wrong with you people? Why is my picture linked to some murder! I'm an upstanding citizen, and you'd better clear this up in a hurry. I'm calling my lawyer right now . . ."

An innocent man would do that, wouldn't he? Come forward to clear his name?

Yes, he would. If the Face didn't call, that had to mean something.

But he wouldn't call. He *was* involved, no matter what Edgar Sybee claimed.

All the same, I still couldn't dismiss the blankness on Sybee's features when he looked at the composite. He hadn't recognized it. He *hadn't*.

I sighed aloud. This morning was progressing as ambivalently as the previous night. I'd tossed and turned, mentally going over and over every detail of the case. Reliving the moments as I sketched alongside Erin . . . Remembering Edgar Sybee's denials—and the expression upon his face.

My only positive thought during the night was a thankfulness that Stephen had called me at dinnertime from Nate's. The boys had returned as instructed.

By five a.m. I'd known it was no use trying to sleep. Numbly I folded up my bed, punched down the three couch cushions, and pulled the forensic art book onto my lap. For the next three hours, until I heard Jenna making coffee in the kitchen, I read. In the airplane the previous day, I'd skimmed the beginning chapters. Now I read every word, soaking in the material like a dry sponge. The more I read about past cases, how composites and face sculptures had helped apprehend suspects, the more the information grew and formed within me. I felt like some strange creature taking in sustenance, readying myself to metamorphose. Details I'd blitzed over the first time now stood out to me. The muscles and bones of the face. Different head shapes. Parts of the ear, the nose, the mouth. Dental aspects. The great importance of proportions.

Many of these things I studied years ago in art school. I used my understanding of faces for a decade in the courtroom. Reading this information in the book now, I felt more aligned with forensic art than ever.

Okay. So I've had no training in the field. But I do have a lot of pertinent background education and experience.

Then reality hit.

Pressing my knuckles into my chin, I began to reread the chapter on interviews and composite imagery. My confidence, like a fledgling sparrow flying from its nest, tumbled to the ground as I lingered on all the details I had done wrong. Still I pushed on, telling myself I would lift my wings once more. By the time I heard Jenna, I'd already begun the chapters on age progression, a technique used to update photos of suspects who have been on the lam for years.

Now I sat with Jenna over coffee, telling her about all I'd read. I rehashed with her the events of the interview with Sybee. Went over once again all the possibilities, the problems. The newspaper sat between us, refolded so the Face could not stare in defiance, mocking me. Jenna stuck to her belief in the composite. It was simple, she said—Sybee was lying. Because everything else fit.

But Jenna hadn't been there. She hadn't seen Sybee's face, his eyes, as he denied recognizing the drawing.

The morning paper seemed my last resort. Either it would yield leads . . . or it wouldn't.

By nine o'clock I'd waited all I could wait. I wanted to call Chetterling, see if he'd heard from his colleagues in Redding. After all, most newspapers were delivered by six a.m. People had already had three whole hours. Surely *somebody* had called.

"Annie . . ." Jenna gave me one of her looks. "It's Saturday. Most people are still in bed."

How could the world sleep at a time like this?

Somehow ten o'clock rolled around. Just to keep occupied, I sat at the kitchen table and read more of the forensics book. In spite of my nervousness, I found the chapters on skull reconstruction fascinating. Imagine being able to take bones from the grave of an unknown victim and reconstruct the face. I read stories of how forensic artists had accomplished this time and time again, helping to give an identity to an unknown victim. How through this process, grieved families had been given closure on their missing loved ones, and in some cases the murders had been solved.

At ten-thirty my head snapped up to check the time once more. And in that instant the concentration I'd summoned melted away. I stared at the clock, my fingers tightening on the book's cover, then closing it. Had I lost my mind? Reading about death and skulls and *savoring* it?

The phone rang. I dashed like a madwoman to answer it. "Hello?"

"Annie, it's Helen."

Nate's mother did not sound right. At her tightened tone, my emotions shifted into a new tilt, like the world heaving itself on its axis. Worries about the Face dissolved as I steeled myself for some new disaster. "What's wrong?"

"Well, I don't want you to get too concerned." She gave a forced little laugh. "Boys are boys, you know."

I waited, silent.

"Anyway. I let them go out again with some friends last night after they came back for dinner. You know T. J.? He picked them up in his car."

Oh yes, I knew T. J. One of Stephen's druggie friends. My mouth opened and I slowly, purposefully, took a breath.

"I told them to be back at ten, but they didn't come back until almost three in the morning. I got up when I heard them come in. Of course, I couldn't sleep. They were high. I could smell the marijuana."

A dozen accusations bombarded my brain. How could she have let them go with T. J.? How could Stephen have done this, when I'd warned him time and again about the danger of drugs? How was I going to raise this kid? There I was, trying to help search for a murderer who may have killed *twice* because of drugs. Like an auto careening out of control, my thoughts swerved down the winding mountain highway of my son's teenage years. I could only imagine the inevitable grind of gears and wreckage at the bottom.

My son was destroying himself and I could not help him. My son would end up like Edgar Sybee, caught in a world of violence that could not be escaped.

Nausea roiled through me as I bent over the counter. From a distance came Jenna's voice, asking what had happened. I shook my head and pressed the phone deeper into my ear, as if pushing calmness into my brain.

Somehow I found my voice. "Where are they now?"

"Still sleeping."

Bitter words leapt up my throat. I forced them back down. What was the point of blaming her? What was done was done.

"Wake Stephen up. I'm on my way to get him right now."

"Okay." She hesitated. "Annie, I'm sorry. I shouldn't have let them go."

I flattened my hand against the counter as if to compress the tile, drive it into the cabinet below. Part of me wanted to rail at her. But the other part could not forget that she, like I, was a single mother. I knew what it was to feel overwhelmed. I knew what it was like to say yes to my son's wrongheaded demands out of sheer exhaustion. Hadn't I done the same thing in allowing him to go to Nate's in the first place?

"I don't blame you, Helen. It's just ... too much to handle sometimes, you know? Parenting—especially for *our* sons—we shouldn't have to do it alone."

She blew out air, clearly relieved. "I know."

Five minutes later I pulled out of Jenna's detached garage to pick up Stephen, my cell phone stuck in the car's center cup holder in case Detective Chetterling called. My parting words to Helen rang in my head. *We shouldn't have to do it alone.* It seemed that my whole life, not just parenting Stephen, was destined to be done alone. Even when I was married to Vic, deep inside I'd sensed a loneliness that not even the best of husbands could fill.

And Vic had been anything but the best of husbands.

Stephen slumped in the seat on the way back to Jenna's, chin set, eyes narrowed into slits. He no doubt planned to make life as miserable as possible for me. I'd taken him away from his friends, and that was inexcusable.

We talked little. There was nothing to say. He knew what he'd done, and I knew that if I asked him about it, he'd only deny, deny. I gripped the steering wheel, my imaginative brain conjuring up my composite of the Face, the man's features fading, fading ... and Stephen's replacing them. In rapid succession my personal projector threw more pictures from the past week on the walls of my mind, as if to prove the theory that Stephen's choices were setting him on the worst of courses.

"I won't stay here, you know." He climbed out of the car and slammed the door, his expression twisted with a heightened rebellion I had not seen before. "I can sneak out anytime I want."

I shouldered my purse, the infuriatingly quiet cell phone clutched in my hand. "What do you want from me, Stephen? Just to let you go your own way and do whatever you like? Let you ruin your life?"

"If anyone's ruining my life, it's *you.*" Yanking open the back door of the car, he grabbed his duffel bag of clothes and stalked out of the garage.

His words knifed me in new and cruel ways. For a moment I stood still, my eyes closed, feeling the pain. Then I leaned against the car, a plaintive chant of *Why, why, why?* echoing in my head. How was I going to raise my children on my strength alone?

From nowhere Gerri's words about God's peace swirled into my mind. Was it only two days ago that her prayers had brought some strange, supernatural calm into my being? I puffed out air. Whatever I felt, it hadn't been God. Because he sure didn't seem to be worrying about me now.

Summoning my willpower, I pushed away from the car. By now Stephen would be in the house, and Jenna didn't need to deal with him alone. I left the garage, pressing the controller on Jenna's key ring to close the door, and headed for the town house.

Please let this be over soon.

The prayer raveled through my mind like the strands of a fraying rope. I seethed at the betrayal of my thoughts. I told myself I prayed to no one. But deep inside I could not quite believe my own denials. Something seemed to be shattering within my soul, something hard and brittle and stubbornly chaotic.

Reaching the stairs, I grasped the rail with one hand and pulled myself up them, still holding my cell phone. As each step drew me closer to facing Stephen, my way became clearer. We had to leave the Bay Area as soon as possible. I needed to separate my son from the temptations that surrounded him here. It had been a wretched mistake to come in the first place. I'd known that, even as I made the decision. Who did I think I was, running around, trying to catch the elusive killer of my neighbor when my own child was falling apart? At least Grove Landing offered a certain respite. There we could lock our doors, turn on the burglar alarm to safeguard us from predatory danger. But here the danger lurked within, clattering about my recusant son's head, pushing him to make choices that could haunt him for years.

The only other thing to do was send Stephen away, maybe to some camp or wilderness program. But where? I had no idea where they were, which ones were trustworthy and which were not. And the proper research would take time. I needed to guard Stephen against himself *now*.

Stephen would not make this easy. I felt sapped by exhaustion just imagining his biting arguments.

Sighing, I stepped over the threshold into Jenna's town house. Before I could close the door, my cell phone rang.

Chapter 40

Annie, it's Sid Haynes."

Sid. Disappointment softened my muscles. Why couldn't this be Chetterling with good news?

I shut the town house door and sagged against it. The sound of rap music from the living room assaulted my senses. Stephen was watching videos on TV.

"Hi."

"Sorry it took me so long to get back to you. Things have just been busy around here, as always."

My mind scrambled to recall why he would be phoning. So much had happened since our last conversation. "Uh, no problem."

"You all right?"

My eyes closed. "Yeah. Fine."

Gary—Sid's investigator. The memory popped into place. "Everything safe at your house?"

"Yes. I mean, no. I mean, I don't know. We left. We're in the Bay Area right now, staying with my sister."

He took a breath. "That was probably a good idea. Look, I'm calling to tell you I asked Gary about your man on the street. He says he doesn't know the guy. He's never even seen anyone fitting that description."

No kidding. Gary could get in line with everyone else. "Yeah, well. I expected as much."

I wandered into the kitchen. Through the back sliding door I could see Jenna sitting on her deck, an open novel in her hands. But she gazed into the distance. Poor Jenna. My son had driven her to retreat from her own house.

Stephen's poor excuse for music grated in my ears. "Excuse me, Sid." I covered the mouthpiece. "Stephen, turn the television down."

He ignored me.

"Turn it *down!*"

A disgusted grunt erupted from my son's mouth. Grabbing the remote off the couch, he smacked a button. The music lessened one degree. I retreated into the office and closed the door.

"Sounds like you've got a lot going on there," Sid commented.

If he only knew. "Yes. But, Sid, thanks for calling. I appreciate the follow-up. The composite's in the *Mercury News* this morning; have you seen it? We're expecting some leads soon. We'll figure this out."

My voice held not the slightest bit of confidence.

"Look, Annie, it'll be all right. They'll catch your man. I know I'm not talking like a defense attorney right now, but . . . these guys are all the same. It's some kind of masquerade with them. They think they're mighty and cunning and above the law. That they'll never get caught. But none of them are as smart as they think."

Masquerade.

"Thanks, Sid. I'm sure you're right. I'll let you know what happens." My gaze fell to my suitcase. The symbol of my family's having been forced out of our new home. "One thing, though. And you have to promise me. When this guy's caught? Don't you dare represent him."

He emitted a chuckle. "Little chance of that, Annie, under the circumstances."

I clicked off the phone and placed it on Jenna's desk, checking the time. It was past noon. Where was Chetterling?

The forensics book sat on the desk, where I'd left it since early that morning. Distractedly I flipped it open, then turned away. I couldn't stand to look at that stuff for another minute.

I paced the office, mulling. Telling myself I should make Stephen turn off that awful music video station. Telling myself I should plead with Jenna to take us back to Grove Landing for Stephen's sake. I needed to make arrangements to pick up Kelly at Emily's house. And when we got back home, Erin and Dave would need my emotional support.

Need, need. I had a dozen obligations and didn't feel the strength for any of them.

My phone sounded again, the ring creating a vibration that sent it inching across the desk like some live creature. I snatched it up.

"Hello?"

"Hi, Detective Chetterling here. Thought it was about time I checked in with you."

"Yes. What's happening?"

Please, please tell me something good!

"Not much of anything. I've spent the morning talking to more detectives here, showing them the composite. None of them recognizes it."

"What about phone calls from people reading the papers?"

"Nothing."

"*Nothing?*"

"Not one."

"Have you had your cell phone on?"

Good grief, Annie, what a stupid question.

Chetterling retained his patience. "Yes."

Questions and fears crowded my mind but I could not voice any of them. I didn't want to ask Chetterling if he'd lost all faith in the composite. Because I couldn't bear to hear his answer.

"What are you going to do now?"

Air seeped from his throat. "I want to stay here another day in case calls come in. But I'm being summoned back to Redding. One of our detectives had a death in the family this morning, so he's got to take off immediately, which leaves us shorthanded up there. I can't justify waiting around if nothing is happening."

"I see." My heart sank. Our one big potential break in the case and nothing was going to come of it. True, the composite had only been printed in the *Mercury News* that morning, but the past few hours were the most critical. The time when people were reading their papers, seeing the Face staring at them from their breakfast tables. Someone should have recognized him by now.

Still . . .

"But we both *know* I saw that man here. Even if he doesn't have anything to do with our case, why wouldn't someone recognize him?"

"Annie, I just don't know. If I had time, I'd go back to Sybee again, see if I could get anything more out of him. But it may make no difference anyway. He's under no obligation to talk to me and probably wouldn't."

I had to agree. We would get no more out of Edgar Sybee. And I still couldn't help but believe he told us the truth about the composite. "Yeah. Probably not."

"What about you all? You staying a few more days?"

"No, we have to leave. Stephen's giving me trouble here. We'll be going in the next couple hours."

"Oh. Sorry to hear that." He sounded empathetic. "We may reach Grove Landing about the same time then. Let me know when you've arrived back home."

"I will."

Shoulders sagging, I clicked off the line and placed my cell phone on the open forensics book. We'd tried our best. I wanted to hang on to that but felt no comfort whatsoever. Who cared how hard we'd tried? We hadn't succeeded. And we still were not one step closer to the truth.

With both hands I buffed my eyes. When they opened, my gaze landed on a large bold heading in the book. I blinked at it, unseeing, trying to gather the energy to start the process of returning to Grove Landing.

Until the word filtered into my consciousness.

Disguises.

I tilted my head, staring. What was it Sid Haynes said? The word that resonated within me?

Masquerade.

Disguises.

A thought bloomed in my head like a flower in the desert.

Wait. What if . . .

My finger reached out to touch the printed word as if to draw meaning from it. Barely breathing, I reread the short section on criminals and their disguises. Sunglasses and hoods like that of the Unabomber were only the beginning, it said. Suspects had changed their hair color, grown beards and mustaches. They'd used makeup to create amazing alterations, changing the shapes of noses, eyelids, cheeks, and lips.

I leaned over the desk, thinking of my interview with Erin . . . Sybee's adamant assertions . . . Springer's cynicism . . . the Face . . . the lack of leads from two different newspapers . . .

Pieces of conversations and facts skittered through my brain like tumbleweeds.

His hair . . . got messed up . . . it had come down his forehead . . .

The eyes are so blue, they don't look real . . .

I've never seen this guy before . . .

The single brown hair found at Barry Draye's house—

A small cry escaped me.

I reached for my cell phone to call Chetterling but my hand stalled in midair. Why on earth would he listen to me now? He'd think this was another wild goose chase. And maybe it was. If he convinced his superiors to let him stay in the Bay Area and check this out, only to again come up with nothing, wouldn't he find himself in real trouble—thanks to me?

Besides, I had no idea how to investigate my suspicions. Chetterling was right—Edgar Sybee wasn't likely to talk to him again. And I wasn't about to try seeing him alone.

Plus I needed to get Stephen out of the Bay Area—soon. But . . .

I had to drive over to Emily's to pick up Kelly. Which would place me within one block of Sybee's home. What if his wife, Crystal, could help? Maybe at some point she'd caught a glimpse of Tip. The dealer had sold her husband drugs. Maybe she would talk to me, mother to mother, for the sake of a third who now lay in the grave. If I showed her the composite—just in case she hadn't read the newspaper. And the notes of the interview between her husband and my father. If she could admit to seeing Tip in the past, yet like her husband didn't recognize the Face . . .

If there was even the remotest chance . . .

I spun on my heel to leave the office.

Hurrying through the living room, I ignored Stephen and his music. With each step arguments crowded into my head like clamoring children. What was I doing? Hadn't I concluded that my priority was taking care of my own children? That I needed to get Stephen out of the Bay Area—now?

I told myself that what I planned to do would not delay our leaving for very long. Five minutes on the way to Emily's house—that's all I needed. Just five minutes.

Stepping onto the back deck, I thrust the sliding door closed behind me and launched into an animated explanation to Jenna.

"Wow, that's amazing!" She tossed her novel aside. "Sounds really good! Oh, and yes, I agree we need to get Stephen out of here. But right now—go see Crystal Sybee."

"You sure? This isn't crazy?"

"No, it's not crazy. I'd do it."

Of course she would. But she was Jenna.

"Do you want me to come with you?"

I hesitated. "Yes. But you can't. You've got to stay here and keep an eye on Stephen. If we leave him alone, he'll be out of here."

She nodded. "Does he know we're leaving?"

"No. And I don't want to tell him until I get back. Less time for him to get mad and storm out."

"Yeah, you're right." She raised her eyebrows at me. "Good luck."

"Thanks. I'll need it."

As I slipped out the front door without a word to Stephen, the raucous sound of rap music assailed my ears.

Chapter 41

The circular drive in front of Crystal Sybee's house lay empty. Three garages were attached to the left side of the house, all their doors closed. I drove up near the front walk and stopped, praying Crystal was home, half hoping she wasn't. On the drive over, I'd started thinking of all the reasons I shouldn't be here. Now that I'd arrived, I dreaded knocking on the woman's door. A confrontation was the last thing I wanted. And it now seemed possible that I would be anything but welcome.

Gathering my purse and the file folder containing Sybee's interview and the drawing of the Face cut from the newspaper, I slid out of Jenna's car and closed the door. The air seemed eerily quiet. Not the slightest breeze rustled the old oaks in the front yard. My eyes grazed over Sybee's house, left to right. It was a modern-looking two-story stucco with wide steps leading up to a deep porch and recessed front door. Beveled glass graced the top half of the door, but I could not see inside the foyer, due to the shadowed porch.

For some reason my skin tingled at the lack of noise. Atherton is a quiet and stately neighborhood, the massive homes far apart on large lots—worth a fortune in the Bay Area. The community is much like Hillsborough to the north, where Jenna and I grew up. I understood peaceful neighborhoods. Grove Landing was quiet, too. Except for the airplanes.

Maybe Crystal Sybee wasn't home. After all, it was a Saturday in July.

Yet in the back of my mind a disturbing thought broke free: *There is nothing normal about this silence.* The air seemed pendent, heavy with some strange portent.

Oh, good grief, Annie. My active imagination was gearing up, that was all. Best pull the plug before it got started.

My anxiety increased as I walked around the car. Strangers did not just drop in on people in the Bay Area, not unless they were solicitors. Crystal Sybee would probably answer the doorbell through an intercom, hear my spiel, and refuse to let me in. I started up the front walk, trying to gear myself up. I had to get in that house. Had to talk to her. Crystal was my last hope.

I would not listen to the voice warning me I was grasping for straws.

Mounting the five porch stairs, I focused on the door. With each step I strained to see through the glass, to perceive some grayed motion suggesting a living presence.

Nothing.

A chill teased my arms as I moved from sunlight into shadow. I reached the ornately designed doors and pushed the bell—a lighted circle surrounded by a gold-filigree plate. Rich tones of Westminster chimes rang through the house.

A wail from inside the house arose in answer—the high, frightened cry of a toddler. This was not good. I'd awakened the little boy from his nap. Crystal would not be pleased. For a second I considered leaving, fleeing like some salesperson before the wrath of a mother could descend.

The wail increased in intensity. Then it rose and fell like a lament at a funeral, wrapping around my head, reaching the very core of my being. My mind flashed a close-up of a child's face, his

head tipped back and eyes squinched shut, cheeks ruddy, a flush on his neck. A few small teeth shining white with spittle against the redness of an opened mouth . . .

I waited. What should I do? Crystal would not immediately answer the door. She would go first to her child, calm him. Quiet him.

No footsteps sounded within the house. No door opening or closing. And the little boy continued to cry as if he could not be comforted.

I hunched forward, an ear toward the door. Part of me felt like an intruder, a voyeur. What would I think as a young mother, opening my door to some stranger who strained to hear inside my home? And yet the child's cries were soul-searing, the wails licking at the back of my neck like tongues of fire. I waited and waited for some sign of their lessening, but the sounds remained tortured, without the least interruption. I found myself inhaling and exhaling, an audible whine in my throat, as if my own body were in tune with the keening. As if I could in some telepathic way soothe the quivering screams.

The child's dirge rose and fell, rose and fell. What mother would allow her child to become so frenzied? Why wasn't Crystal Sybee picking him up, consoling him? I closed my eyes, listening for some variation in pitch or projection, something to indicate that the little boy was being held, his hot little face pressed against a loving chest.

The fingers of my right hand cramped as they clutched the folder. The toddler's howls pulsated within me, an energy begging to be dissipated.

And still he cried.

Anger flared next, my nerve endings prickling with a sense of injustice. Poor little boy. His father a druggie and a liar, and his mother so neglectful. I had a mind to turn on my heel and head straight for the Atherton Police Station, merely blocks away, and report what I heard. Most likely the mother wasn't even at home. Who could sit in a house with that kind of racket and not try to stop it? It would take less energy to tend the child than to block out the ear-splitting sound.

Unless she was unable to help.

The thought rose within me like a rogue wave, fizzling out the heat in my nerves. Leaving me practically shivering. What if something had happened to her?

I edged toward the center of the door, forgetting all etiquette. Tucking the file under my arm, I cupped both hands around my temples and leaned into the door, my eyes sweeping the foyer left to right. I saw a spacious hardwood-floor entrance. To the left a doorway led into an area too darkened to see. To the right was a staircase carpeted in light rose. The far side of the staircase ran along a wall. A banister lined the near side, ending at the bottom of the stairs in a snail-shell curve. Beyond the stairs stood another open doorway to what looked like a formal living room.

I turned my head from side to side, listening. Although I couldn't be certain, it seemed the little boy's cries were flailing down that staircase from the second floor.

Spine taut, I straightened, filling my lungs with air. I felt suspended, wanting to leave but afraid for the child. A minute or two must have passed as I hung there, undecided. The longer I wondered what to do—and the longer the little boy howled—the harder it became to force myself to leave, even though everything within me said, *Go, get out of here, something isn't right!*

My imagination began filling in all sorts of scenarios. Crystal Sybee, lying on the floor, overdosed on drugs. Or she'd hit her head and lay unconscious. Or she'd left her little boy alone and he was hurt.

Of its own accord my hand veered to the doorknob. The metal against my palm had almost a numbing affect, stalling my fingers. After some hesitation I twisted the knob the slightest bit, expecting it to be locked.

It turned to the right.

I stared at it, feeling betrayed. Now I would have no excuse to leave the toddler wallowing in his misery.

Holding my breath, I pushed open the door.

The wailing assaulted me at once, like multilegged bugs crawling into my ears. The door had muffled far more of the sound than I would have imagined. I could hear the intake of breath between the cries, the staccato grinding of air in the little boy's chest. And, piercing my heart, I could now make out the single word wrenching from his mouth.

"*Mmmmmaaaaaa-mmmmmaaaaaa! Mmmmmaaaaaaaaa-mmaaaaaaaa!*"

I leaned across the threshold, scanning as far as I could see. "H–hello?" At my quivering voice I felt foolish. What was a half whisper next to the boy's screams? If he could not make his mother materialize, I certainly wouldn't.

In brilliant Technicolor, my mind flashed to young Erin Willit. All alone in her house, facing horror with no one to help her. Had I known the danger she was in, I'd have been by her side in a heartbeat. Because of her, no choice existed here. I could not leave this little boy to cry alone.

I stepped into the house and closed the door.

Illogical though it was, fear bade me make no sound. I tiptoed across the hardwood foyer until I reached the bottom step. Raising my chin, I allowed my gaze to travel up the stairs to what I could see of the hallway on the second level. Which wasn't much. Apparently, one had to turn either right or left at the top of the staircase.

The unending wails were coming from the right.

Clutching the folder in one hand and the banister with the other, I placed a foot on the stairs. As I raised myself up the first step, my ankle shook. By the time I gathered the courage to take the second step, my knees were trembling as well.

Between the mind and body exists the most diaphanous of walls. In times of alarm—*poof!*—it disappears. Apprehension may start in the mind, but soon it starts to play with the body. Hands tremble. Palms sweat. The heartbeat sputters. With the first shake of my ankle, I knew I was doomed. No longer would I be able to tell myself that this ill-begotten scene would end well. The projector in my head spun into frenzied mode, churning out disordered sequences from every movie I'd ever watched that included a misfortunate in stealthy movement through a house fraught with danger.

I climbed the third stair. Already my hand failed to glide over the banister, the wood sticking under the wetness of my palm.

"*Mama! Mama!*" The wails ululated until my pulse pounded in my head.

Leave, leave! The voice of reason echoed in my ears. *Something isn't right here and you know it!*

I struggled for rational thought. I could turn around and go. Head for the Police Station, tell them what I heard. They could come back and investigate. Or I could go outside and call 911.

The idea chummed the waters of my brain. Arguments broke the surface like predatory sharks. I could practically hear the officers now: *You mean you just left a kid alone in the house, screaming? You didn't even go upstairs to see if he was hurt?*

No. They wouldn't say anything like that. Police officers would never advise someone to walk alone through a house that could hold danger.

Maybe so, if a child wasn't involved. But this was a two-year-old, no less, completely unable to help himself.

I took the fourth stair. And the fifth.

My heart beat double time as I strained to listen for something, anything, other than the little boy's cries. Footsteps in the entryway behind me. A door closing. Maybe Crystal had been out in her backyard and now finally heard her son's torment. Perhaps she was doing laundry in a room off the garage and still couldn't hear him at all.

Surely that was it. Crystal *was* here, safe and sound, somewhere. All I needed to do was pick up her child and take him to her. As awkward as that would be—coming upon her in her own home, her son in my arms—it was far more comforting than the alternative.

I wiped my left palm against my pants and climbed three more steps.

Only then did I see it.

A mark on the wall straight ahead. No, more than a mark. It looked like a long smudge of something. Before I realized it, I'd taken another stair, focusing, squinting at that smear, knowing deep within what it was even as I could not let my mind believe it.

All I could see of the hall was that area at the top of the stairs. To the right and left it looked so dark, built as it was in the middle of the house. Why hadn't they put a skylight in the hall ceiling? Why hadn't they knocked out one of the front walls and just run a banister across instead, allowing light to filter up from below?

My chin raised. I sucked in my top lip and stared at the smudge on the wall. A vague thought made its way through my mind. This kind of hallway, though dreary, would be the safest for a crawling baby. A mother could wedge one of those portable safety gates at the top of the stairs. But a long banister with its supporting posts was dangerous. A baby could get his head stuck between those posts.

A possibility blew across my mind like a thundercloud. Maybe Crystal had chosen this home because of its safe design. If so, she was a careful mother. A mother who would not go off and leave her child alone. Who would not leave a toddler this long to do laundry in a far-off room.

Air dragged in and out of my throat. I dropped my jaw to pull in more oxygen. When I rose one more step, I saw another smear on the wall, below the first one. As if two fingers had trailed along, leaving the telltale sign of violence in their wake.

Blood.

The raw truth washed over me, weakening my knees.

"Ma-ma!"

I was over halfway up the stairs. So close to the screaming toddler. I knew I should sprint up the rest of the steps,
tear down the hallway, and rescue him. Whatever evil had
happened to his mother may have touched him as well.
Maybe he wasn't just lonely and mad; maybe he was *hurt*.

My heart told me these things, begged me to run, to help
him. But I could not move. I stared at the dual tracks of
blood—darker on the right side, fading to the left. I tried to
force my body into gear as my internal movie projector
flashed one manic picture after another of the destruction
down that hallway, waiting to be found.

Jesus, help me.

The name sounded in my head as if I had called upon it
all my life. In that horrifying moment I could think of nothing else. I felt no strength within me to do what needed to be
done.

A force outside myself pushed my legs into action. I
mounted the rest of the stairs, heart in my throat, following
the sounds of the terrified child. When I reached the hallway,
my head turned left first, as if to put off the inevitable sight
of what lay at my right. That end of the hallway ran about
twenty feet, ending at a closed door. Another door about ten
feet from me was also shut. If these were open, surely light
from windows in those rooms would fill the hall. But I could
not take the time to open them. The boy's cries peaked and
rasped, and I had to follow them—*now*.

Gathering my courage, I turned to the right.

In perfect symmetry the hall ended in another closed door
twenty feet away. Halfway down, to my left, lay another room,
the door wide open, light spilling through it to pool on the
hall carpet, the walls. Like a mocking spotlight, one sunbeam

aimed itself at a large blot of blood on the door frame, glistening a surreal red.

From that room came the earsplitting screams of the toddler.

Air clogged in my windpipe, threatening to suck back into my lungs. My eyes followed another sunbeam down to the floor of that room. Something solid lay just within my line of sight. I could not tell what it was. I managed one step forward, hugging the wall to my right, to peer closer.

A sandaled foot. Tilted outward, toes pointing in accusation toward the blood on the door frame.

My fingers loosened on the folder. It slid down the wall and onto the carpet in front of me.

"Mmmaaaaa, mmmaaaaa . . . aaaahhhh!"

The little boy gasped and choked. Then raised his wails once more.

His screams pulled me forward. I pushed away from the wall, stepping over the folder and down the hallway. My legs moved beneath me through no will of their own. At the entrance to the room, I reached out to steady myself as I peered inside.

The metallic-sweet scent of fresh blood invaded my nostrils.

Crystal Sybee lay on her back, arms extended, fingers curled. Her neck twisted to one side, her eyes staring lifelessly at the bottom drawer of a dresser painted in sky blue and dotted with puffy clouds. Blood saturated the front of her T-shirt, sprayed across her arms, and oozed from self-defense cuts in her hands. She'd been stabbed. Multiple times. A red-glazed kitchen knife lay by her left knee. Her little boy hunched on the floor to her right, vainly smacking his fists into her hip.

Trying, *trying* to wake his mother. His cheeks flamed red; mucus ran from his nose, over his lips.

With a groan I flung myself into the room, a dozen voices clamoring in my head.

You're in a crime scene, Annie; don't touch any more than you have to!

Is the boy hurt? He's spattered with blood but is it his?

How long has she been dead?

Run, leave! The killer could still be here!

As I sank to my knees beside the boy, he turned to me, bewildered, terrified eyes wide. His cries sputtered, then died in his throat. My purse strap fell off my shoulder and I shoved the bag aside. I reached out, running my hands down the boy's arms, exploring his head, his legs, his chest. No wounds that I could find. His forehead creased. *"No!"* He scrabbled backward, his bare heels digging into the carpet. He did not stop until he hit a leg of his wooden crib. "I want my *mama!"*

"It's okay, it's okay," I soothed ridiculously. "What's your name?"

"Tommy! Go away!"

"Tommy. Okay."

Clearly, he'd not been hurt. Ignoring him for the moment, I turned my attention to Crystal. Laying the backs of my fingers against her throat, I felt for a pulse. Nothing. Next I tried her wrist. Still nothing. She was dead. I'd known it the first second I saw her. But she felt so warm. She couldn't have been gone long. Minutes maybe, no more.

How long had I been there? Time seemed so distant since I drove up, got out of my car, saw no one and heard nothing. Only when I reached the front door had the toddler begun to cry. Only then.

That couldn't have been more than five minutes ago.
Where was the killer?

Before I knew it, I'd thrust to my feet, crossed the room, and snatched the boy off the floor. He squirmed in my arms, pulling my hair, kicking my hips. I pressed him tighter against my chest, ignoring his cries, smearing tears and mucus and blood into my shirt. Teeth clenched, I fought my way back over the carpet, around Crystal Sybee's still form. Somehow I managed to grab my purse. Out the door and into the hall I fled. I had to get myself and the child away from this house of death. I would throw him into my car, lock the doors, screech out the driveway to the Atherton Police Station . . .

Adrenaline ricocheted through my veins. I overshot the hallway and banged into the opposite wall, turning sideways just in time to save the boy from hitting it. My left hip and shoulder took the blow. I bounced off and staggered, blinking hard, trying to regain my equilibrium. My eyes focused on the floor before me—those ten feet leading to the top of the stairs.

Something had changed.

Deep within my brain the knowledge shouted, struggling to be heard over the pain in my side, the kicking toddler, the terror in my limbs. *Something isn't right! What is it?* The question careened against the walls of my mind.

My eyes squeezed shut, then opened to stare again at the carpet near the top of the stairs. The truth hit, cutting through me as keenly as the blade of a knife.

The folder was gone.

My heart turned over in my chest. No . . . no . . . the file must have somehow slipped onto the stairs. It lay out of my sight, that was all. I only had to move a few steps and I'd see it. But my denials rang false. That folder had fallen in front of me, *in* the hall. I'd stepped over it to get to the nursery.

In that instant I knew. The Face was here.

Who else would care about that file? This scene—the blood smeared on the wall, Crystal Sybee's death—was his doing. Why he had done it, I did not know. But suddenly the hall, the house, reeked with his presence.

"Shhh, shhh." I tried to silence Tommy, putting a hand over his mouth. But he only cried harder. There would be no silent slinking from this house. Wherever the Face lurked, upstairs or down . . . he would know our every move.

My mind on hold, my body moving on someone else's legs, I skulked down the hall, clutching the toddler, my purse, and whatever courage I had left.

I'd nearly reached the stairs when the door twelve feet away opened and a figure materialized before me.

Chapter 42

A gurgle sounded in my throat as needle points pricked down my legs. Weakness washed through me and I almost dropped the little boy.

"Annie Kingston."

The man spoke my name in sneering disgust.

I stood frozen, staring, my suspicions gelling into reality. This man—with blood on his hands, his shirt, spattered up his bare arms—was not the Face. I had never seen this man before. Brown hair, gaunt cheeks. But the shape of his eyes . . .

Tommy twisted in my arms, seeking the source of the voice. One look at his mother's killer and he pitched his screams higher than ever. He pounded my shoulders with both fists, struggling to free himself. Somehow, in sheer desperation I hung on. If he were to slip from my arms and run now, I would not be able to save him.

If I managed to make it out of here alive.

"Kid!" the man blared. "Shut *up!*"

In two seconds he'd closed the distance between us. His large hand drew back, fingers extended to slap the boy's head. With a small cry I swiveled away. The vicious blow landed on my shoulder blade. I flew forward, Crystal Sybee's terrified son slipping from my arms. As I hit the wall, I felt him scramble across my feet and around my legs. My purse fell to the floor.

"*Mama!*" He darted back down the hall toward his dead mother.

Stunned, I pushed myself upright. The man grabbed my arm from behind, fingertips sinking into the flesh above my elbow. I jerked around, aiming a fist at his face. He caught that arm at the wrist and yanked it downward, then shoved me into the wall. His leering face thrust within inches of mine.

"Forget the kid. You and I have some talking to do."

I could do nothing but look into his eyes. They were light gray and ice-cold. I had not seen them before . . . and yet I had.

He pulled back with a smirk and watched the recognition play across my features. Time uncoiled itself, like a deadly snake, in what would surely be the last few seconds of my life. These *were* the eyes I had drawn. The eyes that had locked with Erin's in the desperate second before she fainted. The eyes that watched as Lisa gasped for breath . . . died. Tip. The Face who wasn't the Face. The killer who had effected such a disguise that all of his features, save for the shape of his eyes, were radically changed.

"Stared at me enough?" He pushed me sideways. "Get moving, we're going downstairs. That kid's about to drive me crazy."

I stumbled down the steps before him, one of his hands clamped around my arm. My mind raced through a thousand thoughts. No one but Jenna knew I was here. How long would it take before she became worried? Kelly—my daughter who needed her mother. I couldn't leave her like Lisa left Erin. Stephen. He needed my protection. Without me fighting for him, what would he become?

We hit the foyer. Tip pulled me right, into the family room, and shoved me down on the couch. I lay on my spine, breathing up at him, unable to make a sound.

Upstairs Tommy's cries stopped. Surely he had worn himself out.

Jesus, help me stay alive and save that boy . . . and I promise I'll seek you. The plea washed through me like frigid blood.

"W–were you going to kill him, too?" I was amazed I could utter a word.

A slow, almost charming smile spread across Tip's face. "You'll never know, will you."

I licked my lips. Somehow I had to keep him talking, stall for time. "They'll find you for sure. You've left fingerprints in blood. All kinds of evidence. Not neat like the Draye's house."

The smile faded. "I'm in control. I'll clean the place up. I wasn't planning on your little interruption."

Distantly I heard my cell phone ring. It still lay inside my purse, somewhere near the top of the stairs.

Tip's eyes cut toward the sound. "Too bad you're busy."

Was it Chetterling? Jenna? What would she think when I didn't answer?

It rang a second time.

I pressed back into the couch. "What do you want from me?"

"*I'll* ask the questions, hear?" He sat down hard on the massive coffee table and leaned toward me, hairy arms crossed. "What are you doing here?"

What had he done with the file? I could not deny that I'd brought it to show Crystal Sybee.

A third ring. After five my answering message would click on.

"Talk to me!"

Air caught in my windpipe. "I came to see if Crystal recognized you. N–not you, I mean. Your disguise."

A satisfied expression narrowed his eyes. "My mask."

I could only look at him, feeling the questions flicker across my face.

My phone stopped ringing.

He pushed his tongue under his top lip, then pulled it away with a sucking sound. "I used to work in Hollywood. Know all about making casts of faces. Silicon masks that look so real, nobody can tell they're not." His lips stretched into an ugly smile. "Not even a fancy face-artist like you."

Even as my body shook, I couldn't help but think of that evidence. Had he been cunning enough to destroy the mask? Or was it still sitting in his house somewhere, with a blond wig and blue contacts?

None of them are as smart as they think. Sid Haynes's comment blew through my mind. *Smart.* The word throbbed in time with my rapid heartbeat. Clearly, Tip liked to think of himself as intelligent. Above the next man. But he was also paranoid and volatile. If I could reach the egotistical part of him, get him to keep talking . . . without losing his temper . . .

"I can't believe you planned all this. You put on that mask just to talk to me on the street that day. You used it when you came to Grove Landing to find the file. Just in case somebody saw you."

His features darkened. He jumped to his feet, finger pointing inches from my cheek. "It wasn't *my* fault it was the wrong house!"

"No, no, of course not. I wasn't even thinking—"

"I was smart enough to find out the address, wasn't I? To plan the whole thing, wasn't I?"

"Yes, you w—"

"So many houses in the dark, how could I tell? I wouldn't have needed to go, anyway, if baby Eddie had been convicted. If it wasn't for *your father!*"

At the last two words his face purpled. A vein on the side of his neck pulsed. He slapped his hands around my arms and yanked me off the couch like a rag doll. My head snapped back, sending pain jolting down my neck.

"By the time I got home, I wanted to kill somebody. I *needed* that file." He dragged me across the family room, spewing venomous, crazy stuff about wanting to kick his cat to death, and all I could think was, *You did kill somebody; you killed Lisa, just like you're going to kill me now.* He slammed me against a door frame, pinning me with an arm across my throat. "Then you and that detective start nosing around, trying to get Sybee to talk. And now you're *here*, in this house."

He leaned into me, pushing his arm against my throat. I could smell Crystal's blood on his hands. My mouth fell open as I began choking. Black spots danced before my eyes. In desperation I pummeled him with both fists, struggling to push him away. My knees weakened. I slid a few inches down the wall. The projector in my mind ground into gear, flashing scenes of Lisa's death mixed with images of my own.

Abruptly Tip pulled away.

I slumped over, gasping. My fingers splayed across my throat as if to stretch it wide, pull in oxygen. I felt spittle run down my chin.

"No, no, you're not dead yet." His voice turned to hard-edged steel. "Not until I find out what I need from you." He forced my head up. "Look at me."

I turned bleary eyes upon him. His face swam before me.

"What did Sybee tell that detective?"

I fought to answer, but the only sound was air raking down my windpipe.

"What did he say!"

I shook my head, swallowing hard, trying to form the words.

Tip erupted in curses and wrenched me away from the wall. He hauled me across the room, then turned and dragged me back. Around the couch we went, my feet nearly slipping as he forced me between it and the coffee table. Tip raved and cussed in wild streams of consciousness, ranting about how he'd read all the Redding newspaper articles, and about some snitch at the jail with Sybee, and his sick sister, and how he'd never, ever, *ever* go to prison. The more he vented, the more agitated he became. When he tired of the family room, he shoved me into the kitchen, into a chair at the table. A second later he jerked me out of it, ramming me against the counter, my head bouncing back into an upper cabinet.

"We're gonna try this one more time. What did Sybee tell you?"

Tears spilled down my cheeks. "Nothing, really! He wouldn't say anything."

He tore himself away from me and backed up to lean against the stove island, glaring. His arms crossed and I could see his biceps pumping. For the first time I noticed a bulge underneath his T-shirt, at the waistband of his jeans.

He had a gun.

Yet he'd cruelly chosen to stab Crystal with her own kitchen knife.

Wildly I wished for Jenna's gun. Why hadn't we brought it to the Bay Area? Why didn't I have my own—and know how to use it?

"Where's the original file?" he demanded. "That thing you brought looks like a copy."

I hesitated, my legs trembling. If I told him the truth, no telling what he would do.

"You gave it to that detective, didn't you?"

My head moved in the slightest of nods.

A black cloud formed over Tip's face. He slammed a palm on the cabinet next to my ear. Terror surged and I jumped, falling away from him. My hand flung out, catching the handle of a drawer and pulling it open. My fingers twisted in the handle and I cried out in pain.

Tip jerked forward, ramming into the side of the drawer. I fell to one knee, then shoved to my feet. The drawer crashed shut behind me. A voice rang in my head, telling me this would be my only chance. I had to *move*.

In one Herculean motion I sprang forward, grabbed a kitchen chair, and spun it around. Its legs whooshed through the air, catching Tip full in the face with a resounding smack. He staggered back with a cry, one hand covering his crushed cheekbone. I hoisted the chair and launched it again. The edge of its seat crunched into Tip's right temple. He didn't even have time to scream. His cold gray eyes bulged, then rolled back into his head.

With a loud thud he dropped to the tile floor.

The chair slipped in my sweaty palms. Tip's arms trembled, his hands clawing the tile as he struggled to rise. "No!" I summoned the strength from I knew not where to raise the chair a third time. It smashed into the back of his head. His chin cracked against the floor, bounced up, then hit again.

He lay silent, unmoving.

I threw the chair aside, stumbled to the table, and leaned into it. Every muscle in my body shook. Sweat and tears trickled down my cheeks. I wiped them away with the back of a hand.

The phone—where was it? I should call 911. The police could be here in minutes. I saw the empty base of a cordless phone on the counter and swung my head back and forth, seeking the receiver. There it lay, on the other side of the sink. I lunged for it, hit the power button, and listened for the dial tone, keeping my eyes on Tip. *Come on, come on.*

No tone sounded. I smacked the phone off, then on again. Waited.

Nothing.

I jabbed the power button so hard, it sent jolts up my hand. Off, on. Off, on. Listened once more for that sound I needed so badly.

Silence.

Tip lay still. My eyes cut from him back to the phone. He may be unconscious but the damage was already done. He'd made sure Crystal couldn't call for help.

I set the receiver back down on the counter.

My purse lay upstairs with my cell phone and Jenna's car keys inside. And Tommy was up there, too. I could not hear him but I knew he was still there, hunched by his mother's bloodied body. I had to rescue him. If Tip woke before I could bring help, surely he'd kill the toddler in sheer rage.

I aimed a piercing stare at Tip, watching for the slightest movement. Nothing, save for his breathing. He was alive but out cold. Who knew how long I would have? A minute, maybe two.

That was enough.

God give me wings!

I turned away, ready to bolt from the kitchen and up the stairs. But an unseen hand seemed to push my focus back to Tip. The gun. I should take it, just in case he woke too soon.

The weapon's shape was barely visible through Tip's T-shirt. Half of it lay underneath his heavy body. I would need to raise his shirt, perhaps move him a little, to slide out the gun. At the mere thought of touching him, my mind flashed a scene of

Tip waking, his beefy hand jerking up to catch my wrist, pull me down, down . . .

"No." The word formed on my lips. I could do this. I *would* do this. For my sake, and for Tommy's, and for Crystal's and Barry Draye's—and most of all for Lisa and Dave and Erin.

Tip's head lay close but I could not bring myself to approach it. Summoning energy to my tremulous legs, I inched away from the table. Around the stove island opposite where Tip lay. Down around the back corner and up toward his feet. There I stalled, my courage draining away. One quick move of his foot, one savage kick, and I would go down.

What if he was ready for this? What if he heard my every move and lay waiting to strike?

I pulled my top lip between my teeth. My fingers clung to the tile of the island, my knuckles turning white. Tip did not move.

Two shuffled steps to the right, giving ample room between me and his body. My back to the cabinets, eyes never leaving Tip, I eased sideways until I was even with the gun.

His right hand lay so close to his waist. He could grab me so easily when I stooped down, reached for the weapon . . .

My heart pounded like a jackhammer. I could hear the blood whooshing through my ears.

My cell phone rang. A muffled sound emanating from the depths of my purse, flowing downstairs and into my being. Summoning me. My body jerked, wanting to run and answer it. Pleading to use the excuse to get away from the murderous beast at my feet. Maybe it was Chetterling. He could have Atherton cops here within minutes.

But what if Tip woke before they came? When I was still upstairs, gathering my purse and Tommy? We would be trapped.

My jaw hung open as I forced myself into a slow bend, my mouth dry. Incoming air felt like fragments of glass across my tongue. I bent over farther, making no sound, reaching out my right hand. Bending . . . reaching . . . My arm shook so badly, I did not think I could control it. How would I ever operate my fingers efficiently enough to get the gun?

The fabric of Tip's shirt was a hair's breadth away. An internal warning screamed that the mere touching of it would spring him into action like some evil jack-in-the-box. I hesitated, my hand hovering, quaking. Through sheer determination, a will outside myself, I grasped the hem of his T-shirt and began to lift.

He did not move.

Pain vibrated through my back. I was bent at an odd angle, my body as tense as a coiled spring. But I would not bend my knees. I would not place myself that close to the floor.

The shirt rose above the top of his back pocket. Up to his waistband. My fingers clenched the fabric as if glued to it. My calf muscles began to twitch. I could not hold this position much longer.

I pulled farther. The barest patch of skin appeared above Tip's jeans. And a glimpse of black metal.

The shirt stopped. I could tug it no more without pushing against Tip's body to relieve the weight. For that I would need my left hand. My thigh and back muscles screamed. I couldn't stay bent long enough to do that, nor could I gather enough strength at this angle.

I would have to crouch beside him.

My feet shuffled closer to Tip. Slowly my knees folded until I sat on my haunches. If he were to snatch at me now, I would not get away.

I lay the back of my left hand against the cool floor and slid it toward Tip's waist. My hand came to rest against his body.

Okay, Annie, here goes. One. Two. Three!

In one motion I thrust my hand beneath him, heaved at the dead weight, and jerked up his shirt with my right hand. The handle of the gun lay exposed. I grabbed it and tore it away from Tip with such force that I fell backward, banging down hard against the floor. Panic-stricken, I crabbed away from the hands that could grasp for me at any moment.

They didn't move.

I pushed to my feet and, with a final glance at Tip's silent form, turned and ran from the kitchen.

Again I miscalculated the doorjamb, ramming into it with my right shoulder. Shock waves jolted down my arm. My fingers sprang open and the gun rattled to the floor. I reared back, afraid it would go off. Then I lunged to pick it up.

I sprinted out of the kitchen, down the hall, skidded left and across the foyer. My fingers wrapped around the curled end of the banister, whipping my body around and onto the stairs. I took the steps two at a time, clutching the gun with all my might. At the top of the stairs I ignored my purse, heading first for the boy. Crystal's still foot came into view as I ran toward the nursery. I froze in the doorway, my eyes sweeping the room.

Tommy wasn't there.

Had he crawled back into his crib, seeking comfort in his blankets? Toddlers could do that—climb right over the bars. I jumped over Crystal's body and hurried to the bed.

Nothing.

"Ah!" I backed up, then ran around Crystal and out of the room. Farther down the hall the door to what looked like the master bedroom stood ajar. Had it been open before? I plunged into it, knocking it back. It hit the wall with a bang. Panting, I pulled to a halt in the middle of the room. My gaze lurched across the carpet, the furniture, the king-size bed. Empty.

"Tommy, where *are* you? Please come out!"

Silence.

Think, think, Annie.

He would be hiding. That's what a frightened toddler would do. Where? Under the bed? In the closet?

I ran around the bed. Nothing there. Falling to my knees, I raked back the covers and checked underneath. A pair of shoes. A small tote bag. No boy.

"Tommy!"

On my feet again, heading toward the closet. Yanking open the door to a large walk-in. Multiple shoe racks, all full. Edgar's clothes on one side, Crystal's on the other. Tommy was nowhere to be seen.

Gun still in hand, I ran. Into the dressing area, the bathroom. Relief flooded me at the sight of a small shadow behind the shower curtain. I stopped, willing myself to slow, take this easy. I could not frighten him any more.

I pushed back the curtain. Tommy huddled against the back corner of the tub.

"Come on, honey, let's go. I'm going to get you out of here."

"No! I want my mommy!" He wilted away from me, head down.

I reached out. "Come on, now. We've got to hurry. I promise, someone will be here to help your mom."

"No."

He would not move. I begged and pleaded. He only pressed himself harder against the white porcelain. I would have to step inside and lift him. But that was impossible with one hand. What would I do with the gun? I looked down my body, knowing I would have to shove it into my pants, just as Tip had done. What if it went off? Had he put the safety on?

Why hadn't I learned more about guns?

Lifting my shirt, I slid the gun into my waistband, at the small of my back, then stepped one foot into the tub. I grabbed Tommy and hoisted him. He wriggled and fought but I clung on for dear life.

With his hot body pressed against my chest, I stumbled out of the bathroom . . . through the master suite . . . down the hall toward the stairs. My purse lay like a golden prize upon the carpet, ready for me to snatch it up. I reached it, gasping for air, started to bend over to retrieve it. The minute I let go of Tommy with one hand, he squirmed out of my grasp and slid to my feet.

"No, Tommy, *don't!*" I jammed my purse on my shoulder and grabbed for him just as he started to dart away. He fought like a tiger, hitting, kicking.

My cell phone rang. No way could I answer it.

I swiveled toward the stairway. So close now. I needed to get down it, through the front door, and into my car.

Tip hunched at the bottom of the stairs.

Waiting for me.

Blood oozed from his battered cheek and down onto his collarbone. One of his hands pressed into the wall for support. The other gripped the banister. He lurched there, weakened but clearly determined. I would not get by him.

"Come on," he mocked through clenched teeth. "You got no way out." He managed a gruesome grin. "Did you really think you'd get out of this alive?"

All energy drained from my body. My arms loosened and Tommy slipped to the carpet. Bawling for his mama, he crawled away.

I backed from the stairs, breathing hard. My brain scrambled for ideas but none came. Even the projector in my head had fallen silent.

"Come on, Annie," Tip taunted. "Nnno waaay to go but dowwnnn."

I shifted and metal pressed against my skin.

The gun.

Like someone else's appendage, my right arm reached behind me, and my hand extracted the weapon. I brought it around and raised it, the barrel wavering before me. My shaking fingers could not hold it still. My left hand came up to clutch its other side. Willing, *willing* my arms into steadiness, I stepped forward and aimed the gun down at Tip's muscular chest.

His lip curled. "You'll never do it, Annie. You don't even know how to shoot the thing. Probably never held a gun in your life."

No answer would form. I clung to the metal . . . and breathed.

"Besides, there's no bullets in it." He pushed himself up one stair. "You think I'd tote it around loaded, so I could shoot my own foot?" A second step slid beneath him. "You'd better run. It's your last chance. I'm gonna reach you in a minute— and then what will you do?"

Was he bluffing about the bullets? I could turn and run. I *should*. Anything to delay his approach. Maybe I could find something else to hit him with. I had hurt him badly the first time, hadn't I? He lurched and winced as he took the fourth and fifth stair.

"You're making me real mad, Annie." He climbed the sixth step. "*Real* mad. It's only gonna go worse for you when I get there."

"*Mama!*" Tommy's sudden cry tore through my ears. Involuntarily I turned my head toward the sound. Feet pounded in front of me and I wrenched my gaze back. Tip had mounted three more stairs. He hulked scant feet away, a mere two steps between us.

"No!" I shuffled backward.

He drew his tongue across his lips. "You wouldn't kill me, Annie, even if you had bullets. I'm the only one who knows the truth. You think you've got everything figured out, but you're wrong. With me dead, how would you ever know who really killed that neighbor of yours? How would you ever feel safe in your house again?"

He lifted his foot and climbed a stair.

"*Stop!*" I adjusted my aim toward his heart.

He held up both hands. "You can't do it, Annie. You *can't*."

Could I? If I didn't shoot, he would kill Tommy and me both. If I tried and failed . . . he would still kill us. What did I have to—

He pulled himself up the last stair.

"No, *please!*" I wilted back against the wall.

My finger jerked.

And squeezed the trigger.

Crack!

The bullet rent the air, slamming into Tip's chest. His black expression flattened into one of utter shock. His hands flew up, his body jerking like a yanked puppet.

I pulled the trigger again. Tip's neck tore away, blood spurting on his shirt, his face, the wall. He collapsed and fell backward heavily, tumbling, shaking the staircase. At the last step his head twisted sideways, his body flipping over and skidding across the hardwood floor.

He crunched into the wall, convulsed, and lay still.

I stared in total disbelief, unable to move.

Time blurred into one frantic series of events. I remember throwing down the gun. Somehow I managed to race back into the nursery, pluck Tommy from his dead mother's body, clutch him as I lowered my trembling legs down the stairs. Miraculously, my purse still hung from my shoulder, and I could only pray that my keys had not fallen out. We clomped across the foyer, well away from Tip's still form. I threw open the front entrance, clattered down the steps and front walk. Ran around my car, opened the door, and shoved Tommy across the console. Sliding into the driver's seat, I hit the button to lock the doors.

Less than a minute later my car screeched to a halt outside the Atherton Police Station. I scooped up Tommy and flung myself inside the building, still clinging to the boy as if Tip would rise from the dead any minute and snatch at our throats with bloodied hands. "Help! *Help!*" My screams bounced off the walls of the station like ricocheting bullets.

Three officers sprang to our aid at once. Just in time. Instant shaking overtook my limbs until I could not hold up myself, much less Tommy. One of the men caught the boy as he slid from my arms. I sank to the floor in swallowing darkness.

Monday, July 28

Chapter 43

A slight jostle, the feel of the Grove Landing runway beneath our wheels. Jenna had executed a perfect landing. The midmorning air felt stifling hot. I popped open my window as soon as the plane turned onto the taxiway, sending a furnace-like wind around our bodies.

"Good job, Sis," I said into the mouthpiece of my headphone. "As always."

"Thanks." Jenna shot me a meaningful look. "Goodness knows, *somebody* had to get you home safe. No thanks to your crazy self." She pushed the button to talk to other pilots in the area on the 122.8 frequency. "Six-eight-four-Mike-Charlie leaving the active. Grove Landing."

I made no comment. Jenna still hadn't forgiven me for venturing into the Sybees' house alone. Not that I could blame her. "Even I wouldn't have done *that!*" she'd spouted Saturday upon arriving with Chetterling and a wide-eyed Stephen at the Atherton Police Station.

Maybe not. But she wasn't a mother. To her credit, she'd hugged me first, ignoring the smears of blood, little-boy mucus, and sweat on my shirt. She'd clung to me like she never wanted to let go. Even my belligerent son wrapped his arms around me for a brief moment, whispering into my neck that he was glad I was okay.

"Yeah, Mom." Kelly's voice came from the plane's back-seat. "Crazy is right."

Stephen just grunted.

"Okay, Jenna—" I nodded—"and everybody else. For the millionth time, I *hear* you."

The forensics book lay in my lap. I'd picked it up as soon as we took off from the Bay Area and had closed it only moments ago as we began our descent. I had moved on to new chapters, fascinated to read more about the techniques of aging the faces of victims or suspects who'd been missing for years. I also read a chapter on ethical conduct for forensic artists. One of the author's points hit me right between the eyes: never, never interfere in an investigation.

Oops.

"Fine, but I'm going to keep reminding you," Jenna retorted, her feet working the pedals to steer the plane.

"No doubt."

In a flicker, her expression morphed to the one I knew so well—that I-told-you-so firming of her mouth, the slight raising of her right eyebrow. "Else you might get too big a head. 'Never seen a composite so right-on.' Jenna perfectly mimicked Chetterling. She ran her tongue over her teeth. "And you refused to believe you'd done it at all."

"Okay, okay." I raised both hands. "You're right about that, too. You're right about *everything*. Happy now?"

Despite my tone, I found myself looking out my window, feigning keen interest. I could not keep the satisfaction from my face and did not care to display it to my ever triumphant sister. She'd quoted the detective correctly. When the police searched the home of John Berengeti—Tip's real name—they found the multiple-layered silicon mask of the Face in his dresser drawer. It proved an exact replica of my drawing. Beside it lay the blond wig. A pair of bright-blue contacts were in his medicine cabinet.

Also now in Chetterling's possession were a pair of Berengeti's shoes, which the detective believed would match the footprint taken from the Willits' back deck. And a long-sleeved black shirt with the high probability of yielding fibers like those found underneath Lisa's fingernails.

Jenna guided the plane off the taxiway and down the wide Grove Landing streets, turning onto Barrister Court. At first sight of my father's house, I felt tears sting my eyes. Never had it looked so much like home.

I climbed out of the plane and unlocked the front door. The high-pitched whine of our burglar alarm keened through the great room. Mouthing a prayer of gratitude for our safe return, I punched in our code on the kitchen keypad and shut it off.

By the time I opened the hangar door, Kelly had already slipped from the plane and into the arms of a waiting Erin. They stood on the Willits' front walk, rocking back and forth. My heart wrenched at the sight. As Jenna cut the plane engine and slid off her earphones, I saw Dave emerge from his front door. I took a deep breath. *Oh boy.* No time to even prepare myself. But there could be no pretending that I hadn't seen him. I lifted a limp hand and waved. He waved back. Then started down his steps.

Jenna stepped onto the pavement. Stephen perched on the edge of his seat in the back, impatient for my sister to move her seat forward so he could get out.

"Hurry up, it's hot in here," he complained.

"Do you need me to help push the plane back, Jenna?"

My sister gave me another look. She'd been doing that a lot lately. "You know I don't need your help. Go talk to him, Annie. No excuse for delay with me."

I nodded.

God, are you there? Would you mind helping me with this, too?

Cutting across the street, I aimed myself toward the girls. This would not be easy. Erin and Dave both knew the whole story now. Chetterling told them before night fell on Saturday. But Dave and I hadn't talked yet. When I asked Chetterling about his conversation with Dave, the detective assured me Dave wasn't angry. "Blame you?" Chetterling had repeated in surprise. "After everything you did? How could anyone possibly blame you?"

Easy.

"Erin." I reached her side and put a hand on her shoulder. She pulled away from Kelly, threw her arms around me, and burst into tears.

"I'm so glad you're okay." Her voice was muffled against my shoulder. "It would be so awful to lose you, too."

Her words wrung my heart. "Thank you, honey, I'm just fine. Don't you worry." I patted her back, my eyes squeezing shut. I did not deserve this devotion from her.

Footsteps sounded to my left. I looked around to see Dave approaching. "Hi, Annie." Pain jolted through me at the gentleness in his voice. Erin stepped back and he held out his arms. I hesitated, then let him hug me tightly. Slowly my arms went around his back.

"Thank you." He breathed the words into my hair. "Dear God, I'm so glad you're all right."

My throat locked up. I could make no response. I could only feel his arms around me, this man whose beloved wife was killed a week ago because of what had lain hidden in my house. His chest jerked as he dragged in a ragged breath, mixing gratitude and grief. That did it. For the first time since Lisa's death, I abandoned myself to a good cry.

Dave didn't seem to mind. He just held me tighter.

After a few minutes I got hold of myself. Embarrassed, I eased away, one hand sheltering my eyes like a visor. I couldn't look at him. "Sorry. I just . . ."

Someone touched my arm. I glanced over to see Kelly peering at me anxiously. I couldn't remember when she'd ever seen me cry like that. "Are you okay, Mom?" Her forehead crinkled.

"I'm fine," I lied. "Really." I glanced toward our hangar. "Why don't you and Erin go help Jenna unload the plane. I'll be over there in a minute."

"Okay."

Erin shot me a parting, sad smile, then she and Kelly headed across the street, arms around each other's waists.

I turned back to Dave. Things still needed to be said—before I lost my nerve. Perhaps I wouldn't have possessed the courage without the events of the last few days. But so many emotions now swirled in my head, so many questions. Two days ago I'd faced down a multiple killer. I could certainly face Dave now.

"Want to come inside?" Dave gestured toward his house. His eyes told me he perceived my need to talk—and my reticence. I saw no judgment in them at all.

"Yes."

We walked up his porch steps and through the front door without speaking. Inside he extended a hand, inviting me into the family room. I lowered myself onto the couch. He sat in an armchair, hands clasped between his knees. I could not find the words I needed to begin. He filled the silence.

"How's the little boy—what's his name?"

"Tommy Sybee. He's okay. I mean, as best as can be expected. His mother's parents live in the area. They're taking care of him."

"And his father?"

I pressed my lips together. "In jail for another three months. And absolutely heartbroken, from what I hear. His mistakes—they cost him so much."

"Yeah." Dave bounced his hands off one knee. I knew he empathized with Edgar Sybee, thinking about his own loss. "What about all the logistics with you? Everything going to be all right?"

Logistics. He had chosen a tactful word. In the eyes of the law, there is nothing simple about fatally shooting another human being, even if it is clearly in self-defense. I'd had to give numerous statements. The police went over and over the crime scene. Much paperwork remained, not to mention meetings with the D.A. over whether or not they would charge me with a crime. Chetterling told me not to worry. "No way they're going to charge you with anything. You solved our murder as well as theirs—that is, *if* they're smart enough to reexamine their evidence."

I nodded at Dave. "I'm sure everything will be fine. After all, they let me come back today. And Jenna can fly me down if I need to put in a final appearance."

"Or I could. And she could stay with the kids."

Was there no end to this man's gracious spirit? "Thank you."

Dave focused on his feet. "Speaking of the kids . . . Detective Chetterling mentioned that Stephen was giving you trouble." He glanced up and, seeing my expression, added hastily, "I don't think he meant to say it, but it slipped out when he talked about how you planned on coming back as soon as they'd allow it." He looked down again for a moment, then lifted his eyes to mine. "I don't know much about raising boys, but if I can be of any help . . ."

My heart panged at this second generous offer. He had enough problems of his own. "Thank you. Stephen's going to be a handful, I know. Already is." As it turned out, Stephen was the one who'd called me three times while I was at the Sybees' house. He'd figured out I was picking up Kelly so we could leave the Bay Area, and wanted to harangue me about it. "But I must say, when he really understood that he almost lost me, he did soften up a bit. He didn't even give me a hard time about coming back here."

"Don't ever think he doesn't love you, Annie. I wasn't that easy to raise myself. Went off the deep end a few times, and my mother nearly despaired over me. I treated her so terribly, even when I needed her the most."

I could find no response to this. Never would I have imagined Dave being as difficult to raise as Stephen. "And look how you turned out. Gives me reason to hope."

He drew in a deep breath. "There's always hope."

We fell silent. I gathered my nerve. "Dave, I—"

"Look, I just want to thank you again." His words ran over mine. "Oh, sorry."

"That's okay. Go ahead."

He spread his hands, then clasped them once more. "I just couldn't believe it when I got the call from Detective

Chetterling. How you insisted on helping. What you did. How you almost lost your *life.*" He glanced away, unable to continue.

"I had to." As if a dam had broken, the apologies gushed from me. "I'm so sorry we left without saying why. Detective Chetterling didn't want me to tell you, but I felt just terrible about it. And I'm so sorry that file was in my house. If I'd only known about it, if I hadn't waited so long to clean the office—"

"Annie." He laid his hand on mine. "Stop. *None* of this is your fault. Nobody blames you, certainly not me or Erin. I can't even imagine your apologizing to me. We can only thank you for all you've done."

I held his gaze, searching for the slightest hint that he did not believe his own declarations. And finding none.

"Does God make you like this?" I blurted.

Surprise flicked across his face. "Like what?"

"So . . . forgiving."

"Like I told you, there's nothing to—"

"That's just what I mean." His hand still lay on mine, and I put my other one over it and squeezed. "Because after being at Lisa's funeral, and seeing how you and your friends prayed, and talking to Gerri Carson . . . I found myself praying, and I've never done that before. And then when I was in that house, so sure I was going to die . . ." My throat tightened again. "I prayed then, too. I told Jesus if he'd just get me out of there, I'd . . . pay more attention to him. Find him somehow."

Dave smiled. "You don't need to go looking for him, Annie. He's been right here all along."

Self-consciousness rose within me. I pulled my hands away. "Somehow I knew you'd say that. But I'm just not ready to . . . I mean, I have to think all this through."

"Well, I don't mean to push you. But let me say just one more thing on the subject, and then I'll leave it alone. What are you going to do about that promise you made?"

Promise. Somehow I'd never quite thought of it in those terms. At the time, quivering upon the brink of death, I had considered it more a desperate bargain. Yet the word pulsed within my spirit. I managed a weak smile.

"I aim to keep it."

# # # #

Well-wishers and grateful neighbors called throughout that afternoon. It seemed every time I put the phone down, it rang again. Around two o'clock Gerri Carson called from the Sheriff's Office. She'd heard the details—they were all the department was talking about, she said—but she wanted to check in with me, make sure I was all right.

I pulled out a chair and sat at the kitchen table. "Tell you the truth, I have my moments. Sometimes I'm okay. Sometimes I just want to bawl. Even though I had no choice but to pull that trigger, even though in my head I know he deserved it . . . Still, never would I have imagined killing somebody." I traced a circle on the table with a finger. "Did you hear he has a sister who's a quadriplegic? She was the one person he cared about, I guess, and he visited her all the time. Now she's left without her brother." My eyes stung. "This is hard, Gerri. I don't think I've sorted out all my emotions yet."

"That takes time, Annie, so go easy on yourself. In fact, it's the main reason I'm calling. I'd like to meet with you, give you a chance to talk about it."

"You don't have to do that, Gerri."

"Hey, no problem." I could hear the smile in her voice. "It's part of my service. I've debriefed a lot of police officers and sheriff's deputies who've experienced a tragedy on the job. You've been through no less, and I want you to know I'm available. In the meantime I'll be praying for you."

Her help—and the prayers—were something I was going to need. "Okay. Thank you. Yes, I would like to meet."

"Great."

We set up a time for the following day.

"Hey," she said, "Ralph Chetterling just walked up. He wants to say hello to you."

I heard the clunk of the phone being passed.

"Hi, Annie Kingston, heroine of the decade. Glad to hear you made it home."

I couldn't help but smile. Never in a million years would I have expected to hear such a statement from the detective. "Not to worry. We're all fine."

"Good, good." He paused. "So. Your sister tells me you're going to study forensic art."

My mouth dropped open. "She *what?*"

"Sounds great to me. No doubt we'll need your help again someday. That is, at your drawing table. From now on you can leave chasing the bad guys to us."

No kidding.

"Just when did Jenna tell you this?"

"I don't know. I think before you went to the Bay Area. But we talked about it again down there yesterday."

Before we even left Grove Landing. I shook my head. How had Jenna known? I hadn't even realized how much the field was luring me in until last night in her town home. Exhausted as I was, I'd nevertheless chosen to read three more chapters of the book instead of going to sleep.

"I can give you plenty of information, you know," Chetterling continued, paying no heed to the tone of my voice. I swear, he could be as pushy as my sister. "There are all kinds of workshops you could attend. After all you've done for us, I'd be willing to bet that our department would even sponsor you to take classes back at FBI headquarters in Quantico. Although it can take a long time to get in, I hear. Would you be interested in that?"

Whoa, this was happening too fast. "I . . . I . . . yeah, sure, why not? I mean, it wouldn't hurt for you to get me the information, at least."

"Will do."

We said our goodbyes and I clicked off the line, placing the receiver on the table. When I pushed back my chair to rise, Jenna materialized from the laundry room. Of course.

How much had she heard?

Oh, no, no, no. I was *not* going to let her argue this subject with me. If I'd stood up to Tip, if I'd faced Dave, I could deal with my own sister. For once, she would not have the satisfaction of knowing she'd pushed me into some new venture.

This one was going to be on *my* terms.

She opened her mouth but I cut her off.

"Jenna." I pulled out a second chair. Pointed to it. "Sit down. I've been thinking about something . . ."

Cast a Road Before Me

Brandilyn Collins

A course-changing event in one's life can happen in minutes. Or it can form slowly, a primitive webbing splaying into fingers of discontent, a minuscule trail hardening into the sinewed spine of resentment. So it was with the mill workers as the heat-soaked days of summer marched on.

City girl Jessie, orphaned at sixteen, struggles to adjust to life with her barely known aunt and uncle in the tiny town of Bradleyville, Kentucky. Eight years later (1968), she plans on leaving—to follow in her revered mother's footsteps of serving the homeless. But the peaceful town she's come to love is about to be tragically shattered. Threats of a labor strike rumble through the streets, and Jessie's new love and her uncle are swept into the maelstrom. Caught between the pacifist teachings of her mother and these two men, Jessie desperately tries to deny that Bradleyville is rolling toward violence and destruction.

Softcover: 0-310-25327-6

Pick up a copy today at your favorite bookstore!

ZONDERVAN™

GRAND RAPIDS, MICHIGAN 49530 USA

WWW.ZONDERVAN.COM

Color the Sidewalk for Me

Brandilyn Collins

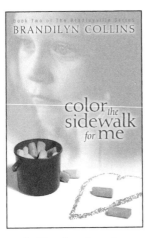

As a chalk-fingered child, I had worn my craving for Mama's love on my sleeve. But as I grew, that craving became cloaked in excuses and denial until slowly it sank beneath my skin to lie unheeded but vital, like the sinews of my framework. By the time I was a teenager, I thought the gap between Mama and me could not be wider.

And then Danny came along. . . .

A splendidly colored sidewalk. Six-year-old Celia presented the gift to her mother with pride—and received only anger in return. Why couldn't Mama love her? Years later, when once-in-a-lifetime love found Celia, her mother opposed it. The crushing losses that followed drove Celia, guilt-ridden and grieving, from her Bradleyville home.

Now thirty-five, she must return to nurse her father after a stroke. But the deepest need for healing lies in the rift between mother and daughter. God can perform such a miracle. But first Celia and Mama must let go of the past— before it destroys them both.

Softcover: 0-310-24242-8

ZONDERVAN™

GRAND RAPIDS, MICHIGAN 49530 USA

WWW.ZONDERVAN.COM

Eyes of Elisha

Brandilyn Collins

The murder was ugly.

The killer was sure no one saw him.

Someone did.

In a horrifying vision, Chelsea Adams has relived the victim's last moments. But who will believe her? Certainly not the police, who must rely on hard evidence. Nor her husband, who barely tolerates Chelsea's newfound Christian faith. Besides, he's about to hire the man who Chelsea is certain is the killer to be a vice president in his company.

Torn between what she knows and the burden of proof, Chelsea must follow God's leading and trust him for protection. Meanwhile, the murderer is at liberty. And he's not about to take Chelsea's involvement lying down.

Softcover: 0-310-23968-0

Pick up a copy today at your favorite bookstore!

ZONDERVAN™

GRAND RAPIDS, MICHIGAN 49530 USA

WWW.ZONDERVAN.COM

Dread Champion

Brandilyn Collins

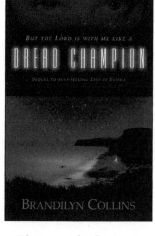

Chelsea Adams has visions. But they have no place in a courtroom. As a juror for a murder trial, Chelsea must rely only on the evidence. And this circumstantial evidence is strong—Darren Welk killed his wife. Or did he?

The trial is a nightmare for Chelsea. The other jurors belittle her Christian faith. As testimony unfolds, truth and secrets blur. Chelsea's visiting niece stumbles into peril surrounding the case, and Chelsea cannot protect her. God sends visions—frightening, vivid. But what do they mean? Even as Chelsea finds out, what can she do? She is helpless, and danger is closing in. . . .

Softcover: 0-310-23827-7

Pick up a copy today at your favorite bookstore!

ZONDERVAN™

GRAND RAPIDS, MICHIGAN 49530 USA

WWW.ZONDERVAN.COM

We want to hear from you. Please send your comments about this
book to us in care of zreview@zondervan.com. Thank you.

GRAND RAPIDS, MICHIGAN 49530 USA

W W W . Z O N D E R V A N . C O M